SHOT IN THE BACK

SHOT IN THE BACK

WILLIAM W. JOHNSTONE
with J. A. Johnstone

PINNACLE BOOKS
Kensington Publishing Corp.
www.kensingtonbooks.com

PINNACLE BOOKS are published by

Kensington Publishing Corp.
119 West 40th Street
New York, NY 10018

PUBLISHER'S NOTE
Following the death of William W. Johnstone, the Johnstone family is working with a carefully selected writer to organize and complete Mr. Johnstone's outlines and many unfinished manuscripts to create additional novels in all of his series like The Last Gunfighter, Mountain Man, and Eagles, among others. This novel was inspired by Mr. Johnstone's superb storytelling.

All Kensington titles, imprints, and distributed lines are available at special quantity discounts for bulk purchases for sales promotions, premiums, fundraising, educational, or institutional use. Special book excerpts or customized printings can also be created to fit specific needs. For details, write or phone the office of the Kensington sales manager: Kensington Publishing Corp., 119 West 40th Street, New York, NY 10018, attn: Sales Department; phone 1-800-221-2647.

PINNACLE BOOKS, the Pinnacle logo, and the WWJ steer head logo are Reg. U.S. Pat. & TM Off.

ISBN-13: 978-0-7860-3448-2
ISBN-10: 0-7860-3448-3

First printing: June 2015

10 9 8 7 6 5 4 3 2

Printed in the United States of America

First electronic edition: June 2015

ISBN-13: 978-0-7860-3449-9
ISBN-10: 0-7860-3449-1

CHAPTER ONE

Granbury, Texas—December 7, 1941

J. Frank Alexander limped into the living room, turned on the cathedral radio, and tuned it to a program of music. Sitting in a nearby rocking chair, he began eating the bowl of chocolate pudding he had brought with him while tapping his foot to the music. To the casual observer he might look like a very old man sitting in a rocking chair, but in his mind he was twenty-five years old and dancing with "the prettiest girl in Clay County, Missouri."

Suddenly the music stopped and Alexander glanced toward the radio, aggravated that the melody had been interrupted. From time to time the radio did that, and he could generally bring it back by giving it a hard slap on the arched top. He was about to do that when the sound returned. It wasn't music, though; it was an announcer's voice.

"Ladies and gentlemen, we interrupt this musical program with a news bulletin from NBC News in New York. President Roosevelt said, today, that the Japanese have attacked Pearl Harbor from the air."

"Where the hell is Pearl Harbor?" Alexander asked.

As if responding to Alexander's question, the announcer continued.

"Pearl Harbor is a U.S. Navy base in the American islands of Hawaii. After attacking the ships in the harbor and setting several of them on fire, the Japanese planes, hundreds of them, then attacked the army air corps at Hickam Field and army troops at Fort Shafter. Continuing on, the Japanese planes bombed and machine-gunned civilians in Honolulu.

"The loss of life is said to be very heavy, but no numbers are yet available. It is believed that a state of war will be declared between the United States and Japan.

"Again, Japanese planes have attacked the United States in Hawaii. We will have more information for you as it comes available. And now, back to our regularly scheduled programming."

The music returned, but Alexander was no longer listening. He had never been to Hawaii, but he knew where it was and had seen pictures of it. He knew that it was a very beautiful place, and for a while he had even contemplated going there after his first "retirement."

"You Japanese sons of bitches have stepped in it now."

Granbury—February 2, 1942

Alexander parked his 1937 Ford convertible on Crockett Street, two blocks north of the post office, which was the closest parking space he could find. He put a nickel into the parking meter.

"Good morning, Mr. Alexander."

"Mornin', Clem," Alexander replied.

Clem had called out to him from inside a sidewalk newsstand, on which were spread newspapers and magazines. Alexander stepped up to glance at the headlines.

FLEET SMASHES JAP SUB BASE

MacArthur's Men Take Heavy Toll On Jap Attackers in the Philippines

"Looks to me like we're already givin' those Jap bastards a good lickin'," Clem said.

"Yeah, but we're a long way from whippin' 'em yet, I'd say."

"People from all over are joinin' up to go fight 'em," Clem said. "I'm fifty-eight years old, but if I was younger, I'd be one of the first in line. I was too old for the first world war, and too young to go off 'n fight agin' the Spanish. I was only sixteen then, but I tried."

Alexander bought a newspaper, then with a wave good-bye continued on.

The recruiting office was just inside the post office, and there were two recruiting posters on the wall, one on either side of the door.

One had a picture of a muscular, shirtless sailor, wearing a sailor's cap and shoving an artillery shell into a big gun.

MAN THE GUNS!
Join the Navy

On the other side of the door was an army recruiting poster, featuring a uniformed soldier who was blowing a bugle as he stood in front of a furled American flag.

THE CALL
TO DUTY
Join the Army
For Home and Country

Inside the office there were two soldiers and two sailors. All four were sitting around a table playing cards.

"Gibson, you better watch Martell, he's goin' to try and shoot the moon," one of the sailors said.

"Ha! You, don't have to worry none about that, Calvin. You wait until somebody drops the ole bitch on 'im. Then we'll see how he does," Gibson said.

An army sergeant glanced up from the game and saw Alexander standing just inside the door.

"Yes, sir, something we can do for you?" the sergeant asked.

"Is this where you join the army?" Alexander asked.

"It sure is. If your grandson is looking to join, why you just bring him right on down here, old-timer, and we'll sign him right up."

"Come on, Sergeant Kilbride, you know that boy isn't going to want anything to do with the army. Tell you what, mister, you bring him here, the navy will treat him right," Calvin, who was a navy chief petty officer, said.

"No, sir, it's the army I'm interested in."

Corporal Martell, who put his cards on the table facedown when Alexander walked in, laughed. "Ha!

What do you think about that? He knows what's good for his grandson."

"No, sir, I'm not askin' about my grandson. I'm askin' about me."

Sergeant Kilbride got a confused look on his face. "I don't understand. What do you mean, asking about you?"

"Joinin' up," Alexander said. "I want to join the army."

The sergeant laughed. "You want to fight for Uncle Sam, do you?"

"You're damn right I do. And I'll fight as hard for the Yankee government this time as I once fought against it."

"As you once fought against it?" Seaman Gibson asked. "What do you mean, you fought against the government?"

"When I rode with Quantrill."

"Holy crap! Are you telling us you were with Quantrill?"

"Damn straight I am."

"How old are you?"

"I'm ninety-five."

"You are ninety-five and you want to enlist in the army?" Martell asked.

"Yes."

Sergeant Kilbride laughed. "So, you rode with Quantrill, did you? Next you'll be telling us you're Jesse James."

"How did you know?"

The four men looked at him with eyes opened wide in shock.

"Wait a minute. Are you going to stand there, flat-footed, and tell us that you are Jesse James?"

"Well, if I'm going to enlist, I will need to use my real name, won't I?"

The four recruiters laughed.

"I tell you what. The army can have him," Calvin said, laughing out loud.

"You men don't believe me, do you?"

"What about you, Sergeant Kilbride? Do you believe this is Jesse James?" Calvin asked.

"Mister, why don't you leave now? You're wasting our time," Sergeant Kilbride said.

"But I want to join the army."

"If you don't leave now, I'll call Sheriff Baker," Kilbride said, reaching for the phone.

"Yes, sir, you do that. Call Oran; I'll just have a seat over here and wait for him," Alexander said.

"Tell me, old-timer, do any of your friends want to join? Billy the Kid? Doc Holliday? Bill Doolin?" Martell asked, laughing as he spoke.

"Bill Doolin?" Alexander said. He made a hacking sound of disgust deep in his throat. "Hell, Doolin wasn't nothin' but a joke."

Kilbride asked the operator to get him the sheriff's office. A moment later he said, "Sheriff Baker? This is Sergeant Kilbride down at the recruiting office." He looked at the others and smiled. "We've captured a notorious outlaw, and we'd like to turn him over to you for the reward."

The others laughed.

"Oh, yeah, we'll hold him here for you," Kilbride said before he hung up.

"While we're waitin', old-timer, would you like a cup of coffee?" Corporal Martell asked.

"Make it black," Alexander said.

Martell poured a cup of coffee and handed it to

him. "Today was the navy's turn to make the coffee," he said. "So I can't guarantee this. It probably tastes like bilge water."

"I've had coffee, chicory, even ground-up parched corn. I reckon I can handle your coffee," Alexander said. He took a sip, then smiled. "This is good."

"Well, I'll say this for him," Gibson said, "he likes navy coffee, and that means that he does have taste."

A few minutes later the sheriff arrived.

"Hello, Sergeant Kilbride. You said you had someone I should meet?"

"Yes," Kilbride replied. "I've got someone here who says . . ." He laughed. "Are you ready for this? He says he is Jesse James."

"Hello, Oran," Alexander said.

"Hello, Jesse. I thought you weren't ever going to tell," Sheriff Baker replied.

The gasps of the four recruiters were audible.

"Why not? What are they going to do to me now?" Alexander replied. "It's been more'n sixty years since the last paper was out on me. And if I get one last chance to serve my country, I want to do it."

"Wait a minute, Sheriff! Just hold on there! Are you saying this fella really is Jesse James?" Gibson asked.

"That's exactly what I'm saying."

"You're putting us on, aren't you?" Martell asked.

"My pa saw Jesse James once, and he told me about it. Ever since then I've been interested in Jesse James, and I reckon I've read just about ever'thing that has ever been written about him, which, in a court of law, would qualify me as an expert witness."

"But what makes you think this old man is Jesse James?" Calvin asked.

"There are seven bullet wounds on this man," Sheriff Baker said. "That is the same number of times Jesse James is known to have been shot, and the bullet wounds are in precisely the same places. There is a scar on his neck, consistent with the same type scar that would have been left by the rope that a sixteen-year-old Jesse James had from an aborted attempt to hang him. There are also several burn marks on his feet, from where Union soldiers tortured him, trying to get him to tell them where Frank was hiding. If you notice, his left ring finger is missing below the knuckle. I don't think someone would chop off a finger just to promote a lie. And last, but not least, I have questioned this man extensively. He knows things that only Jesse James could possibly know."

"All right, let's say you are Jesse James. I'm not buying that, but let's say that you are. You're ninety-five years old. Just what is it that you think you could do for the army?" Sergeant Kilbride asked.

"I can teach 'em how to fight behind the lines."

"Behind the lines?"

Jesse laughed. "Sonny, I spent most of my career behind the lines, be it Yankee lines or the law. There's a lot I could teach your soldier boys."

"Yes, well, even if you are who you say you are, I don't think we can actually enlist you," the sergeant said. "But let me talk to Captain Kirby. Maybe we can find some way to use you as a civilian consultant. We'll be in touch with you soon."

"You'd better make it very soon. At my age, I don't even buy milk. I might expire before the milk does," he added, laughing at his own joke.

"Sheriff, uh, let's say this is Jesse James. Is there still a reward out for him?" Sergeant Kilbride asked.

Baker laughed. "I don't think so." He turned to Jesse. "Jesse, I was going to look you up today anyway. It just so happens that there is someone in town I would like for you to meet. Would you mind coming with me?"

"Don't mind at all."

"Would you ring Mr. Faust's room for me?" Sheriff Baker asked the hotel clerk.

"Yes," the clerk replied. He made a connection on the switchboard, then pointed to a white telephone on the counter. "Pick up the courtesy phone please, Sheriff."

"Mr. Faust? This is Sheriff Baker. You know the gentleman I told you about? I have him with me. All right, we'll be right up."

"Who is this man we're meeting?" Jesse asked as they waited for the elevator.

"His name is Frederick Faust. But he writes books as Max Brand."

"Max Brand. Yeah, I've heard of him."

"I've read your book *The Outlaw*," Jesse said a few moments later after Sheriff Baker introduced them in Faust's room.

"Oh? What did you think of it?" Faust asked.

"Don't know as I can say, seein' as I never met Billy the Kid. Have you ever done one on me?"

"By 'me,' do you mean J. Frank Alexander? Or Jesse James?"

"Have you?"

"I've borrowed from the Jesse James story of course, but no, I've never done a book specifically about Jesse James."

"But now you're wantin' to. That's why you're talkin' to me."

"It might be, Mr. Alexander, or Mr. James, whichever is your real name."

"Actually, I've gone by the name Alexander a lot longer now than I went by the name of Jesse James, or Tom Howard. But I reckon you know about such things, seeing as you have two names, Frederick Faust and Max Brand. I mean, they are both your real names, wouldn't you say?"

"I suppose you could say that."

"Well, you may as well call me Jesse. I mean, the cat's out of the bag. And it's like I told Oran, there's been no paper out on me for more'n sixty years now. Why, I'd be willin' to bet there isn't a dodger out on me in any sheriff's office anywhere in the whole country."

Faust laughed. "I'd say that's a safe bet. But, before I start calling you Jesse, you're going to have to convince me that you are who you say you are."

"Ask Oran. He knows who I am."

"I know that you have convinced him. But I'm asking you to convince me."

"How am I supposed to convince you who I am? All I can do is tell you who I am and I reckon you're just going to have to believe me."

"Maybe it would help if you told me a few things that I can verify, things that have been recorded in the history books. I want to hear your version of it."

"There's only one problem with that," Jesse said.

"What would that be?"

"My version and what's written in the history books might be somewhat different. My version is always right. The history books aren't always right."

"I'll take that into consideration."

"All right, what do you want to hear about first?"

"The Northfield Raid."

Jesse sighed and shook his head. "You would choose that."

"I'll admit, it wasn't your finest hour," Faust said. "At least, it wasn't the finest hour for Jesse and Frank James. But let me hear your side of the story."

"It was the worst day of my life."

CHAPTER TWO

Clay County, Missouri—May 10, 1876

"Why go all the way to Minnesota to rob a bank?" Frank James asked his brother.

"We're too well known here," Jesse said. "There's not a bank in the state we can go into and not be recognized. Nobody in Minnesota knows us. We could pick out a town, any town in Minnesota, and walk up 'n down the street without anyone ever paying any attention to us."

"We've also got friends here, Jesse," Frank said. "We've got places to go to hide out. We know where those places are, and we know who to trust. Neither of us have ever even been to Minnesota. We wouldn't even know our way around up there."

"Bill Chadwell is from Minnesota. He knows his way around, and he swears he can get us in and out real easy."

"Who do you have lined up to go?"

"Bill Chadwell; then there's Bob, Jim, and Cole Younger. Also Charlie Pitts, Clell Miller, and of course you and me."

Frank shook his head. "You can't count me. I haven't decided yet that I'll go."

"Frank, you've been saying you want to quit, haven't you?"

"Yes, you know I have. Annie doesn't like this. She doesn't like it at all."

"Neither does Zee. Don't you see, Frank? We can rob that bank up in Minnesota, maybe come away with a hundred thousand dollars or more. Even splitting it up among all of us, we'd have twelve thousand, five hundred dollars apiece. Can you imagine what we could do with that much money? We'd have enough to start over anywhere we wanted. We could go to some place like Tennessee, or Kentucky, or maybe Virginia and buy a farm. I mean a good farm, with good dirt." Jesse smiled. "We'll buy two farms, right next to each other, and we'll be gentleman farmers. Our kids will grow up together, and some day, we'll just sit on the front porch and rock. What do you say, Frank?"

"I know I'm crazy for saying this," Frank said. "But I have to admit that the idea of having enough money to buy a farm and settle down does sound good to me."

"Then you're in?"

"All right, Jesse, yeah, I'm in. I'll go along with you this one last time."

"Good!" Jesse responded enthusiastically.

"What's the plan?"

"First, we have to raise some money, enough money to finance the operation."

"So, what do you have in mind? Are we going to rob a bank so that we have enough money to rob a bank?"

Jesse smiled. "No. We're going to rob a train."

Otterville, Missouri—July 7, 1876

It was ten o'clock at night when Jesse and Frank James; Bob, Jim, and Cole Younger; Bill Chadwell; Charlie "Chuck" Pitts; Clell Miller; and Hobbs Kerry rode into town. Most of the townspeople were home in bed, though the saloon was still open and the splashes of light spilling through the windows were the only source of illumination in the entire town. An off-key piano was rendering some tune in discordant notes, and a man's loud laughter could be heard.

"The rest of you, go on up to Rocky Cut and wait," Jesse said. "Frank and I will take care of the night guard."

Rocky Cut referred to the gash just beyond the edge of the town that had been blasted through the hill when the tracks for the Missouri Pacific Railroad had been laid.

Jesse and Frank dismounted, then went inside the depot. The night guard was sitting in one chair with his legs propped up on one another. He was reading a newspaper by lamplight, and he looked up as the two men came in. His eyes grew large when he saw they were both pointing their pistols at him.

Fifteen minutes later, with the guard tied to the chair he had been sitting on, and with one of his socks stuffed into his mouth held in place by his kerchief, Jesse and Frank joined the others at Rocky Cut. Jesse had the guard's lantern, with a red lens, and when they heard the train coming, he lit it and stood alongside the train, swinging the red lantern back and forth as a signal to the engineer to stop.

Hearing the vented steam, then the squeak of the brakes as they were applied, Jesse knew that the engineer was complying with his signal.

"Get out of sight, boys," Jesse said. "He's stopping."

Only Jesse remained alongside the track, and when the train stopped, the engineer stuck his head through the cab window.

"What's up? What did you stop me for?"

"Why, we stopped you so we could hold up the train," Jesse said, almost jovially.

The others came out of hiding then, and, boarding the train, held the passengers and the conductor at gunpoint while Jesse and Frank climbed into the express car. There were two safes in the car.

"Listen to me just real close, Messenger, because what you do next could mean the difference between whether you live or die. I see there are two safes. Would you please be kind enough to open them for me?"

The messenger didn't respond right away, and Jesse pointed his pistol at the messenger's head and pulled the hammer back.

"Because if you can't open them, we'll just kill you now and blast them open. But blasting is so messy, I'd rather not do that, and I know you don't want a big mess in your car. Oh, what am I talking about? It wouldn't make any difference to you, would it? I mean, after all, you would be dead."

"No! I can open them, I can open them!" the messenger shouted.

"Good. I was hoping you might see it my way."

The entire operation was over within ten minutes, and Jesse and the others were on horseback, galloping away.

The robbery netted fifteen thousand dollars, and it would have been an unmitigated success had Hobbs Kerry not been captured a month later. He gave the authorities the names of everyone who participated in the robbery. Fortunately for Jesse and the others, they were already on the train on their way to Minnesota. Jesse, Frank, Clell Miller, and Jim Younger were on one train. Bob and Cole Younger, Bill Chadwell, and Chuck Pitts were on a second train. They had shipped their horses up on the stock cars that were attached to each train.

It was the middle of August when they arrived in Minnesota, and they had no idea what bank they wanted to rob, so they split up into four pairs to scout out several small towns before finally deciding that they would rob the First National Bank of Northfield, Minnesota.

"These Yankee bastards ain't never run in to the likes of us," Clell Miller said. "When it goes down, they won't know whether to scratch their ass or pick their nose."

On the morning of September 7, the eight men met just outside Northfield.

"We'll break up into three groups. Frank, Bob, and I will be the ones who actually go into the bank," Jesse said as he laid out the plans. "Cole, you and Clell stay out front of the bank to stand guard. Jim, I want you, Chuck, and Bill to cover our escape route. Any questions?"

"We're all wearin' our guns," Chuck Pitts said.

"Well, yeah, don't you think we might need them?" Clell Miller asked.

"It's just that, if you notice, there ain't nobody in any of these towns we've been through that's been wearin' guns. Don't you think maybe we ought to put on our dusters so as to cover them?"

"Good idea, Chuck," Jesse said. "Yes, let's do that."

"All right, Frank, Bob, and I will ride into town first. We'll have lunch and sort of scout the town over. Cole, you and Clell give us about an hour or so before you two come in. When we see you two arrive, we'll go on into the bank. Jim, you and your group stay back at the bridge. Don't let anybody block it, because after we come out of the bank, this is where we'll gather up. Cole, that's when you and Clell will cut the telegraph lines, so they can't get any word out about us."

The others nodded, then all of them put on their dusters. With a little wave, Jesse, Frank, and Bob rode across the bridge and into town.

The town was busy, with men and women walking up and down the boardwalks on either side of the street. A wagon carrying beer barrels was backed up to a saloon, and a couple of white-haired and bearded men were playing checkers on the front porch of a hardware store. From the far end of the street came the ring of a blacksmith's hammer.

The three went into a restaurant that was on the same street as the bank. A man wearing an apron came over to their table.

"Fried chicken, or ham and potatoes?" he asked.

"I never pass up fried chicken," Jesse said with a smile. "Especially if you've got biscuits."

"No biscuits. Fresh baked bread, though."

"That's good enough."

Frank also ordered fried chicken, but Bob ordered the ham.

"Haven't seen you gents before. Just get into town, did you?"

"We're just passing through," Jesse said. "Looks like a nice town, though."

"We like it."

When the three finished their lunch, they walked across the street to the Lee & Hitchcock Dry Goods Store. This was right next door to the bank, and they sat casually on some crates that were stacked up in front of the store.

"It doesn't look to me like the bank is doing all that much business," Frank said.

"I hope that doesn't mean they don't have much money in it," Bob said with a little laugh.

"All right, get ready, boys. There's Cole and Clell," Jesse said.

As soon as the two men arrived, Jesse gave them a nod, then he, Frank, and Bob went into the bank.

There were three men inside the bank, all three behind the counter. Jesse, Frank, and Bob immediately pulled their guns and aimed them at the three bank employees.

"We're robbing this bank. Don't any of you shout out!"

The three robbers jumped over the counter.

"Which one of you is the cashier?" Jesse asked.

Jesse saw two of the men glance quickly toward the third man. "Mr. Heywood isn't here," the third man said.

The other two men, who had glanced momentarily toward the third, looked away, pointedly.

Jesse smiled. "I think you are Heywood," he said. "Open the safe for me, Mr. Heywood. And be damned quick about it. The sooner this is done and we get out of here, the safer it will be for you."

"I can't open the safe," Heywood said.

"I don't believe you. What bank would have a cashier who can't open the safe?" Jesse asked.

"Maybe the safe is already open," Frank suggested. He walked over to the open vault door to inspect the safe inside, and as he began to enter the vault Heywood suddenly bolted toward the vault door and pushed it shut, attempting to lock Frank inside. Frank managed to get out just in time, but his arm and hand were caught by the vault door as it slammed.

"Damn!" Frank called out.

"Damn you!" Bob shouted, and he brought the butt of his pistol down over Heywood's head.

Outside the bank at that moment, J. S. Allen, who owned one of the town's two hardware/gun stores, noticed that two men he had never seen before, both wearing long, identical dusters, were standing suspiciously in front of the bank, looking up and down the street. Curious, Allen approached the bank, but Clell grabbed his wrist.

"What's going on here?" Allen asked. Then, looking through the window, he saw men holding guns. "The bank is being robbed," he said.

"Get out of here, mister, and keep your damned mouth shut!" Clell said, pushing him away.

Allen walked merely a few feet away, then he began running and shouting, "Get your guns, boys! They're robbing the bank!"

Allen's shout was picked up by Henry Wheeler, the young medical student with whom Allen had been walking.

"Robbery! Robbery! They're robbing the bank!" he shouted.

Clell pulled one of his pistols and fired at Wheeler, but he missed.

After Clell's first shot, he and Cole mounted their horses and began charging up and down the street firing into the air and shouting.

"Get off the street! Everyone, off the street!"

Jim, Bill, and Chuck, on the bridge, heard the shooting and hurried down to offer assistance. At first, it seemed to be working. The citizens got off the street but only to arm themselves. Within minutes, dozens of armed townspeople were shooting at the five outlaws, and the street became a battlefield with bullets flying from every direction.

Inside the bank, Jesse knelt down by Heywood, who was still on the floor. He held a knife to Heywood's neck. "Open the safe, or I'll cut your damn throat from ear to ear."

"I can't open the safe," Heywood said. "It has a time lock."

"It has a what?"

"A time lock. It can't be opened until four o'clock this afternoon!"

Cole stuck his head in through the front door. "Hurry up! All hell's breaking loose out here!"

Outside, Clell Miller took a load of birdshot in the face, not enough to kill him but opening up wounds that bled profusely. Cole and Jim both took slugs through the shoulder.

One of the townspeople, seeing three horses tethered in front of the bank, shot one of them in the head. The horse, which belonged to Bob Younger, dropped dead instantly. Cole Younger's hat was shot off, while Bill Chadwell was shot through the heart and he fell from his saddle, dead before he hit the ground.

Clell Miller, still screaming in pain and rage from being shot in the face with a load of light birdshot, was hit again, this round severing his subclavian artery. With blood gushing out of his eye, face, and shoulder, he attempted to lift himself up on his arms, but after about three seconds of this, his strength gave and he toppled over. Cole saw this and raced toward him. Reaching his body, he dismounted and, using his horse for cover, knelt to examine Clell. Discovering that Clell was dead, Cole grabbed Clell's pistols and cartridge belts and attempted to remount. As he was doing so, another bullet tore through his left thigh. He winced in pain but managed to pull himself up on his horse and make another charge. He ran past the bank door again and yelled inside, "We're being killed out here! Come on, now!"

As they were leaving the bank, Frank saw that Heywood had pulled a pistol from somewhere and was aiming it at Jesse.

"No!" Frank shouted and, aiming at Heywood, pulled the trigger. Blood, brains, and bone detritus exploded from the side of Heywood's head.

"Where the hell did they all come from?" Frank shouted as they ran from the front of the bank.

"My horse!" Bob shouted, seeing his mount lying dead.

"Let's go!" Jesse said as he and Frank mounted. Frank was shot in the leg, and Bob was shot in the arm.

"Don't leave me, boys!" Bob called.

Cole came racing back for his brother, while Chuck covered them with his pistol. By now everyone was firing at Cole and Bob. One bullet hit Bob in the left leg and he stumbled. Another took off Cole's saddle horn and another cut his reins. Despite that, he managed somehow to reach down, and, with almost superhuman strength, he lifted Bob off the ground and onto the back of his saddle. Bob then wrapped his left arm around Cole's waist and, with Cole holding his horse's mane, they took off after the others. The townspeople kept firing, and Cole was hit three more times. Following this, he and Bob met up with Chuck at the end of town and the three of them rode at breakneck speed after Jesse, Frank, and Jim.

CHAPTER THREE

Granbury—February 2, 1942

It had grown dark outside, and now the three men, Jesse James, Sheriff Oran Baker, and Frederick Faust were sitting in Faust's hotel room, which was dimly lit by a single lamp that sat on the bedside table.

It had taken Jesse several minutes to tell the story, and now he sat in the chair, staring ahead silently.

Faust got up and walked over to the table, where he dropped some ice into three glasses; then he poured a shot of whiskey into each of the glasses. He handed one to Sheriff Baker, then another to Jesse.

"I thought you might need this," he said.

"Thanks," Jesse said.

"Is there more to the story?"

Jesse drained the glass before he spoke again.

"Yeah, but not much more," he said. "You want to know how much money we got from that robbery?"

"It didn't sound like you got anything," Faust said.

"Oh, we got something," Jesse said. "Before we left

the bank, Bob scooped up twenty-six dollars and seventy cents. He grabbed it from an open drawer behind the teller's cage. Twenty-six dollars and seventy cents. And for that, we left behind Bill and Clell dead, one dead horse, and two dead Northfield citizens. Truth is, though, Heywood is the only one we killed. The other fella, the Swede, Nicholas Gustavson, was killed by a stray bullet from one of the townsmen. Five out of the six of us who actually made it out of town were wounded; I was the only one who wasn't. We split up then, and within two more weeks, all three of the Younger brothers were captured."

Faust had not taken a swallow of his drink until then, and now, he raised the glass to his lips and drank.

"I must confess that you told that story most convincingly," he said. "I would be inclined to believe you, but there is one more hurdle we must get over."

"You want to know about me being killed," Jesse said.

"Yes, that's a rather major incident, wouldn't you think? That's going to have to be dealt with before we can go any further in this narrative. To begin with, I would be very interested in knowing how it is that you managed to get up and walk away after Bob Ford shot you."

Jesse chuckled. "Well, that's easy enough. It wasn't me that Bob Ford shot."

"Who was it?"

"It was a man by the name of Charlie Bigelow."

St. Joseph, Missouri—April 2, 1882

When Jesse James, known by everyone in town as Thomas Howard, stepped into the Missouri

Cattlemen's Bar on Mitchell Avenue, he was greeted by the bartender.

"Hello, Mr. Howard. There are two cattlemen from Kansas City here to see you. They're sitting in that table in the corner."

"Thanks, John," Jesse said.

Jesse smiled as he recognized the two "cattlemen." They were the brothers Bob and Charley Ford. In September, Charley Ford had ridden with Jesse and Frank James when they robbed the Chicago and Alton Railroad at Blue Cut, near Glendale, Missouri.

"Hello, Jesse," Charley greeted as Jesse approached the table.

Jesse glared at him. "My name is Howard," he said. "Tom Howard."

"Sorry, Tom."

"You sent a letter, asking me to meet you here today. What's up?"

"Have you seen this?" Bob Ford asked, pulling a folded-up piece of paper from his jacket pocket.

Jesse unfolded the paper.

PROCLAMATION
of the
Governor of Missouri

$25,000 REWARD
JESSE JAMES
DEAD OR ALIVE

$15,000 for Frank James

"Why are you showing me this?" Jesse asked, shoving the poster back across the table.

"I'm showin' you this 'cause I got me an idea as to how I can collect this here reward."

Jesse inched his hand toward his pistol.

"Now, hold on, hold on there!" Bob Ford said, reaching his hand out toward Jesse. "Hear me out."

"All right, what is it? What's your idea?"

"Tell 'im about Bigelow, Charley," Bob said to his brother.

"Bigelow? You mean Charlie Bigelow?" Jesse asked.

"Yeah. Since you've heard of 'im, then you prob'ly know that he's been robbin' stores, stagecoaches, and even held up a bank, claimin' to be you," Charley Ford said.

"That's how come there's been all these robberies that you've been blamed for that you didn't do," Bob said.

"Like you say, I have heard of him, but I've never met him," Jesse said.

"Well, if you was to see him, you'd think you was lookin' in a mirror," Bob Ford said.

"He looks that much like me?"

"Yeah, he does. That's how come he's been able to convince ever'one that he's you," Charley said.

"So, when I say I'm goin' to collect the reward on you, what I'm actually goin' to do is collect it on him," Bob said, "and pass him off as you. That way, the law will think they've got their man, and you'll be free and clear. Nobody will be looking for you again."

Jesse shook his head. "That won't do. If you take him in, he'll just say that he isn't me. And there are enough people who actually do know me that they'll know he's tellin' the truth."

"He won't be tellin' nobody anythin' if he's dead," Bob said.

"You plan to kill him?"

"At your house," Bob said.

"At my house?"

"It has to be done at your house, if we are to pass him off as being you."

Jesse shook his head. "Not with Zee and the kids there."

"You'll just have to get them out of the house for a while."

"How are you goin' to get Bigelow to come to my house?"

"I know that he would like to join up with your gang," Bob said. "He's asked me a couple of times to talk to you about it. All I have to do is tell 'im that we're goin' to pull another job 'n you want him to join us."

Jesse drummed his fingers on the table for a moment or two. "All right," he said. "Go see him, and the three of you come over to the house for breakfast tomorrow morning."

"I thought you weren't going to do any more jobs," Zerelda said as she cut bacon for their breakfast.

"I've got to, Zee. We didn't get but three thousand dollars from the last job, which I had to divide that up with the others. And that was six months ago. We're running out of money."

"When, Jesse? When are you going to stop? We have two kids who don't even know their real names. Jesse and Mary think they are Tim and Mary Howard."

"For now it's best that they don't know their real names. We can't take the chance on one of them saying something. In fact, why don't you take them down to the park this morning before the men come? You don't need to know what's going on anyway."

"All right," Zerelda said. "But, Jesse, please promise me. After today, no more jobs."

Jesse put his hands on Zerelda's shoulders and looked straight into her eyes.

"I promise you, Zee," he said. "After today, Jesse James will pull no more jobs."

"Nor Tom Howard," she said.

Jesse nodded. "Nor Tom Howard," he promised.

Shortly after Zee left, Bob Ford arrived with his brother and Charlie Bigelow.

"Thanks for agreeing to take me into your gang," Bigelow said.

"I'm not taking you into my gang," Jesse replied. "I no longer have a gang."

"But, Bob told me—"

"He told you that so that you would come," Jesse said. "Bigelow, what were you thinking, killing and robbing, and passing yourself off as me?"

"I . . . I only did it out of respect for you," Bigelow said.

"But the twenty-five-thousand-dollar reward isn't being offered for you, is it? It's being offered for me. Now every law officer, every private detective, and every bounty hunter in America is looking for me.

I've promised my wife that I was going to quit, that I was going to lead a quiet life from now on, but you've made that impossible."

"Oh, no, you don't," Bigelow said, shaking his head. "You can't blame me for that. You was robbin' and killin' long before I ever started."

"The difference is, Bigelow, I only killed people who were trying to kill me. You robbed a train near West Plains last month, and you killed three of the passengers for no reason. I can't afford to have you around anymore."

Bigelow pulled his pistol and pointed it toward Jesse.

"I don't know what you've got in mind but—" That was as far as he got before there was the sound of a shot. Bigelow fell with a bullet in the back of his head.

"I did it!" Bob Ford said, holding the smoking gun. "Now all we have to do is get the sheriff here so we can claim the reward."

"Move his body over there by the chair," Charley Ford said.

"Why?"

"Nobody is going to ever believe that you could just walk up behind Jesse James and shoot him. Move him over there by that chair, then set that picture crooked, like as if he was standin' up on the chair straightenin' it out."

"Yeah," Bob said. "Yeah, that's a good idea."

Bob and Charley Ford moved Bigelow's body into position.

"If you're goin' to get the sheriff, I need to be out of here," Jesse said.

"Zee needs to be here, though," Charley Ford said.

"Why does she have to be here?"

"She needs to be here so she can identify the body."

"No, I don't want her to have to go through that."

"She has to, Jesse. Don't you see? The only way this is going to work is if she identifies the body," Charley said.

"And you're going to have to leave Saint Joseph," Bob added. "Without her."

"How is she supposed to look after herself and the kids with me gone?"

"We'll split the reward money with her," Bob promised. "With half the reward money, she and your kids will be in good shape."

Jesse found Zee sitting on a bench, looking out at young Jesse, who was pushing Mary on a swing.

"Have they gone?" Zee asked.

"Yes."

"And did you plan another robbery?"

"No."

"You didn't? Oh, Jesse, I'm so pleased!" Zee said happily. "Let me get the kids and we'll go back to the house. You may have eaten breakfast, but the kids and I haven't."

"I'm not going back to the house, Zee," Jesse said. He paused for a moment, then added, "ever."

"What? Jesse, what are you saying?"

"When you return to the house, you will learn that I have been killed."

"What?" This time the question was a gasp.

"There is a man who looks just like me. He has been on a robbing and murder spree, passing himself off as me. Zee, did you know that the reward on me has reached twenty-five thousand dollars?"

"No, I didn't know."

"All because of the crimes this man has committed."

"That's awful. But, what do you mean I will learn that you have been killed?"

"The man's name is Charlie Bigelow. Bob Ford killed him, and he is now lying in the floor in the living room of our house."

"Jesse! How dare you do such a thing, in our own home!"

"I told you, I didn't do it. Bob Ford did it. Zee, it was the only way, don't you see? You are going to tell the sheriff that Bigelow is me. That way the law will be off my back, I can start over, and I'll be free forever. Bob Ford will get the reward money, half of which will go to you."

"You mean half will come to us."

"No. Just to you."

"What do you mean, just to me?"

"This . . . this is the hardest part of it, Zee. In order for this to work, I'm going to have to disappear. Forever."

"We can go to California," Zee said.

"No," Jesse said, shaking his head. "You don't understand. You are going to stay here as the grieving widow. That is the only way this can work. Zee, we can never see each other again."

"No! Jesse, what are you saying?"

"Don't you understand, Zee? It could have been me, lying dead on that floor. And it will be me, someday, if I don't leave now. Yes, you and I will never see each other again . . . but at least you will know that I'm still alive."

"Jesse, no, I can't," Zee said. "I just can't. Please don't ask me to do that."

"Zee, this is my life we are talking about," Jesse said. "Don't you love me enough to save my life? Even if it means that we can never see each other again?"

"It won't work anyway," Zee said. "There's no way I can cry over the body of some man that I don't even know and make people think it's you."

"Yes, you can, Zee. Because to you, I *will* be dead. Don't you understand what I'm saying? I will be out of your life forever."

Zee put both hands to her face and began crying.

"I will always love you, Zee. And if you love me, you can take some satisfaction in knowing that I'm still alive, somewhere, and that I'm not about to hang or spend the rest of my life in prison. Will you do it, Zee?"

"I . . . I'll do it," Zee said, her voice so weak it could barely be heard.

"Don't let the children see the body. Tell them that if they do see it, it will haunt them for the rest of their lives. It's very important that they don't see the body. If they do, they'll know that it isn't me, and it would ruin everything."

"All right," Zee said.

Jesse reached out for Zee, but she pulled away from him. "No," she said. "Don't kiss me, Jesse. Don't hug me; don't even touch me. I don't think I could stand it. Please just go. Go now."

Jesse looked at her for a long moment, then turned and walked out of the park, in the opposite direction from their house.

CHAPTER FOUR

Granbury—February 2, 1942

Jesse James stopped in the middle of his story, then got up and walked over to the window of Faust's hotel room. He looked down onto the traffic on West Pearl Street, at the white headlights coming one way and the red taillights going the other.

"Do you want to take a break here," Faust asked, surprised by the unexpected show of emotion.

"It's been sixty years," Jesse said. "You'd think that, after sixty years, it wouldn't mean anything to me."

"Mr. James—"

"Call me Jesse. It's been a long time since anyone has, and I'd sort of like to hear the name used again."

"All right. Jesse, as a writer, I well know that long buried emotions can reemerge, and when they do, they can be as strong as they were on the day they were planted in your soul."

"Yes. I loved her, you know. Oh, I've had another family since then, and I loved my second wife, Molly, and the children we had. But, talking about how it was when I had to leave Zee, well, it was harder than I thought."

"Do you want to call the whole thing off, Jesse?"

"No," Jesse replied. He closed his eyes and pinched the bridge of his nose for a long moment; then, dropping his hand, he looked straight at Faust. "No, I've lived a lie all these years, I think it is time I put things straight. I want to go on . . . I want to tell you everything."

"All right."

"Only there's too much to talk about in a hotel room. I've got me a nice little cabin down on the Brazos, along with an extra bedroom. Why don't you move in with me till the tellin' is all done?"

"Sounds like a good idea," Faust agreed.

"I've done my job, putting the two of you together," Sheriff Baker said. "I'll be leaving you two to work together. But if you need me for anything, just let me know."

"Thanks, Sheriff, for setting up the meeting," Faust said. He smiled at Jesse. "I think this may wind up being the most interesting project I've ever worked on."

The cabin on the Brazos—February 3, 1942

After breakfast the next morning, Jesse and Faust went out onto the porch. The Brazos River broke white over rocks in front of the cabin, and sun jewels danced on the rushing deep blue water. Jesse sat on a cushion on the porch and leaned back against the wall. Faust sat at a small table with a pencil and writing tablet. He had brought a cup of coffee out with him.

"Where do you want to start this morning?" Jesse asked. He asked the question between puffs as he lit his cigar. Soon a cloud of smoke rose around him.

"Let's start with where you left off," Faust suggested.

"Look here, Faust, some of these things I'm goin' to be tellin' you could get me in trouble," Jesse said.

"How? It's like you said, Jesse, there's been no paper out on you for sixty years."

"I've read up on it," Jesse said. "I know there's no statute of limitations on killing."

"That's true, but as far as anyone you might have killed during your outlaw days, well, those cases were all closed the day Bob Ford shot you, or, Bigelow. I wouldn't worry about those."

"I'm not talking about those cases," Jesse said.

"Oh? You mean you didn't leave your life of crime then?"

"It wasn't as easy as I thought it would be."

"I see."

"While I'm telling you my story, what would keep you from going into the law and giving me up?"

"Oran Baker is the law. He's the sheriff here, and he is your friend. If he planned to arrest you, don't you think he would have done it already?"

Jesse shook his head. "I'll be telling you things that not even Oran knows. I just need to know if I can trust you."

"You can start right now by telling me the last time you had to kill someone."

Jesse was silent for a moment. "I'd rather not say, at least not now. As I'm telling you my story, and when I get a bit more comfortable with you, well, any killin' I did since 1882, which is when the whole world thinks I was killed, I'd rather just let it come up in the story. Is that all right with you?"

Faust drummed his fingers on the table for a long time as he looked at Jesse.

"You said there is no paper out on you. But you also said that there is no statute of limitations on murder?"

"I wouldn't exactly call it murder," Jesse said. "I mean, it's not like I shot anyone in cold blood. It was more like self-defense."

"Jesse, you've been around long enough to know that killing someone in the act of a felony is first-degree murder, even if the killing is accidental. Say that you are in a shootout with the police, and one policeman accidentally shoots another policeman. You would be the one charged with that murder, even though you aren't the one who actually shot the police officer. A perfect example is the story you told me about Northfield. You said that Nicholas Gustavson was shot by one of the townspeople."

"That's right. Neither I nor anyone in my gang killed him."

Faust shook his head. "Technically, all of you are guilty of murder in Gustavson's case. He was killed during the perpetration of a felony."

"That doesn't seem right," Jesse said.

"It may not seem right, but it is the law. That one, you don't have to worry about, because like I said, it was closed when the world thought Jesse James was killed. Though, in truth, if your identity as Jesse James is established, beyond a reasonable doubt, even that case could be reopened. I just doubt that it would be."

"Yeah, well, I sort of knew that. About the law never forgetting about a murder, I mean."

"Jesse, at this point it is your call," Faust said. "I'm not going to physically tell anyone. But if you are going to tell me your story, your whole story, it's going to wind up in a book. When it does, it is likely to get the attention of the law. Especially since it will be events that happened in your current life. You see, the law won't care whether you are really Jesse James or not. They will only be interested in what you have done as Frank Alexander."

"I know, but I'm just going to have to take that chance," Jesse said. "I have a story that needs to be told, and I want you to tell it."

"All right." Faust picked up the pencil again. "Let's pick up from where you left off. Where did you go after you left Zee in the park?"

April 1882

Jesse had nothing with him but his guns, the clothes on his back, and three dollars in cash. He did have a fast horse, though, and he rode the horse at a gallop for the first four miles, then he walked him four miles, then ran him another four miles. Not until he had left the state of Missouri did he begin to ride at a more leisurely pace. He reached Lawrence, Kansas, just before nightfall the next day.

At first he felt a little hesitant about riding into Lawrence. He had been here before, with Quantrill during the Lawrence raid. But that had been nineteen years ago, and he hadn't been back since then. Also he had been much younger then and was but one of a large group of men. He was absolutely certain nobody would recognize him as Jesse James, and certainly not from having seen him during the Quantrill raid.

Jesse stopped in front of the hotel on Main Street. During the raid, Quantrill had recognized the proprietor as an old friend, and during the time his men were in town, Quantrill had remained in this very same hotel to protect him. Tying off his horse, Jesse went inside and looked around the lobby but saw nothing that he could remember from before.

"Yes, sir, do you need a room?" the clerk asked.

"I do, sir," Jesse replied. He started to sign his name as Thomas Howard but when he picked up the pen, he hesitated.

"Go ahead and sign in, sir. We have a room available."

"How much?"

"Fifty cents."

Jesse signed the register as William Clements, taking "Bloody" Bill Anderson's first name and "Little" Archie Clements's last name. These were two of the men he had ridden with, in addition to Quantrill.

"Where is the friendliest saloon?" he asked as he received the key.

"Why, just next door, sir, the Jayhawker," the clerk said.

Jesse felt a quick flash of anger. The Jayhawkers had been his bitter enemy during the war, and the idea of going into a saloon by that name didn't sit well with him. On the other hand, if he intended to completely disguise his identity, this might be the perfect place to start. He smiled at the clerk.

"Now, there's a good name if I ever heard one."

"Indeed it is, sir," the clerk replied.

Leaving the hotel, Jesse went into the Jayhawker and stepped up to the bar to order a beer.

"It come by telegram today," someone said. "The *Tribune* put it in the paper this afternoon. Jesse James is dead, shot down by one of his own, the story says."

"Well, good riddance, I say," one of the others replied. "It's just too bad it took so long to kill the son of a bitch."

"I don't know," another said. "He never done any of his robbin' or killin' here in Kansas. And they say he was mostly ag'in the railroads. Well, I ain't none too happy 'bout the railroads my own self. If they want your land, they just take it."

"What do you mean, he ain't never done nothing here? Are you forgettin' the time Quantrill come here? He left a hunnert and eighty dead, he did."

"That was Quantrill."

"Jesse James rode with Quantrill."

"Oh? I reckon I didn't know that. Anyhow, if he was just one of Quantrill's men, who would take notice of him?"

"Ha! I'll bet ole Marv Montgomery is glad Jesse James ain't here now," the first man said.

"Why's that?"

"Ain't you heard? He's got fifty thousand dollars in his bank right now."

"Lord all mighty, why's he got so much money?"

"The First Security Bank in Kansas City had a fire. Didn't burn down the buildin', but it did make a mess of things, and they've transferred all their money out to several different banks until they get ever'thing all cleaned up again. Marv says the money that he's holdin' will probably be here for near a month or so. The bank is makin' five hunnert dollars for holdin' it for 'em."

The next morning Jesse left the hotel before day-break. He rode out of town, then made a wide circle and came back into town from a different direction. He tied his horse off in front of the building that was next door to the Lawrence Trust and Savings Bank, then crossed the street and stood in the gap between two other buildings, all the while keeping his eyes on the bank.

Just before eight o'clock, he saw a man walk up to the front door and take a key from his pocket. Jesse crossed the street quickly, glancing both ways to see who might be out. He was happy to see that the street was deserted.

"Mr. Montgomery?" Jesse said as he stepped up onto the porch of the bank. "I'm glad to see you are opening the bank early. I've some business to conduct."

"I'm not open yet," he said. "The tellers won't be here until eight o'clock."

"Oh, we don't need any of the tellers for the business I have to conduct," Jesse said. He shoved his gun into the banker's side. "Let's go on in, shall we?"

With shaking hands, Montgomery opened the door, then stepped inside. He started to lift the shade.

"Leave the shade down," Jesse said.

"I'm afraid you are going to be disappointed. We are a small town; our citizens aren't wealthy people. We don't have that much on deposit."

"I tell you what. Let's not bother with any of your

depositors' money," Jesse said. "I wouldn't want to take anything from the poor people. I'll just take the fifty thousand dollars you are holding for the First Trust in Kansas City."

Montgomery gasped. "How did you know about that money?"

"Word gets around," Jesse said. "Just give me that money, and I'll be on my way. None of your depositors will be hurt."

"I can't give you that money. I've been entrusted with it. I gave them my word that I would keep it safe for them."

"Did you give them your word that you would die before you let it go?"

"What? No. Why would you say such a thing?"

"Because if you don't give me the money, I'll kill you." Jesse cocked his pistol, the hammer making a frightening clicking sound as it came back and the sear engaged the cylinder.

"No! Please, I have a wife and children!"

"Then you don't want to make your wife a widow and your children orphans, do you?"

"No."

"They are going to be if you don't give me the fifty thousand dollars."

With his hands shaking so badly that he could barely turn the combination lock, Montgomery got the vault open.

"There's all the money I have, take it, please take it," Montgomery said.

"I don't want all of it. I just want the fifty thousand."

Montgomery took out two cloth bags. "Here," he said.

Jesse smiled. "It's been very nice doing business with you. Do you have a telephone in this bank?"

"Yes."

"Where is it?"

"It is over there, on the wall." Montgomery pointed to the wall-mounted instrument.

Jesse walked over to the phone, then, using his knife, pulled the box away and cut the line.

"Now, I want you to lie down on the floor, face-down."

"Why? What are you going to do?"

"Nothing, if you behave yourself."

The banker lay down as instructed.

"Mr. Montgomery, I think you should know that my partner is on the roof, just across the street. He has a rifle and a very good view of this bank. The moment I leave, he is going to start counting. If he sees you come through that door before he gets to one hundred, he will shoot you dead. Do you understand that?"

"Yes," Montgomery replied in a small voice.

"I suggest that as soon as you hear the door close, you start counting. I take it you do have an extra key, because I intend to lock the door behind me as I leave."

"Yes, I have another key."

"Good for you."

Jesse draped his coat over his arm, effectively covering the two bank bags. He stepped outside, locked the door behind him, then mounted his horse and rode off.

The most money he had ever gotten in all his years as an outlaw was sixty thousand dollars from the Clay County Savings Association, back in 1876.

All of that money wasn't easily negotiable, and it had to be divided up among the entire gang.

This fifty thousand dollars was all his. It was enough to start a new life.

He thought about Zee and wondered if there was some way he could send some of the money back to her, but he knew it wouldn't be possible. Anyway, she wouldn't need it. Bob Ford was going to give her half of the reward money, and Zee was frugal enough that she would be able to make that money go a very long way.

CHAPTER FIVE

The cabin on the Brazos—February 3, 1942

"Did Bob Ford split the money with her?" Faust asked.

"No, the son of a bitch didn't give her one cent. Not only that, he went to New York and put on a play as to how he killed Jesse James. He became famous and made a lot of money, but still, he never gave Zee one cent."

"How do you know that? Did you get in touch with Zee?"

"No, I never did get in touch with her. I didn't find out that she didn't get any of the money until after she had already died. She wound up being kicked out of the house in Saint Joseph and had to go live with her sister in Kansas City. She sold a couple of old guns of mine and some of my clothes to folks who wanted them as souvenirs. But according to what I've read since then, when she was offered money to tell her story, she turned them down."

"She sounds like a good woman with a lot of pride."

"She was both, a good woman and she had a lot of pride. Like I said, I didn't find out until much later that Bob Ford never gave her any of the money he promised. And by the time I found out, Ed O'Kelley had already killed the son of a bitch. And of course, Charley Ford killed himself."

"Well, shall we pick up the story where we left off last night?" Faust asked.

"Where was that?"

"You had just stolen fifty thousand dollars from the Lawrence Trust and Savings Bank."

"Oh, yeah." Jesse smiled. "That was the easiest job I ever pulled, and it was for the most money."

Jesse continued on with his story.

April 1882

In Ellsworth, Jesse sold his horse and saddle, then bought clothes, a suitcase, and a valise. He put clothes in the suitcase and the money in the valise. He also bought "notions," bits of material, sewing needles, thimbles, and scissors, which he put into the valise to cover the money. After that, he bought a train ticket to Denver.

"We can check your luggage through for you, sir," the ticket agent said. "It'll be on the baggage car and you won't have to deal with it. It'll be there when you arrive."

"Oh," Jesse said. "Yes, I would like to check my suitcase through. But I'll hang on to my valise."

"It will be just as safe as your suitcase and there's no extra charge."

Jesse opened the valise to show its contents. "But this has all the tools of my trade," he said. "If I lose my clothes I can always buy more. But I'm a salesman, you see. And if I lose my notions, why, I may well be out of a job."

The ticket clerk chuckled. "I understand," he said. "You salesmen are all alike. None of you want your valise to get out of your hands."

Jesse was glad that his insistence on keeping the valise didn't come across as being odd. He wondered what the clerk would think if he knew there was fifty thousand dollars in the valise.

Jesse had intended to go all the way to Denver, but when the train stopped at a small town called Wild Horse, he saw a For Sale sign on the front of a gun store, and that gave him an idea.

"Conductor," he called.

"Yes, sir?"

"I bought a ticket all the way to Denver, but I want to get off here."

The conductor shook his head. "Well, of course you can get off here if you want to, but the railroad isn't obligated to return any funds from the unused portion of the ticket."

"That's all right; I'm not looking for that. But my suitcase is in the baggage car, and I would like to take it off here."

"Do you have your baggage claim?"

"Yes, I have it right here," Jesse said, showing it to him.

"Very good, sir, I'll hold the train long enough for you to get your suitcase. If, after you detrain, you'll step up to the baggage car, it will be handed down to you."

"Thank you," Jesse said.

Fifteen minutes later, Jesse was standing on the

depot platform with his suitcase in one hand and the valise in his other, watching as the train pulled away.

Turning toward the town he saw a hotel, so he walked across the street to register. He started to write the name William Clements, then stopped. There was a possibility that name could be associated with the bank robbery back in Lawrence, so he registered under the name he would use for the next sixty years.

J. Frank Alexander.

"What does the J stand for?" the clerk asked, looking at the book.

"I don't know," Jesse said. "My mama never told me."

The clerk laughed. "Very good, sir. How long do you plan to stay?"

"It depends on whether or not the gun store owner and I can come to an arrangement."

"An arrangement?"

"As the train came into town, I saw a sign that said the store is for sale. It is still for sale, isn't it?"

"Oh, yes, sir, indeed it is," the clerk said. "And Miz Collins is most anxious to sell."

"Mrs. Collins? You mean the gun store is owned by a woman?"

"Yes, sir. Well, it is now. She's the widow of Ken Collins, you see. He died last month, he did. It was the damndest thing. I mean, he was just walkin' down the street 'n fell dead. The doctor said it must've been his heart, but there didn't anybody ever have any idea of him ailin' or anything."

"The heart is a mysterious thing," Jesse said.

"Here is your key, sir. You are in room two oh two.

It's at the top of the stairs on the right, in the very front. You'll have a nice view of the town."

"Thank you," Jesse said. He saw a pile of newspapers on the counter, and he stepped over to look at it.

"I see there's a newspaper in this town."

"Yes, sir, the *Wild Horse Times*. It's quite a nice paper, too, with not only local news, but news from all over."

"I can see that," Jesse said.

OUTLAW JESSE JAMES KILLED BY MEMBER OF HIS OWN GANG.

Shot Dead While Hanging a Picture.

Widow Grieves.

"I guess it is a good thing that outlaw is dead," the hotel clerk said. "But you can't help but feel sorry for his widow, finding him dead in their own living room."

"Yes," Jesse said without further comment.

Jesse took the key from the clerk, then went up to his room. There, he took five thousand dollars cash from the valise, then hid the valise behind the armoire. From the hotel he went straight to the bank, where he stood politely in line until it was his time at the teller window.

"Yes, sir, how can I help you?"

"I recently sold my business back in Kentucky and thought I would come west to buy another. I would like to deposit what I got from the sale of my property, which is five thousand dollars"—he took the money from his jacket pocket and put it in front of the teller—"and ask if you have any idea what the owner of the gun store is asking for that business."

"Oh, I have a very good idea, since we hold the mortgage," the teller said. "She is asking three thousand dollars."

"How much is the mortgage?"

"Well, normally I would say that I shouldn't answer that question. But if you are serious about buying the business, I suppose you have every right to know. After all, it wouldn't do for you to buy the business, only to find out that you still owed a great deal on it, would it?"

"That's why I have asked."

"She owes one thousand two hundred and seventy-five dollars. So the purchase price of three thousand dollars is fair."

"Thank you. I would like to buy the note."

"Oh, sir, I'm not sure I can do that."

"Sure you can; banks sell notes all the time."

"Come over to my desk, Mister, uh, I didn't catch the name," another man said. Jesse had seen this rather officious-looking man when he first came into the bank, and he had a feeling he would wind up talking with him.

"Alexander," Jesse said. "J. Frank Alexander."

"My name is Brown, Douglas Brown. I own this bank, Mr. Alexander, and I couldn't help but overhear your conversation. You want to buy the store from Mrs. Collins, do you?"

"I will, if I can come to some sort of agreement with the owner. Mrs. Collins, you said?"

"Yes, Molly Collins. And you think that if you hold the note, that she'll be easier to convince?"

"Yes. At least, I hope so."

"Mrs. Collins has been a very good and valued customer. I would not like to see anyone take advantage of her."

"I assure you, Mr. Brown, that I have no intention of taking advantage of her. If I buy the store, I plan to make my home in this town. It wouldn't be good business for me if people thought I had cheated a widow, now, would it?"

"Indeed it wouldn't," Brown agreed. "I'm glad you are of that opinion."

"Since we are being honest with each other, I would like to ask about the store. Does it do a good business? Would I be smart to buy it?"

"Mr. Alexander, she is asking three thousand dollars. I must tell you that I advised her to ask thirty-five hundred dollars because it is worth that, and more."

"Good," Jesse said. "I thank you for your honesty, sir."

"I believe you said you would like to open an account with us?"

"Yes, for five thousand dollars."

"I'll be happy to open an account for you, Mr. Alexander. And I'll also sell you Mrs. Collins's note."

With the account opened, and the note in his hand, Jesse went down to the gun shop. The first thing he did was remove the For Sale sign, so that when he walked in, he was holding the sign in his hand.

"What are you doing with my sign?" a woman asked.

The woman had clear blue eyes, auburn hair,

high cheekbones, a smooth, clear complexion, and full lips. This couldn't be Collins's widow, could it? Collins had dropped dead in the street. Jesse had assumed that meant he was a relatively old man. This woman was young, younger even than Zee.

"Are you Mrs. Collins?"

"I am Molly Collins, yes. And I'll ask you again, what are you doing with my sign?"

"The sign says this place is for sale. I want to buy it."

"Three thousand dollars," Molly said.

"I'll give two thousand dollars for it."

"That's not enough. I need three thousand."

Jesse smiled, then showed her the note. "I'll give you two thousand dollars, and this note."

"You . . . you bought my note from the bank?"

"I did."

"And you are willing to give me two thousand dollars and the note?"

"Yes, I am. But on one condition."

"What condition is that?"

"That you stay on for at least sixty days, until I'm sure I've got the hang of running this store. I'll be happy to pay you a salary to do so."

Molly looked at him with a confused expression on her face. "Mister, I don't want to take advantage of you."

"Take advantage of me? What do you mean?"

"I don't know if you can cipher or not, but if you give me two thousand dollars and the note, you will be giving me more money than I'm actually asking for."

"Yes, I know."

The confusion on Molly's face turned to a big smile, and she stuck her hand out.

"Mister . . . ?"

"Alexander. J. Frank Alexander."

"Mr. Alexander, you have just bought yourself a gun store," she said.

"And hired a store manager?"

The smile turned to a little laugh. "Yes. And hired a store manager."

Tuesday, July 4, 1882

Jesse very much missed Zee and his children. But almost as much as he missed them, he missed the very act of having a family. He knew, also, that if he had a wife and a family, that it would be much less likely that anyone would ever be able to find out his true identity.

After three months of working with Molly, he decided that if he was going to take another wife, she was the one he wanted. Molly was a very pretty woman, prettier even than Zee, though he felt a little guilty about thinking that. Like such a thought would be a betrayal.

Jesse thought about it long and hard before he asked Molly to marry him. Technically, he knew that he couldn't marry her, because he was still married to Zee. On the other hand, he was legally dead, and though he wasn't actually dead, he told himself, in all probability, that meant his marriage with Zee had been dissolved as surely as if there had been a divorce.

He also wondered if he should tell Molly his real name. He decided not to, because he didn't want to burden her with that knowledge. Also, he wasn't sure how she would take being married to an outlaw, especially an outlaw with the reputation of Jesse James.

Molly accepted his proposal, and they decided to get married on the Fourth of July.

"Damn, Frank," Sheriff Wallace said. "The Fourth of July is Independence Day. Why are you choosing that day to give up your independence?" He laughed at his own joke, and Jesse laughed with him.

Sheriff Wallace was a good customer of the gun store, and Jesse recognized the advantage of making friends with the law. He had even allowed himself to be sworn in as a deputy on a couple of occasions.

CHAPTER SIX

Sheriff Wallace, his wife, and several other businessmen of Wild Horse gave up a part of their Independence Day celebration to attend the wedding. And now, as firecrackers popped in the street, Jesse and Molly stood before Father Gordon Prouty, the priest of Holy Spirit Episcopal Church of Wild Horse.

Jesse listened to the priest drone on through the litany of matrimony, then Father Prouty looked up from the prayer book he was holding.

"I require and charge you both, as thee will answer at the dreadful day of judgment when the secrets of all hearts shall be disclosed, that if either of you know of any impediment why ye may not be lawfully joined together in matrimony, ye do now confess. Far be well assured, that if any persons are joined together otherwise than as God's word doth allow, their marriage is not lawful.

"Frank, wilt thou have this woman, Molly, to be thy wife? Wilt thou love her, comfort her, honor, and keep her in sickness and in health; and, forsaking all others, keep thee only unto her, so long as you both shall live?"

Jesse hesitated. It wasn't Molly he was seeing, it was Zee, and he saw her as clearly as he had that last day, standing in the park back in St. Joseph, Missouri. If he was going to say anything, if he was going to confess who he was, this was the time and the place to do it, because after this moment it would be too late.

As the delay in his response stretched on, the smile on Molly's face faded, to be replaced by a look of concern and confusion.

"Frank?" Father Prouty prodded.

"What? Oh, sorry. Yes, of course I will," Frank said, smiling at Molly.

Molly's return smile was one of relief.

"Molly, wilt thou have this man to thy wedded husband, to live together after God's ordinance in the holy estate of matrimony? Wilt thou obey him, and serve him, love, honor, and keep him in sickness and in health; and, forsaking all others, keep thee only unto him, so long as you both shall live?"

"I will."

"Join your right hands together."

Jesse turned toward Molly and took her hand in his.

"I declare you man and wife. Those whom God hath joined together, let no man put asunder."

As if on cue, several firecrackers went off outside, just in front of the church. Jesse, dropping Molly's hand, spun toward the front door, his right hand moving quickly to his side, as if reaching for the pistol that wasn't there.

Sheriff Wallace laughed. "Whoa, hold on there, Frank. You're a little jumpy, aren't you?"

Jesse laughed. "I guess I am," he said.

"Come on, folks, we're goin' to have a wedding party for these good people down at the hotel," Seth Parker said. Parker owned the hotel.

From the *Wild Horse Times:*

Wedding on Independence Day

Wild Horse's newest businessman, J. Frank Alexander, married Molly Collins on July 4. The wedding was well attended by all the businessmen of the town.

It was widely thought that when Ken Collins died, the gun store he had begun would go out of business. But to the satisfaction of all who would prefer to do as much of their business in Wild Horse as is possible, Mr. Alexander arrived from his former home in Paducah, Kentucky, bought the store from Ken Collins's widow, and continues to operate it. His extensive knowledge of firearms has been of great benefit to all the citizens of the town.

He kept Mrs. Collins on to help him, and soon, nature took its course. Mr. and Mrs. Frank Alexander are now the newest married couple in our rapidly growing city.

Wild Horse, Colorado—September 1892

Not long after Jesse and Molly were married, Jesse had a house built for them. In one room of the house, he had the carpenter build a setback in the corner, telling him it was for a piece of furniture he was going to buy. Then, claiming he had changed his mind, he had the carpenter take out the setback. The result was a double wall, and that was where he hid the remainder of the fifty thousand dollars he had stolen. Nobody, not even Molly, knew of that money, and over the next ten years he finally managed to get it all into his account at the local bank, making periodic deposits of the stolen money, along with the money his store earned. On a couple of occasions he made deposits that were clearly larger than his earnings from the store, but he convinced Molly, and the banker, that the money was the result of betting on horse races.

Molly had given him two children, twin sons, whom Jesse named William Anderson Alexander, and Frank James Alexander. Though they were twins, they had very different personalities. Billy was the more daring of the two and more apt to get into trouble. He was often a truant, and Jesse, half in jest, and half serious, posted an advertisement in the *Wild Horse Times*.

One Gallon of Black Strap
M O L A S S E S
To <u>anyone</u> who can keep
My son, BILLY, in school
Long enough to advance
To the next grade.
~J. Frank Alexander

Frank, on the other hand, was always on the straight and narrow. He never disobeyed his parents or his teacher, he made very good grades in school, and he was well liked by everyone.

"Oh, why can't Billy be more like you?" Molly asked Frank Jr. one day after Billy had broken a neighbor's window by using a sling to throw a rock.

"Mom, you know that colt that Pa bought? He was hard to break but once he was broke, he was a real good horse."

"Once he was broken," Molly corrected.

"Yes, ma'am. Well, Billy is like that. Yeah, he does things that he ought not to do. But I think that's just because he is young."

"You're twins, Frank. You're both the same age."

"No, we aren't. I was the first one born, that's what you 'n Pa said. That means I'm older."

Molly laughed. "I suppose that's true."

Molly shared with Jesse the conversation she had had with Frank.

"Billy reminds me of myself when I was his age," Jesse said. "I wouldn't worry about him; he's not even nine years old yet. He'll come around. Look at me, I'm a legitimate businessman now."

"I can't help but worry about him. I do wish he would settle down and be more like his brother."

"Give him some time."

Molly sighed. "There's nothing else I can do but give him time, is there? All right, I'd better get to work. I have to get the order filled out for some more ammunition. You know where I'll be if you need me."

Molly kissed him, then went into a small room at the back of the store. They used this room, which wasn't accessible to the customers, as the store office.

Shortly after Molly left the front of the store, the bell on the door tinkled as Sheriff Wallace stepped into the gun shop. Jesse was standing at the workbench in the back of the shop working on a rifle, the pieces of which were spread before him. He looked up as the sheriff came in.

"Hello, Larry. What can I do for you?"

"There was a bank that was robbed up in Mirage this morning," Wallace said. "I just got a telegram that said the bank robbers are more 'n likely heading this way. I'm getting some men together, and I'd like to deputize you."

"All right," Jesse said. "Molly's in the back; let me yell at her so she can mind the store."

Half an hour later Jesse joined the sheriff and five more men to go out in pursuit of the bank robbers. Jesse couldn't help but sense the irony. Here he was, part of a posse, when there were so many times in his past that he had been the pursued and a posse had been the pursuer.

"You got 'ny idea where to look for 'em, Sheriff?" Lindell, one of the members of the posse, asked.

"We got word from someone that they saw four men going into Twin Peaks Canyon."

"Whoa, hold it," one of the others said. "There's four of 'em goin' to be holed up at Twin Peaks, and we're goin' after 'em with just six men?"

"What's your problem, Sarno? There are six of us, only four of them."

"But they'll be there, hidin' behind the rocks in

the canyon. Don't you see? They'll have the advantage. We need more men."

"How many more men?" Jesse asked.

"I'd say at least four more. I mean, without at least ten men, we don't have a chance against 'em."

"A posse that large is hard to handle," Sheriff Wallace said.

"And we may as well be ringing cowbells to tell them where we are," Jesse said. "With a posse that large, all we would do is scare 'em off. We wouldn't have a chance in hell of actually capturing them."

"How would you know?" Sarno asked.

"I've been around a few posses," Jesse replied without being more specific. "Six people is all we'll need."

"Yeah?" Sarno replied. "Well, six may be all you need, but five is all you're goin' to have. 'Cause I ain't goin' with you."

The posse members had been inside the sheriff's office, and they looked on as Sarno walked out.

"Then we'll do it with five," Wallace said. "Unless some more of you decide to leave."

"I'll stay," Lindell said.

One by one the others made the commitment to stay.

"All right, stop by Suzie's Café; I've already made arrangements for her to make lunches for us. Also, make certain that you have water and ammunition." Sheriff Wallace looked over at Jesse. "I'd say twenty rounds each, at the county's expense. Can your store handle that?"

"We can handle it," Jesse said.

* * *

Two hours later, Sheriff Wallace halted the men at the beginning of Twin Peaks Canyon.

"Damn," he said.

"What is it?"

"I think Sarno may have had a point. If we start into this canyon, they'll have cover and position on us. If they start shooting at us, we won't have any maneuvering room. We'll just be hanging out there."

"I've got a suggestion," Jesse said.

"Any suggestion is welcome."

"Suppose I go this way"—he pointed up—"around the mountain."

"Over the top? That's a mile high."

"Not over it, just around it. If I'm lucky, I can get down into the canyon behind them."

"You want someone to come with you?"

"No, if there are two of us that just doubles the chances of being discovered. I'll go alone. Give me about half an hour, then start into the canyon. Make as much noise as you can going in."

"Why would we want to do that?" Wallace asked.

"I know what he means," Lindell said. "If we make enough noise, it will draw their attention toward us and give Frank a better chance of getting in behind them without being seen."

"Exactly right," Jesse said. "Larry, will you keep up with my horse? I'm going to have to do this on foot."

"All right," Sheriff Wallace agreed.

Jesse climbed up the side of the east mountain of Twin Peaks, figuring that the higher he went, the less distance he would have to cover in circumnavigating the mountain. He climbed about a thousand feet, then started working to his right, which he knew would eventually take him all the way around.

At first he could only move by going sideways, finding hand- and footholds wherever opportunity presented them. Then, as he was reaching for a handhold, a rock dislodged underneath and, losing his footing, he began sliding down. The mountain wasn't a perfect cone, and he knew that within another few feet he would go over the edge, then fall several hundred feet to the valley floor below.

At the last minute he managed to grab hold of the trunk of a small but sturdy juniper tree. He hung there for a second, looking down to the ground, far below.

"Damn, that would be something," he said aloud. "All the times I've been shot at and hit, to wind up falling off the side of a mountain?"

Catching his breath, Jesse managed to pull himself up, then finding foot- and handholds he climbed until he found a narrow ledge. The ledge was still not big enough for him to walk on, but it did provide a solid and continuous path for him to work his way around. Then, halfway around the mountain he came upon a trail that would let him walk standing up.

After that he was able to move easily and quickly. He worked his way all the way around the mountain until he heard the exaggerated sound of the others coming in through the front of the canyon.

"Here them sons of bitches come!" someone said, and looking toward the sound of the voice he saw four men in position behind a rock ledge.

"Soon as we see 'em, we start blastin'," another voice said.

That voice caught Jesse by surprise. He could almost swear he had heard it before.

The sound of the posse coming in grew louder, and the waiting outlaws stared toward the point where they would first see the posse.

The distraction worked perfectly, because none of the outlaws saw Jesse walking up behind them. When he got to within fifty feet of them, he called out.

"Drop your guns, and throw up your hands!"

"What the hell!" one of the men shouted.

All four turned and started shooting. But Jesse was already set and aiming. He fired three quick shots, and three men went down. The fourth man threw down his gun and put his hands up.

"Don't shoot! Don't shoot!" he shouted in panic.

The expression of panic in his face turned to one of shock.

"Jesse? No! It can't be! You're dead!"

"Hello, Pete. I didn't expect to see you here. You're getting too old for this sort of thing, aren't you?"

Pete was Pete Arnold, who had ridden with Quantrill and, at one time, with the James-Younger gang.

"My God! It is you! But how is that possible? The whole world thinks you're dead. You was kilt by Bob Ford ten years ago!"

"As you can see, I wasn't."

"But how—?"

"It's a long story. But now we have a problem. You are right, the whole world thinks I'm dead. But now you've seen me, and you know that I'm not. Bud, I can't have anyone know that I'm still alive. You are a danger to me."

Jesse pointed his pistol at Arnold and cocked it.

"Jesse, for God's sake, you ain't goin' to shoot me, are you? I mean, me 'n you rode together with

Quantrill, Anderson, even Little Archie. I ain't goin' to tell no one, I swear I won't."

Jesse lowered his pistol and pinched the bridge of his nose.

"All right," he said. "I'm just going to have to trust you. Go on, get out of here."

"Thanks, Jesse. You won't regret this," Arnold said. He reached for the money bag from the bank robbery.

"Leave that," he said.

"The hell you say. I risked my life for this money. I ain't goin' to just leave it here."

"You've got no choice, Pete. Leave it, and go now. Hurry up, before the rest of the posse gets here."

"The rest of the posse? Wait a minute, are you telling me that you're ridin' with a posse?" He laughed. "Who would've ever thought that Jesse James would be ridin' with a posse?"

"We don't have time to gab, Pete. Hurry up, go, before they get here!"

Jesse looked back toward the curve in the canyon, and that was when Arnold made his move.

"I ain't leavin' the money!" Arnold said, shooting at Jesse. Arnold missed. Jesse returned fire and didn't miss.

Arnold slapped his hand over the wound in his chest, then went down.

"Pete! Why the hell did you do that?" Jesse asked, running to him. "I told you, you were free to go!"

"I had to try, Dingus," Arnold said. "I had to try." He gasped once more, then died, taking his last breath just as Sheriff Wallace and the rest of the posse came riding up.

"Damn!" Sheriff Wallace said. "You did all this?"

"I didn't have any choice," Jesse said. "There's the bag from the bank."

"All this for three hundred dollars," Sheriff Wallace said.

"What?" Jesse asked, looking up in surprise.

"Three hundred dollars. That's all the bank said they got away with."

CHAPTER SEVEN

The cabin on the Brazos—February 5, 1942

"Damn, if I had known that was all the money he got, I would have let him take it," Jesse said to Frederick Faust. "It still bothers me that I shot him."

"The way you're telling it, Jesse, you had no choice. He took a shot at you," Faust said.

"I had a choice," Jesse said. "I could have let him take the money. I should have let him take it."

"That was a long time ago," Faust said. "It's as I told you, I know how verbalizing all of this now can bring it back as real as if it is actually happening at this very minute. You've had to relive the Northfield Raid, leaving Zee, and now, having to kill an old friend. I've no doubt but there will be many more incidents like this, so it's up to you whether or not we go on. But I have to tell you, you've got me into the story now, so I hope that you agree to continue."

"Yeah," Jesse said, "well, I want someone to know. And I need to get it all out. I figure it's a little like pickin' a boil. It hurts while you're doing it, but after, it feels a lot better."

"Picking a boil. Yes, that's a good analogy. I'm glad you feel that way," Faust said. He stood up and walked to the edge of the porch, looking down at the Brazos River. "What kind of fish are in the river, there?" he asked.

"Buffalo, bass, bream, and catfish. Lord, I've seen catfish taken out of there that are five feet long."

"Zane Grey was quite a fisherman, you know," Faust said.

"I didn't know that. I've read some of his books. I like yours better. His books are a little too—"

"Mushy?" Faust asked with a chuckle.

"Yeah."

"He was pretty sensitive about that. But there's no denying his success. He died a few years ago, and I miss him."

"I would think that, what with the two of you bein' Western writers 'n all, that you'd not get along."

"You mean because of competition?" Faust asked. He shook his head. "No, it doesn't work that way. There are a lot of stories to be told, and not that many of us who can write them. We're sort of a close colony because of that. Besides, our readers feed off each other. If they like reading one of us, they tend to want to read others. I see you have a boat, so do you ever go fishing?"

"Not as much as I used to."

"Let's go fishing and see if we can catch something for supper. I'm somewhat of an amateur cook. If we catch something, I'll cook it. And the break will be good for you. You can catch up on your thoughts."

"All right," Jesse said. "I'm having to furnish the

boat; I guess I'm going to have to furnish the tackle as well."

"Unless you want me to drive back into town so I can buy my own."

Jesse chuckled. "No need for you to have to do that."

They caught two bass and three bream, and while Faust was frying the fish for their lunch the next day, Jesse read the paper.

From the *Hood County Herald:*

JAP FLEET WIPED OUT AT BALI ISLAND

ONE SHIP ESCAPES, NIP MEN ISOLATED

(by the ASSOCIATED PRESS) Dutch and American air and naval forces destroyed and scattered the entire Japanese invasion fleet, which invaded Bali last week. Some of the invaders have succeeded in getting ashore, overrunning part of the island and seizing the airport.

"Damn, this war's going to be over before I can get in it," Jesse said. "Why do you suppose it's taking the army so long to get back to me? I know I can teach those soldier boys a few things, if they would just let me."

"I don't think the war is going to be over all that quickly," Faust said.

"But look here, it says the whole Jap fleet was wiped out."

"It also says that the Japanese overran the island and seized the airport. It seems to me like the articles are being written to put a good face on things. I think that's wrong. I think the articles ought to be truthful. And they should be more personal. They should tell the stories of Seth and Tom and Bill and John, the average soldiers who are fighting this war. I think the people at home can handle the truth, and I think they should see what their sons, husbands, and brothers are doing." Faust laughed. "Excuse me, Jesse. It would appear that I climbed up onto my soapbox there."

"Yeah, but I think you're right. You're a writer. After you get through writing this story about me . . . why don't you go over there and write about our army?"

"You know, I just may do that," Faust said.*

"Say, this fish is pretty good," Jesse said. "You know, if this writing business doesn't work out for you, you could always be a cook. I bet there are a lot of outfits that would sign you on in a heartbeat."

"You think so?"

"I'm sure they would."

---

*When World War II began, Frederick Faust did become a war correspondent, despite being well into middle age and having a heart condition. Like Ernie Pyle, Faust became a favorite of the soldiers with whom he served. Then, on May 12, 1944, while with American soldiers fighting in Italy, Faust was mortally wounded by shrapnel. He was personally commended for bravery by President Franklin D. Roosevelt.

Faust chuckled. "I'll keep that in mind. But what do you say after we eat this fish, that we get back to work?"

"All right. I'm going to jump ahead quite a few years, though, if you don't mind."

"That'll be fine. You're the one that's telling the story."

Chandler, Oklahoma—1895

The town of Wild Horse was losing population rapidly, so rapidly that Jesse was unable to find a buyer for his gun store, so he closed it down. He still had some money left, though, enough to start a farm if he could come by the land. Then he read in the paper about the Kickapoo Land Rush in Oklahoma, said by the article to be the last land rush to be held for the fertile land in Oklahoma.

That was what brought him here, just outside the town of Chandler, at five fifty-five in the morning on Thursday, May 23, 1895. The rush was due to start at six a.m. and in preparation for that, Jesse and his twelve-year-old twins were all three mounted on horses. Molly was driving a wagon, loaded with the things they would need to start their new home. Each person, sixteen and older, could claim one hundred and twenty acres of land. Jesse, Billy, and Frank were each going to make a claim. They planned to get around the age limit, if anyone questioned them, by saying that their father had claimed the land and they were just holding it for him while he went back to get their mother and their belongings.

"Remember, we have to have the land next to each other or it won't work," Jesse explained.

At one minute until six o'clock, a soldier carrying

a bugle came out of the Chandler land office. He raised his pocket watch, examined it until just the right moment, then he lifted the bugle to his lips and played "Charge," the notes rising loud and clear in the quiet morning air.

By the time the last note was sounded, the morning air was no longer quiet. It was filled with the thunder of hoofbeats, and the squeak, creak, and rattle of rapidly pulled wagons, buckboards, surreys, and buggies. *Hurrahs* and shouts came from hundreds of voices, and within seconds nothing could be seen but a towering cloud of red dust.

Billy was a better rider than Frank Jr., and because he was lighter than Jesse, he started out ahead.

"Billy!" Jesse called out to him. "Hold on there; we can't get separated! If we do, our plan won't work!"

"Well, Pa, tell Frank to hurry up! He's holdin' us back!"

Jesse had been in this part of Oklahoma before, and he knew the perfect spot for a land claim. It was on Warwick Creek, and last night he had drawn a map for Billy and Frank, showing them where to go. Knowing exactly where to go gave them an advantage over ninety percent of the rushers, because most of the people who were participating were from all over the nation, some even from other countries, and they had no idea what they were looking for.

It took less than half an hour for them to reach the creek. Once there, Billy went west, Frank went east, and Jesse staked out the land in between. All three of them pitched tents, then settled down to make their claim.

Shortly after Billy pitched his tent he threw out a

blanket and sat down on it to wait. Half an hour later, a rider came up to him. He had a scraggly beard, a dirty face, a scar that pulled his mouth to one side, and a cleft upper lip. He rode up to Billy, then spit a wad of tobacco onto Billy's tent.

"You spit on my tent," Billy said. "What did you do that for?"

The man wiped his mouth with the sleeve. "Get on your way, boy," he said. "I'm a' claimin' this here land."

"You can't claim it," Billy said. "I'm already here."

"That don't mean nothin'. Now get on your way, like I told you to."

Billy shook his head. "Like I told you, I'm already here."

"Boy, are you tryin' to tell me you're sixteen? 'Cause I know damn well you ain't."

"It don't matter how old I am," Billy said. "I'm holdin' it for my pa. You don't have to be any certain age to hold it for your pa."

"If you don't get offen this land right now, I'm goin' to throw you off," the man said, dismounting and starting toward Billy. "You can't be a' holdin' it for your pa, or anyone else. If you ain't old enough to claim the land, then you ain't old enough to hold it for nobody, neither. You ain't old enough for nothin'."

Billy pulled a pistol from under the blanket and pointed it at the man, cocking it as he did so.

"How old do I have to be to kill you?" he asked, his voice amazingly calm, considering his age and the circumstances.

"What?" the bearded man asked, throwing his

arms out in front of him. "Hold on here, boy! You better put that gun down now, I'm tellin' you."

"I'll put the gun down as soon as you ride away from here," Billy said.

Startled, and clearly frightened by the turn of events, the bearded man remounted.

"All right, all right, I'm a' goin'," he said. "I doubt this land would raise much more'n rocks anyway."

Billy kept the pistol out until the man was out of sight.

One week later Jesse went into the land office in Chandler, where he filed on all three claims, showing receipts where he had bought the two adjoining claims to his property. There, too, he bought the lumber, glass, and roof tiling he would need to build a house, and he hired some carpenters. Within two months they had a three-bedroom house, a barn, a machine shed, and an outhouse.

Jesse didn't get a crop in until next spring. Frank developed quickly into a very good farmer, but Billy clearly had no interest in it. He found every excuse he could to avoid work, and while Jesse and Frank could plow an acre and a half in one day, it was all Billy could do to bring in half an acre.

"I wish Billy could be more help to you," Molly said as the two of them lay in bed one night. "I feel bad about you and Frank working so hard while Billy is doing so little."

Jesse chuckled. "Don't be too hard on him, Molly. Farming isn't for everybody. The truth is, he reminds me a lot of myself when I was his age, back in Missouri."

"Missouri? I thought you were from Kentucky."

"We moved to Kentucky after my pa died and my ma remarried," Jesse said, recovering quickly.

"Frank Alexander, we've been married for more than thirteen years, and this is the first time I've ever heard you say that you were from Missouri."

"I never told you that?"

"No, you never did."

"Didn't I? Well, my memories of Missouri aren't all that good. Like I said, my pa died there, and my ma tried to make a go of the farm. That's what I meant when I said it reminded me of the time I was in Missouri, no more than a boy, trying to make a living on a piece of worthless dirt."

"Where in Missouri did you live?"

"Ke . . ." Jesse started to say Kearney, but that was where Jesse James was from, and he wanted to keep Molly as far away from that as he could. "Kennett," he said.

"Kennett?"

"It's a little town down in southeast Missouri, in an area they call the Bootheel." Jesse had ridden through Kennett once and remembered how much like Kearney it was. "You can't blame me for never mentioning it to you before. Like I said, when I think of it, all I can remember is dirt and hard work."

"If your memory of farming is all that bad, why did you want to come here to farm?"

"What else were we going to do, Molly? Wild Horse was a dying town. I wouldn't be surprised if it would just go away within another few years."

"I hate to think that. Ken was so proud of that town. Now he, and several others, lie buried back there in a graveyard that nobody will ever tend or visit."*

"You really loved that town, didn't you?"

"I loved it while it was a town. Everyone knew each other; it was almost like we were one big family. I think it was coldhearted of the railroad to kill the town the way they did."

"I'll take you back there one of these days, Molly," Jesse said.

"You aren't just telling me that, are you, Frank? I know there's nothing left there, but I would like to go back someday."

"I'll take you back. I promise," Jesse said.

The cabin on the Brazos—February 7, 1942

"Did you ever take her back to Wild Horse?" Faust asked.

"Yes, I took her back."

"I'm sure she appreciated it."

"I'm sure she would have."

"Would have?"

"I'm sorry to say that I never got around to taking her back until after she died," Jesse added.

"Oh, I'm sorry."

"Thank you. That was forty years ago. I lost both of my wives that year."

"You married again?"

"No. I'm talking about Zee."

---

*Today, Wild Horse is an unincorporated community and a U.S. Post Office in Cheyenne County, Colorado. A few of the structures still stand. It is being preserved as a genuine ghost town.

CHAPTER EIGHT

Wild Horse—1902

Although the train no longer made a regular stop at Wild Horse, arrangements could be made in advance for it to do so. Jesse made those arrangements before they left Oklahoma City, and now he, Billy, and Frank Jr. were looking through the window of the car as the train slowed to a stop. The little white sign on the eave of the roof of the deserted depot was hanging by one end so that to read the name of the town, WILD HORSE, one had to turn their head sideways.

"It sure looks deserted, doesn't it, Pa?" Frank asked.

A gust of wind came up, blowing a bouncing ball of tumbleweed down the middle of the street.

"Yes, it does."

"You know what, Pa? I'm glad Ma never got back. I think it would break her heart to see the town like this," Frank said.

Jesse reached over and squeezed Frank's shoulder. He knew that Frank knew that he was feeling guilty for never bringing Molly back, as he had promised. He knew, also, that Frank was just trying to make him feel better about it.

"You the folks that's wantin' to get off here?" the conductor asked, coming into the car.

"Yes," Jesse said.

"Well, you'd better hurry on off. Your baggage is being set down now. We've got a schedule to keep, and stopping in every little jerkwater town doesn't help any."

The three stepped down onto the platform and stood there as the engine's relief valve opened and shut, venting steam with a loud rush as if it were breathing from the exertion of the run.

The door to the baggage car slid open, and some- one from in the car stepped up to the edge, then squirted a stream of tobacco juice over the side.

"Someone here waitin' on a coffin?" the baggage car man asked.

"Yes."

The reply didn't come from Jesse, or either of his sons. Before leaving Oklahoma City, Jesse had contacted Gene Welch in Mirage, and it was he who responded to the question. Welch, who owned a mortuary in Mirage, had once been the under- taker in Wild Horse. But, like all the other business owners, he had left when the town died.

Welch had brought his hearse down from Mirage, along with a grave digger. It was the driver of the hearse and the grave digger who hopped up into the car to retrieve the casket.

"You boys go help them," Jesse said, and Billy and Frank climbed up into the car. As they were off-loading the casket, Welch came over to speak to Jesse.

"My condolences for your loss, Frank," he said. "Those were your boys that climbed in to help?"

"Yes."

"My, my, how they have grown! Why, they are men now."

"Yes, they are," Jesse said. "And they have been a great help to me on the farm."

"I can certainly believe that. Oh, I haven't made any funeral arrangements," Welch said. "You gave me no specific instructions, so I didn't know but what you might have already had her funeral."

"That's all right," Jesse said. "We just want to get her buried, and then get back to Oklahoma."

"I believe you said you wanted her grave next to that of her first husband?"

"Yes. She never forgot him, and I never held that against her. He was her first husband, and from what the people of the town told me about him, he was a fine man."

"Yes, he was."

"I think that burying her by him would be the right thing to do. I do know that she wanted to come back to Wild Horse one day."

"Well, the grave has already been opened, and I see that the coffin is loaded onto the hearse, so if you're ready, we can get on with it. I brought a brougham as well, so we can all ride to the cemetery."

As the carriage rolled through the main street of Wild Horse, Jesse looked at all the boarded-up buildings.

"Look, Pa," Frank said, pointing to one of the buildings. "There's our old store."

The building, which had been built of brick, was more substantial than most of the others. It had a diamond formed of stone on the false front, just above the porch roof.

Dunnigan's Grocery was still open, Glen Dunnigan being able to remain in business because of the forty or so people who still lived in town, and an equal number who lived in the country around Wild Horse.

Dunnigan, and at least twenty more people, were at the cemetery when the hearse and brougham arrived.

"I didn't think there would be anyone here," Jesse said, surprised by the turnout.

"It's only been seven years since you left," Welch said. "You and Molly haven't been forgotten. And Molly was just real well thought of, even before the two of you got married. I hope you don't mind that they showed up."

"No, I don't mind. I'm glad there are folks who still remember her."

Dunnigan and his wife, Louella, came over to greet Jesse as he stepped down from the carriage.

"Hello, Frank. It's good to see you again, though I sure wish it could be under better circumstances."

"Hello, Glen, thanks for coming out. I see your store is still here."

"I'll hang on as long as any part of the town remains. The people who are still here will need some way to get their groceries. I don't know how much longer that will be, though. The Union Pacific taking us off their regular stop has just about insured that the town won't last much longer."

"Hello, Frank," another man said, stepping up to extend his hand.

"Sheriff Wallace," Jesse said.

Wallace shook his head. "I'm not a sheriff any longer. Wild Horse doesn't need a lawman, and I'm too old to get on anywhere else."

"Nonsense, you aren't that much older than I am."

"Let's just say that I'm old enough not to want to go chasing outlaws anymore, or even lock up drunks. I'm a night watchman at the mill in Mirage. It's a real easy job just perfect for me."

"Thank you for coming, Larry. I appreciate that."

The mourners moved over to the open grave, and the coffin was lowered into the ground.

"Pa, wait," Frank Jr. said. "Don't you think somebody ought to say something?"

"Like what?" Jesse asked.

"I don't know, but it seems to me like somebody ought to say something."

"Would you like to?"

Frank swallowed, then nodded his head.

"All right, son. Go right ahead."

Jesse took his hat off, and all the other men present followed suit. Billy didn't at first, though he did after a stern glance from Jesse.

"We're buryin' my mom today," Frank began. "When I think of her, from now on, and for the rest of my life, I'll always see her workin'. The earliest thing I can remember is her bringin' me 'n my brother into the shop and puttin' us down somewhere, while she did whatever work there was that needed doin' whether it was waitin' on folks, or workin' on the books, or just sweepin' and cleanin' the place. Same thing ever we left here and went to farmin' down in Oklahoma. I don't reckon I ever knew that farmin' was as hard for the women as it is for the men. But Ma was always cookin', bakin', mendin', washin' clothes, and keepin' the house and the yard cleaned and took care of. It's hard for me to imagine her dyin', because to be honest, I didn't think she'd ever take the time it needed to die. She always had somethin' to do.

"And yet, for all the work she did, she was always there for Billy 'n me. If we tore a hole in our clothes, she patched 'em up. If we got a cut, she'd clean it 'n bandage it." Frank smiled. "And when we was both young, she'd kiss whatever was hurtin' on us and make it feel better.

"We've been down in Oklahoma for seven years now, but I want you good folks here to know that Ma never forgot you. She used to talk about this town, and the people that lived here, as if we were just visitin' down in Oklahoma and would be comin' back home soon."

Frank looked down toward the coffin, shining black in the bottom of the open grave.

"Well, Ma, you're home now. You're home in Wild Horse, and you're home with the angels. And don't you worry none about havin' to learn to be an angel. The Lord won't have to be trainin' you, none at all. Ever'one that has ever known you, knows that you're already an angel. You were an angel for your entire life."

Frank looked over at Jesse.

"That's all I got to say, Pa."

"That's all that needs to be said," Jesse replied. "You did a real good job."

"Yes, you did, son," Welch, the undertaker, said. "I've heard a lot of people say a few words at the grave, but I swear to you that I've never heard anyone do a better job."

Jesse looked over at Billy and was pleased to see that even he was moved by Frank's words, so moved that he had to wipe away a tear.

All the others who had come to the cemetery came by to extend their condolences, and wish Jesse, Billy, and Frank well.

As the others left, Billy went over to look at the tombstone for Ken Collins.

KENNETH R. COLLINS

BORN AUGUST 15, 1835
DIED FEBRUARY 10, 1882

*A Union Soldier in
Our Time of Peril*

"This was Ma's first husband?"

"Yes."

"But you never met him, did you?"

"No."

"Says here he was a Union soldier. I don't recall Ma ever sayin' anything about that."

"Maybe it was because she knew I fought for the Confederacy."

"What did you do for the South?"

"Nothing much. I was just a soldier. Come, we need to get back to the depot in time to catch the train."

Glen and Louella Dunnigan, as well as a few of the other people of the town, came down to the depot to wait for the train with Jesse and his two sons.

"You didn't have to come down here, Glen," Jesse said.

"It's no problem seeing you off. Besides, I like the idea of the train stopping here for any reason. It reminds me of a time when this town was alive and we actually thought it was goin' someplace."

"Oh, you poor, motherless children," Louella Dunnigan said, approaching both Frank and Billy to give them a hug. Frank accepted it graciously, but Billy turned away from her.

Seeing that, Jesse frowned at him.

"Oh, you're not too old for a hug," Louella said, and, under Jesse's admonishing glance, Billy allowed the woman to pull him into her oversized breasts.

"Here comes the train," Dunnigan said.

The train was approaching at its top speed, and for a moment or two Jesse was afraid that the word had not reached the engineer and that the train wasn't going to stop.

But as it drew closer, he saw steam being vented through the drive cylinders, and he knew the throttle had been closed. Then he heard the squeal of the brake pads being applied to all the wheels, and the train rumbled into the defunct station, then came to a stop. The conductor stepped down.

"We have a special pickup here?" he called.

"Yes, sir," Jesse said. "That would be my boys and me."

A porter also detrained and picked up their luggage. Jesse shook hands with Dunnigan, then he, Billy, and Frank boarded the train.

They found a seat on the depot side of the car, and they waved again at the people who had come to see them off.

"You didn't want to be hugged?" Frank Jr. teased Billy as the train pulled away.

"No."

"Why not? She has big boobs, and I thought all men like big boobs on a woman," Frank asked with a laugh.

"Those aren't boobs, they're pillows," Billy replied.

"Boys, you ought not to talk about that nice lady like that," Jesse said, but he could scarcely contain his own laugh.

CHAPTER NINE

With the stops, and changing trains, the trip back home would be almost thirty hours. They left Wild Horse at six o'clock that evening. Jesse bought seats in the sleeper car so that, between Wild Horse and Salina, Kansas, they would have berths. They were scheduled to arrive in Salina just after seven the next morning, and reach Chandler by six on the second night out.

It was at lunch in the dining car the next day that Jesse dropped a fork onto the floor, and he reached for it just as someone was walking by. The man tripped over Jesse's foot and nearly fell.

"Watch where you're putting your foot, you clumsy son of a bitch!" the passenger said loudly, and angrily.

"I'm very sorry, sir," Jesse said meekly.

"You damn sure are sorry. You are about as sorry a bastard as I've ever seen. I ought to knock you on your ass."

"You speak to my pa like that one more time and you'll be the one who is going to get knocked on his ass!" Billy said. Standing up, he took a step toward the man.

"Billy, sit down," Jesse said.

"Pa, he ain't got no right talkin' to you like that," Billy said.

"Please, Billy, sit down," Jesse said again.

"You need to get a halter on that boy," the man said angrily.

Jesse smiled at him. "Again, let me apologize for my own clumsiness and my son's action."

"Mister," one of the other passengers said to the loudmouth, "sure 'n if the lad doesn't knock you down, I will. Now, this gentleman has very graciously apologized to you, so would you be for doing us all a favor now and close that mouth of yours, and sit down."

"Yeah? And who the hell are you to tell me to sit down?" the belligerent passenger demanded.

The other passenger removed the napkin from his neck, set the fork down, and stood. He was a big man.

"The name, lad, would be Jim Corbett. And who might you be?"

Realizing that he was talking to the former heavyweight boxing champion of the world, the belligerent passenger turned and left the dining car without another word. The other diners laughed.

"I hope you didn't mind my butting in, sir," Corbett said to Jesse. "And may I congratulate you for the gracious way you dealt with that unpleasant gentleman."

"I didn't mind at all," Jesse said. "I thank you for taking a hand in this."

Corbett nodded and returned to his table.

"Wow," Frank said a moment later. "Pa, that's Gentleman Jim Corbett!"

"We didn't need him," Billy said. "I could have handled him."

"I'm sure you could," Jesse said. "But it is always best to avoid a fight when you can."

"I bet you have avoided a lot of 'em, huh, Pa?" Billy said with contempt.

"Billy!" Frank said. "You got no right to talk to Pa like that."

"I'm not hungry," Billy said. "I think I'll go back to the car."

The Alexander Farm near Chandler, Oklahoma—October 1902

Jesse should have realized something was up when Frank started volunteering more and more often to go into town to pick up seed and animal feed at McGill's Feed and Seed Store. In fact, it became more than merely volunteering; Frank began suggesting that they needed more feed, or seed, even when Jesse knew full well that they didn't.

"They've got this new feed now for cows," Frank said. "It's alfalfa that's been coated with molasses. Maybe I ought to go pick up a bag."

"For heaven's sake, Frank. Cows will eat grass, and you want to feed them alfalfa with molasses?" Jesse asked.

"Well, it might make the milk taste better," Frank suggested.

"The milk tastes good enough as it is."

Billy laughed. "Pa, I can't believe you haven't seen it. Or at least figured it out."

"Seen what? Figured what out?"

"Well now, you remember the harvest dance last month? The one that was held in the Dunn Hotel?"

"Yes, I remember. What about it?"

"Didn't you notice who that girl was that Frank danced with just about ever' dance? And didn't you see the way they were making eyes at each other? Like this?" Billy stuck his head forward and opened his eyes wide.

"You mean the little . . ." Jesse started, then he stopped. "It was Horace McGill's daughter, wasn't it? What's her name?"

"Ethel Marie," Frank said. "Pa, don't you think that is just the prettiest name you ever heard?"

Jesse chuckled. "Alfalfa with molasses, huh?"

"Yes, sir."

"Well, we don't need any of that. But I reckon you could go into town tomorrow and get a couple of blocks of salt lick."

Frank smiled broadly.

"Yes, sir, I surely will."

Chandler—March 1903

"Do you want another biscuit, Frank?" Ethel Marie asked. She and Frank had been married for three months.

"Yes, thank you."

"Me too," Billy said.

Smiling, Ethel Marie put another biscuit on both their plates.

"Pa, I was thinking, we can put all cotton north of the creek and wheat south," Frank said.

"I don't know why you put wheat in at all," Billy

said. "You get three times more from cotton than you do wheat. Why not just put in all cotton?"

"Because cotton wears out the soil," young Frank said. "You have to rotate the crops or pretty soon you won't be able to grow anything at all."

"That don't make no sense to me at all. Dirt is dirt, no matter what you grow in it."

"Frank's right," Jesse said. "I'm not sure I understand why, but if you don't rotate the crops around some, the dirt seems to wear out, somehow."

"Well, it don't make me no never-mind anyway, 'cause I'm not farmin' anymore."

"What do you mean?"

"I'm leavin', Pa. This farm isn't big enough to support all of us, especially now that Frank has got married. More 'n likely they'll be havin' kids, then the farm will have even more to support. Besides which, he's a lot better farmer than me anyhow, so, I'm goin' to give him my part of the farm."

"You don't have to do that, Billy," Frank said.

"Yeah, I do. Me 'n you are different, Frank. You like all this farmin', and I don't think I can stand one more day of it." He stood and looked over at Jesse. "I'm leavin', Pa."

Jesse nodded. "All right," he said. "I want you to write out that you're leaving your part of the farm to Frank. I don't want you comin' back on him later, if things don't work out for you."

"I'll do that."

"Billy, I'll buy your part, you don't have to give it to me."

Billy shook his head. "I ain't done nothin' to earn it. You don't have to buy it."

"All right, then, at least let me give two hundred

and fifty dollars; that's all the cash on hand I have now."

"I'll give you another two hundred fifty," Jesse said. "That'll give you a little traveling money. Where are you going?"

"I don't know. But I'll write."

"Billy, take Dancer," Jesse said.

"That's your horse, Pa. I don't want to take your horse."

"Dancer is a good horse, and if you're going out on your own, I'd feel a lot better if you were well mounted."

"Are you sure?"

"Do you not want Dancer?"

"Are you kidding? I'd love to have Dancer. He's a great horse."

"Then I want you to have him."

"Pa, Frank, I don't know what to say. I mean, here you both are, being so good to me 'n all, 'n I thought when I told you what I was wantin' to do that you'd both try and talk me out of it."

"Would it do us any good to try and talk you out of it?" Jesse asked.

Billy smiled self-consciously. "No, sir, it wouldn't have done you no good at all, 'cause what I would have done is, I would have just left in the middle of the night."

"With no money and a lame horse," Jesse said.

"Yeah," Billy said, his smile turning into a self-conscious laugh. "I would have done just that."

"Wait until morning. You may as well leave with a good breakfast in your stomach."

"I'll make pancakes," Ethel Marie promised.

* * *

The next morning, Jesse, Frank, and Ethel Marie stood on the front porch as Billy led an already saddled Dancer around from the barn.

"Billy, you be careful," Ethel Marie said. "I never had any brothers or sisters until I married Frank. Now that I've got a brother, I sure wouldn't want anything to happen to him."

"I'll be careful," Billy promised. He swung into the saddle. "Uhm, uhm, I ate so many pancakes, I'm just about goin' to make poor old Dancer swayback."

"It'll be a long time before you have another breakfast that good," Frank said.

"You're right about that," Billy said. Then, with a wave, he turned Dancer and rode at a trot down the lane, not looking back once.

"You think he'll be all right?" Ethel Marie asked, her voice reflecting her worry.

"He'll be fine, Ethel Marie," Jesse said. "I've known lots of men like Billy. They have a way of taking care of themselves."

Chandler—March 1904

It was the middle of the night when Jesse was awakened. "Pa! Pa, wake up!"

"What? Who is it?" Jesse asked groggily.

"It's me, Billy."

Jesse sat up and lit the bedside lamp.

"Billy? Boy, you've been gone for a whole year

without one word, and you show up here in the middle of the night?"

"I'm in trouble, Pa."

"What kind of trouble?"

"I, uh, I held up a grocery store. And now the law is after me."

"A grocery store? You held up a grocery store?"

"Damn, I should 'a known better than to come here. You always have been a . . . a goody two-shoes." Billy turned toward the door.

"How much did you get?" Jesse asked.

Billy stopped.

"You heard me. How much did you get?"

"Thirty-six dollars."

"Thirty-six dollars," Jesse scoffed. "Tell me, Billy, just how much did you expect to get? If you're going to rob some place, seems to me like the least you could do would be to rob some place that has money. Why on earth would you hold up a grocery store?"

"I don't know. I didn't have any idea how much I would get. All I knew is that I needed money."

"Did you kill anybody, Billy? Did you kill somebody for thirty-six dollars?"

"No, Pa, I swear. I didn't kill nobody. I didn't even hurt anybody."

"Why did you come here, tonight?"

"I thought maybe, that is, I was hoping that maybe you could give me a little money, enough to get out of Oklahoma anyway."

Jesse walked over to the chest, pulled open the top drawer, and pulled out some money.

"Here's two hundred dollars," he said.

"Pa, you don't need to give me that much, all I need is—"

Jesse raised his hand to cut him off.

"Go to Dallas, Texas," he said. "Check in to the Cattleman's Hotel and wait for me."

"Wait for you? What for? Pa, you don't need to waste your time on me. Just give me the two hundred dollars, and I'll be out of your hair."

Billy reached for the money, but Jesse pulled it just out of his reach.

"Do you want the money, Billy?"

"Well, yeah. I mean, yes, sir."

"Then do what I said. Go to Dallas, check in to the Cattleman's Hotel, and wait for me."

"Wait for how long?"

"It'll take me a couple of weeks to get things turned over to Frank. Surely two hundred dollars is enough for you to get by for that long. You just wait on me."

"All right, Pa. I'll wait."

"Do you still have Dancer?"

"No, I, uh, well, I had to sell him."

"I figured as much. How did you get here?"

"I paid a freight wagon driver ten dollars to bring me to Chandler, and I walked out here from town."

"Take a train to Dallas. Now, get on with you."

"I was thinking maybe I could stay here for the night, and—"

"No," Jesse said. "I don't know yet how seriously anyone is looking for you. But I don't want Frank and Ethel Marie to be involved."

"All right, Pa."

"You've got enough money to get a Pullman berth. You can rest on the train."

"I'm kind of hungry."

"We had ham and biscuits for supper. Leftovers are under a cloth on the kitchen table. Come with me; I'll stand by while you make yourself a sandwich."

CHAPTER TEN

"Frank, I'm going to be leaving here in a couple of days," Jesse said over breakfast the next morning.

"Leaving? Where are you goin', Pa?"

"I'm not sure. I just want to do some traveling around. The thing is, I'm signing the farm over to you, lock, stock, and barrel."

"You don't have to do that, Pa. Heck, I'll keep things going here. And I'll bank your share when I get the crop in."

"You don't understand, son. I'm not going to be here to get the crop out, and I'm not going to be here for the harvest, so I won't have a share. It's all yours," Jesse said. He looked over and smiled at Ethel Marie, who was feeding the baby. "Besides, you'll be needing more money, what with the baby and all. You can handle the farm by yourself, can't you?"

"Well, yes, sir, I'm sure I can."

"I'm sure you can as well."

"You'll keep in touch with me, won't you, Pa?"

"I'm not very good at writing letters, Frank, I never have been. But, from time to time, I'll write."

"That's more than we can say for Billy. We haven't heard a thing from him from the moment he left."

"Maybe I'll try and find him," Jesse said.

"If you do, you'll let me know if he's all right, won't you, Pa?"

"I'll let you know," Jesse said.

Eight days later, Jesse checked into the Cattleman's Hotel in Dallas.

"Frank Alexander," the clerk said as he read the registration book. "That's funny."

"Funny because you have another Alexander registered here?" Jesse asked.

"Yes. How did you know?"

"Because Billy Alexander is my son. What room is he in?"

"He's in room three twelve. If you would like, I can put you in three fourteen, which is next door to him."

"Yes, thank you."

Jesse did not go to room three twelve right away. Instead he went to his own room and changed clothes. No longer wearing the three-piece suit he had worn on the train, he was now wearing blue jeans, a denim shirt, and a belt with two holsters and two pistols. Stepping next door, he knocked lightly on the door.

"Who is it?" a muffled voice called from the other side of the door.

"It's your pa, Billy. Open the door."

The door opened. "I waited here for you just like you—" Billy started, then seeing the way his father was dressed, he stopped in midsentence. "Pa, why are you dressed like that?"

"I've come to take you to school," Jesse said.

"School? Pa, what are you talkin' about? I don't have enough education to go to college. I never got beyond the eighth grade, and at my age, I sure don't plan on ever goin' back. I'm damn near twenty-two years old."

"That's not the kind of school I'm talking about. Get your gun and come with me."

"My gun?"

"You haven't hocked it, have you?"

"No, I've still got it."

"Then strap it on and come with me."

"Come with you where?"

"Out to McKamy Creek. I'm going to teach you to shoot."

Billy laughed. "Pa, come on, really? *You* are going to teach *me* to shoot?"

"I was in the war, remember."

"Yeah, I know you've said that. But I wasn't always too sure you were telling the truth. I mean, sure, you were probably in the war, but I always figured that maybe you took care of the horses, or something."

"Or something," Jesse said. "Speaking of horses, I know you said you sold Dancer. Have you got another one?"

"He's in the hotel stable. Same as yours, I reckon."

"I don't have a horse; I left everything with Frank. Let me take a look at your mount."

Billy led Jesse to the stable, where he examined

the horse's feet and legs. He also looked into the animal's mouth.

"No," he said. "He won't do."

"What's wrong with Patch? He's a good horse."

"You think he could do fifty miles in a single day?"

"I don't know."

"I do know. He can't."

"Well, why would he have to?"

"You never can tell. The time might come when we'll have to cover fifty, maybe even sixty, miles in one day. You need another horse."

"Pa, even with the money you gave me, I don't have enough to buy another horse."

"I do," Jesse said.

An hour later the two men, having ridden out on the just purchased horses, were standing alongside McKamy Creek, a quickly flowing stream just north of Dallas. It was an ideal place to practice shooting, as it was over five miles from downtown.

"Let me see you shoot," Jesse said. "I want to know what I'll be working with."

"What do you want me to shoot at?"

"I'll let you pick your own target," Jesse said.

"All right. Look over there. Do you see that can?" Billy asked, pointing to a rusty can on the other side of the stream. "I'll shoot it."

Billy pulled his pistol, raised it to eye level, aimed, and shot. He hit the can and turned toward Jesse with a broad smile on his face. "What do you think about that?"

"You took too long," Jesse said.

"What do you mean, I took too long? I aimed at it; I hit it. What more do you want?"

"You don't always have time to aim," Jesse said. "Most of the time you just have to pull your gun and fire."

"What good does it do to pull your gun and fire if you can't hit anything?"

"Oh, I'll hit something," Jesse said.

"All right, pick the target. Let me see you pull your gun, fire without aiming, and hit something," Billy said with a challenging smile.

There were a couple of dragonflies hovering about four feet over the edge of the opposite side of the creek.

"See those snake doctors?" Jesse asked, pointing.

Billy laughed. "Don't tell me you are going to try and shoot one of those."

"I'm not going to shoot one of them," Jesse said.

"I wouldn't think so. You couldn't, even if you did aim."

"I'm going to shoot both of them," Jesse said.

"Wha—" Before Billy could get the word out, Jesse drew both pistols and fired. The two dragonflies disintegrated right before Billy's eyes.

"Damn!" Billy said. "How the hell did you do that?"

"Point your finger at me," Jesse said.

"Why?" Billy replied, pointing his finger even as he asked the question.

"How did *you* do *that*?" Jesse asked. "You didn't raise your hand and aim your finger at me."

"No, I didn't have to. I just knew where you were and where my finger was pointing."

"That's how I shot the dragonflies."

Billy shook his head.

"I'll never be able to do that."

"Sure you will," Jesse said.

"Shoot snake doctors out of the air?"

"Maybe not that. But before we go back to the hotel today, I'd be willing to bet that you can put more holes in that can, without aiming."

"I never thought I'd be able to do that," Billy said that evening over supper in the hotel dining room.

Once again, Jesse was wearing a suit.

"You're not very good at it yet," Jesse said. "But I have no doubt that as I work with you, you will get better."

"You know what really surprises me is that you can do that. I mean, I've never known you as anything but a . . . pardon me for sayin' it, Pa, but sort of a milksop kind of a guy. I mean, well, you remember the time on the train when that man tripped over you. It was his fault, but you apologized to him."

"It doesn't hurt to be nice to someone," Jesse said. "And it isn't always good to let people know who you are."

"Ha! You say that, but as soon as Jim Corbett said who he was, that man sure turned and ran away, didn't he?"

"I reckon he did."

"Didn't you feel embarrassed by that, Pa?"

"No."

"Not even a little bit?"

"No, not even a little bit. Did you feel embarrassed?"

"Yeah, I did."

"Why?"

"Why? Because you are my pa, and that man was having his way with you."

"He just thought he was. Being embarrassed about something is just a waste of time."

"I don't know. I guess I just thought you should have done something."

"Billy, if I had gotten into a fistfight with that man, I would have been beaten up."

"There, you see what I mean? And you don't think that would have been embarrassing?"

"No, because I would not have gotten into a fist-fight with him."

"What if Jim Corbett hadn't been there? And what if I hadn't been there? What if it had been just the two of you, and being nice to him wouldn't stop him? What would you have done then?"

"I would have killed him," Jesse said calmly.

"What?" Billy's eyes narrowed as he stared across the table at his father, as if seeing him for the first time. "Pa, are you serious? You really would have killed him?" he asked in a quiet voice.

"Yes."

"Have . . . have you ever killed anyone before?"

Jesse picked up the menu. "Look, they've got black- and blueberry cobbler. I know it isn't as good as the cobbler your ma used to make. But I bet it'll be good enough. What do you say we have that for dessert?"

Billy nodded, knowing that Jesse wasn't going to answer his question.

"You're right, it won't be as good as Ma's. But let's try it anyway."

CHAPTER ELEVEN

Every day for two weeks, Jesse and Billy went out to McKamy Creek to practice shooting. Before long, Billy could shoot at a can, or a rock, or a tree, and hit it, even without taking specific aim at it.

"What do you think, Pa?" Billy asked after they concluded one of their shooting exercises. "I'm getting pretty good, huh?"

"Passable," Jesse answered. "Let's get back to town."

The two men mounted and started out, with Jesse in the lead. A short distance after they got under way, Jesse left the trail.

"Pa, where you goin'? Town's that way," Billy called to him.

"Just follow me, and do what I do," Jesse said.

Shortly after turning off the trail, Jesse broke into a gallop, and Billy had no choice but to match his pace. After about two minutes at a dead gallop, Jesse stopped, dismounted, and led the horse into some grass. There, after leading the horse for a few minutes, he remounted and made a big circle, not getting out of the grass for about a mile. Then, he turned back, crossed the trail and the tracks they had left earlier, and continued to ride for at least a mile before turning back to retrace the path they had taken at a gallop. Then, turning off the trail again, he started back toward Dallas, rejoining McKamy Road about three miles from the creek itself.

"What was all that about?" Billy asked as he moved up to ride alongside Jesse. It was possible to ride alongside him on the road, though it hadn't been possible to do so on the narrow trail.

"Someone was following us," Jesse said.

Billy turned in his saddle. "I didn't see anyone. Who was following us?"

"It doesn't matter whether you saw anyone or not," Jesse said. "As far as you are concerned, from now until I tell you otherwise, someone is always following us."

"Oh," Billy said. "Oh, yes, I see what you mean."

"Do you? Because it might save your life someday."

"Yeah, Pa. I see," Billy said.

"You need to know how to build a fire," Jesse said a few days later.

"Pa, I can build a fire."

"All right, make a fire, right now."

"I don't have any matches."

"Have you ever eaten a rabbit raw?"

"What? No! Why would I want to eat a raw rabbit?"

"Well, if you don't know how to build a fire without matches, the day may come when you have to eat a rabbit, or a squirrel, or a bird, raw. And I can tell you for a fact, raw game isn't very tasty."

"You mean you've eaten raw rabbit?"

"Yeah."

Billy laughed. "So you can't build a fire, either, without matches, can you?"

"Didn't say that. I just said that I ate raw rabbit. It wasn't that I couldn't build a fire, it was because at the time, it just wasn't convenient to build a fire."

"Do you have matches now?" Billy asked.

"No."

"Can you build a fire?"

"Yeah, I can build a fire. What you need is a spark, something to catch the spark, wood, and air. Gather some dry grass and little pieces of dry sticks. Then a few larger pieces of wood so that once the fire starts, there will be something to burn."

It took but a minute to get everything gathered.

"A match is the easiest way to start a fire, and when we start out on our adventure, we'll always have matches with us. You can also use flint and steel. That works, but it isn't really all that easy."

"You've built a fire with flint and steel?"

"I've built a fire by rubbing a stick in a hole, dug out of a piece of wood," Jesse said. "And that's even harder to do."

"You said you don't have any matches, so how are you going to build a fire?"

"Next to having a match, this is the easiest way," Jesse said. "And you'll more than likely always have this way with you."

"What way is that?"

"Just hold your horses and I'll show you," Jesse said.

Jesse took a round from a cylinder chamber of one of his revolvers. Removing the bullet, he poured half of the gunpowder onto the little pile of tinder, then he tore a little piece of cloth from his hand-kerchief and stuffed it back into the cartridge. Replacing the cartridge in the chamber, he held the gun over the powder and tinder, and fired. The little piece of cloth came out burning. Jesse bent over quickly, shielded it from the wind, then started dropping sticks onto it until it was a pretty good blaze. He put on larger, and gradually larger sticks, until finally he added a substantial piece of firewood.

"There," he said with a smile. "We won't have to eat our rabbit raw."

"What rabbit?"

Jesse lay back and, lacing his hands behind his head, smiled up at Billy.

"Why, the one you're going to bring to cook," he said with a broad smile.

An hour later, having finished their meal, Jesse put out the fire.

"Are we goin' back to the hotel?" Billy asked.

"Not yet."

"When are we going back?"

"I'll be going back this afternoon. Whenever you get back depends on you."

"What do you mean?"

"You've got more schooling to do."

It was almost two hours later when Jesse dis-mounted. He had been leading Billy's horse. Billy was mounted, but his hands were tied to the saddle horn and there was a blindfold around his eyes.

Walking back to his horse, Jesse untied Billy's hands. "All right, you can take off the blindfold."

"You didn't have to tie my hands to the saddle, Pa. All you had to do was tell me not to take off the blindfold."

"I was just keeping you away from temptation is all." Jesse slipped Billy's rifle from its scabbard. "Climb down," he said.

"Now what?" Billy asked as he rubbed his wrists.

"You can go back to the hotel now."

"Good." Billy started to remount.

"No. I'll ride, and I'll take your horse. You're going to walk back."

"Walk back? How 'm I goin' to do that? I don't know how far it is. I don't know where it is. I don't even know in which direction I'd need to start out in."

"You'll figure it out."

"What if I don't figure it out?"

"If you haven't shown up at the hotel in three days, I'll come find you."

"What if you can't find me?"

"Then you'll be on your own," Jesse said.

"Pa, that ain't right. I could die out here."

"You're right. Get mounted, and we'll go back."

"Good. They're havin' roast beef at the hotel tonight."

"Oh, we aren't goin' to the hotel. We're goin' back to Chandler, and the farm. Only thing is, the farm isn't ours anymore, so I reckon that means we'll both be working for Frank."

"Pa, no! You know I won't do that! I can't do that!"

"Yeah, to tell the truth, boy, I don't want to do that, either," Jesse said. "But it's either that, or you let me continue to teach you."

"Teach me what?" Frank said. "I mean, I know, you've taught me how to shoot, 'n how to make a fire, but what's all this leadin' to, Pa?"

"Billy, you're the one that chose the owl hoot trail."

"The owl hoot trail?"

"You're wantin' to be an outlaw, aren't you?"

Billy grunted what might have been a laugh. "Yeah," he said. "I guess I do."

"If you were to ask me, I'd tell you don't go down that trail. But you're a man now, full grown, and my telling you isn't going to make that much difference. So, if you're bound and determined to do this thing, the least I can do is teach you enough to keep alive. Now, are you going to listen to me, or not?"

"All right, I'll go along with it," Billy agreed reluctantly. "But, don't you even have any instructions for me? Are you just going to cut me loose like this?"

"You'll need water," Jesse said. "First thing you need to do is find a stream."

"How do I do that?"

"Animals need water, and they'll always go toward it. Use them as a guide, and listen for it. Most water in the wild makes a noise that you can hear. And if it is a fast-flowing creek or river, why, you can sometimes hear it from a mile away. You can smell it, too."

"How do you smell water? Water don't have no smell."

"You can smell fish, and you can smell wet wood, and grass."

"Yeah," Billy said with a grin. "Yeah, you can, can't you?"

"All right, I'm going to leave you now. Billy, if you survive this on your own, you'll be ready for just about anything. If you don't survive it"—Jesse smiled—"well, if you don't survive it, it won't make much difference, will it?"

Despite himself, Billy chuckled.

"I guess you're right, Pa."

"I'll see you in three days."

Jesse put Billy's rifle back in the saddle scabbard.

"Ain't you goin' to leave me my rifle?"

"Nope. It'll just get in your way," Jesse said as he swung into his saddle. "Remember, boy. Find the water."

Billy watched Jesse ride away.

"Find the water," Billy repeated aloud.

"Water. My canteen!" Billy realized then that his canteen was hanging from his saddle.

"Pa!" he called. "Pa! My canteen!"

His pa didn't answer.

For a moment, Billy felt panic, then he closed his eyes and pinched the bridge of his nose. He wasn't going to do himself any good scaring himself to death.

He took a deep breath, let it out slowly, then decided to take stock of the situation. The first thing he needed to figure out was which way it was to the hotel.

Which way was north?

Looking around, Billy saw nothing but trees and low-rising hills. Climbing up to the top of one of the hills, he saw that the sun was directly overhead. That didn't help a whole lot, but at least he knew that he didn't have to wait too long before the sun would show him which way was west. And if he could find west, he could find the other directions.

Not that that would do him any good. What difference did it make if he knew which way was north if he didn't know which way it was to town?

The overhead sun was blistering hot, and the land was radiating the heat back up from the ground. Billy was getting very thirsty, and he believed most of it was because he was just thinking about it.

The vegetation was dry and brown, and as he looked around, waiting for the sun to start its afternoon slide, he saw a little strip of green snaking its way through the brown. For just a moment the sight puzzled him; then he realized what it was.

"Water!" he said aloud. "Glory be! I've found water! And I didn't have to follow any animals or smell it!" He started toward the strip of green.

He could hear the water before he reached it.

"Pa was right," he said. "You can hear the water."

Then he was there, and nothing had ever looked more beautiful to him. Lying down on his stomach, Billy lowered his lips into the water, then sucked it up in big gulps.

"Ha! No wonder he said find water," he said aloud. This, he decided, was McKamy Creek. All he had to do was follow it to where he and his pa had been earlier in the day, then it wouldn't be that much of a walk back to the hotel.

One hour later, he realized he had made a mistake. This creek had run into another creek. Had he gone the wrong way? Was this new creek McKamy? Or was it another creek altogether?

He ate nothing the first day and, because he didn't want to lose the water, spent the first night on the bank of the creek. He thought about making a fire but decided to wait until he had something to cook.

The next afternoon, he managed to snatch a fish up from the water. For a moment or two, he was puzzled as how to cook it. He had no skillet with him. Then he decided to lay it open into two halves, skewer them from head to tail, then put them close to the fire. Soon the air was permeated with a most enticing aroma.

About four hundred yards away from where Billy was cooking his fish, Jesse was watching him through a pair of field glasses. He had kept Billy under observation from the moment he rode off the day before. He put the glasses down.

"Well, I'll tell you this, Billy," Jesse said quietly, "you're eating better than I am."

Jesse took out a piece of jerky and began to eat. In anticipation of this very exercise, he had packed enough in his saddlebags to sustain him for the three days he had allowed.

It didn't take three days. Billy followed the new creek east for a while, then he saw something that gave him a big smile. It was the rusted-out tin can he had shot the first day he and his pa had come out. He knew exactly where he was, and he started south, toward Dallas.

CHAPTER TWELVE

The cabin on the Brazos—February 24, 1942

"Did he ever find out that you had been keeping an eye on him?" Faust asked.

"No, I thought it best not to let him know that," Jesse replied. "At least not then. There was a time, some later, when I let him know what I had done."

"How did he take it?"

Jesse chuckled. "It was long enough later that he laughed about it."

The two men had been sitting at a table in a kitchen that was filled with the aroma of Jesse's cooking. "I'd say it smells like it's about done."

Jesse walked over to the stove and stirred something in the pot. "Oh, yeah," he said. "It's done."

"I'm just here to do your story," Faust said. "You don't have to feed me."

"I learned how to make chicken and dumplin's from my ma," Jesse said as he began spooning them onto Faust's plate. "Zee could make them, too, but Molly never got the hang of it."

Not until both plates were piled high did Jesse take his seat across the table from Faust. He put so much pepper on the dumplings that they were covered with little black specks.

"You told your son you were going to take him to school, and I see now what you meant by that," Faust said. "You were conducting the school yourself. Did you say you were teaching him how to be an outlaw?"

"Yeah, that's what I was doing, all right," Jesse replied. "Want some pepper?"

"No, thanks. You're serious, aren't you? You really were teaching him how to be an outlaw."

"Remember, the boy had already robbed a grocery store. Who robs a grocery store, anyway? You take a chance on somebody shooting you, all for thirty-six dollars? That made absolutely no sense at all."

"Jesse, excuse me for bringing this up. But didn't you get your men all shot up in Northfield for ten dollars less than your son got from robbing the grocery store?"

"I reckon you got me on that one, Fred," Jesse replied. "But the difference is, thirty-six dollars is all there was in that grocery store. The bank in Northfield had a lot more money than that; we just didn't get it is all."

"Yes, I can see the difference. I suppose you do have a point there."

"Anyway, I decided to teach Billy everything that I knew, from shooting, to how to live out in the woods when you're on the run, to how to plan a holdup. And, when you do plan one, plan one that is going to be worthwhile. I mean, why steal thirty-six dollars, when for the same amount of risk, you could steal thirty-six thousand dollars?"

"That makes sense. In a rather bizarre way," Faust agreed.

"You've been listening to all this. Don't you think I could teach the army something?"

"Yes, I could see that," Faust said. "Maybe you could design a course of escape and survival for soldiers who have been captured, or perhaps for airmen who have been shot down behind enemy lines."*

"Yes! Exactly!" Jesse replied enthusiastically. "That's exactly what I could do. You're a famous writer and all, Fred. Why don't you talk to the army and tell them what I could do. I think they would listen to you."

Fred chuckled. "I'll speak with them, but I think you are assigning far more effectiveness to my words than they are likely to have."

"You will at least try, won't you?"

"I'll try," Faust said. "Jesse, earlier you alluded to the idea that it made no sense to steal thirty-six dollars when, for the same risk, you could steal thirty-six thousand dollars."

---

*The global nature of World War II created new escape and evasion (or "E & E") challenges for airmen. For the first time, U.S. Army Air Forces (USAAF) airmen received specialized equipment and formal instruction in escape and evasion techniques. During WWII the techniques were just being developed. Today SERE (Survival Evasion Resistance and Escape) classes are much more thorough.

"Yes."

"Did you explain that to your son? What I mean is, did you actually pick out a target for him?"

"Not for him," Jesse replied. "For us."

Cattleman's Hotel, Dallas, Texas—June 1904

Jesse spread out two pieces of paper on the bed in his room. One was a broad sheet and the other was a small pamphlet.

"All right," Jesse said. "You've been a pretty good student; it's time we put it to a test."

"You're goin' to give me a test?" Billy complained. "I never was very good at tests when I was in school."

"I'm not talking about that kind of a test," Jesse said. "This is a real test. We're going to put to real use what you've been learning."

The frown left Billy's face to be replaced by a smile.

"All right!" he said. "What have you got in mind?"

"A train robbery."

"Pa, I don't know. Robbin' a train? I mean, I've read about people robbin' trains, only it was people like Jesse James that done it. But that was a long time ago, and we sure ain't Jesse James. I mean, people don't actually rob trains anymore, do they?"

"I don't know," Jesse replied. "Maybe not. But if they don't, that just means they probably won't be expecting it."

"All right, if you say so. What are these things?" He took in the items on the bed with a wave of his hand.

"One is a map, and one is railroad timetable."

Jesse spread out the map.

"Now, the best place for us to do this thing is as far

from a town as you can get. That way, by the time the train gets into town where they can send telegrams out, or make telephone calls to tell that they have been robbed, we'll have a good lead on them."

"So, that's what the map is for?"

"Yes. Also, the locomotives have to go take on water every forty miles. So what we are looking for is a place that is about forty miles from its last stop, and some distance before the next stop," Jesse said, studying the sheet that was spread out before him. After a few minutes of rather intense scrutiny, he pointed to a place on the map.

"Here," he said. "This is on the Texas and Pacific. It's about forty miles west of San Angelo, which means there will be a water tank here, or very close by. And it is at least another twenty miles before they reach San Martin, so that means it'll give us almost two hours to get away after we hold up the train."

"Pa, it's not goin' to take that train two hours to go twenty miles. It can do that in an hour, easy."

Jesse smiled. "I know. But it is going to take the fireman at least an hour to get the pressure back up after we have the fireman put out the fire in the firebox, then bleed off all his steam."

"Ha! I hadn't thought of that. That's a good idea, Pa. I'll bet not even Jesse James ever thought of doin' something like that."

Jesse examined the schedule for several minutes.

"What are you lookin' for, Pa?" Billy asked.

"I just want to see how many trains come through, and what times they'll come by the water tank. Here's one, for example. It's a westbound, due to arrive at San Martin at eleven in the morning. That means it would be at the tank at about ten in the morning."

"Wow," Billy said. "I can't believe you know how to figure all this out. I mean, I've never known you as anything but a gunsmith and a farmer. But here, you've got this all planned out like as if it is a battle or something."

"In a way it is a battle, us against the people we are going to rob, and us against the law. Only, in this battle, if we do everything right, nobody gets killed. Especially us," he added with a little chuckle.

Billy looked up quickly.

"Yeah, I reckon that is possible, isn't it? I mean, us getting killed."

"It's always possible," Jesse said. "Do you want to back out?"

"No."

"All right, once we decide which train we want to hit, we'll also figure out what time we need to be there."

Billy examined the distance on the map between Dallas and the spot pointed out by his father.

"That's going to be a long ride," he said.

"We'll make arrangements for our horses and go as far as San Angelo by train," Jesse said. "I want to get to San Angelo a couple of days early because we need to decide which train we are going to hit."

"How much money do you think we'll get?"

"That depends on how much money there is in the express car."

"Pa, we're doin' all this, what if —"

"What if what?"

"What if we hold up a train and it's not carrying any money?"

"Then we won't get anything."

"If that's the case, then I think we should rob the passengers."

"There are only two of us. Too many things can go wrong when you start through the cars, and we probably wouldn't get that much money anyway. It isn't worth the risk."

"How is that more of a risk?"

"The engineer and the fireman aren't carrying guns. The express agent probably has one, but there's just one of him, and we can handle him. On a passenger car, any one of half a dozen men could be armed, maybe even more. And if one of them tries to be a hero, we may have to kill him."

"Would you?" Billy asked.

"Would I what?"

"Kill him. Would you kill him?"

Jesse sighed, then put his hand on Billy's shoulder. "Son, you've got to get something straight, right now. Understand this, and understand it good. Anytime you pull your pistol from its holster, and you point that gun at someone, you have to be one hundred percent committed to killing that person if it comes to it. Do you understand that?"

"Yeah, I guess so."

"There is no 'guess so' about it. Listen to me. When you pull a gun, you have to have it in your mind that you are ready to kill someone. You can't shoot someone just to wound them, and you can't stop and think about it. If it comes to that point, and believe me, we are going down a road now where it may very well come to that point, you have to be willing to kill. Are you ready for that?"

Billy hesitated.

"Don't hesitate, boy. It's yes or no, there is no in between. And if it is no, we need to stop this, right now, before we go any further. Now, what will it be?"

"Pa, do you remember during the land rush, when that man tried to run me off the blanket where I was waitin' for you?"

"Yes."

"I pointed my gun at him and made him leave."

"I remember that."

"When I told Ma about it, I said I wouldn't have really killed him. But I would have, Pa. I would have killed him sure, if I had to. So yes, if it comes right down to it, I am ready to kill."

Jesse nodded. "Good. I know that sounds harsh, boy, but life is harsh. And your being ready to kill, if you have to, could very well save your life someday. Or mine," he added with a smile.

"You can depend on me, Pa. I promise, you can depend on me."

"I will depend on you."

Two days later, with their horses in the attached stock car, Jesse and Billy were on a train bound for San Angelo. Both were wearing suits, though Jesse had to buy a suit for Billy since he didn't have one.

"Remember, if anyone asks, we are cattle buyers, and we are going to San Angelo to look at stock," Jesse said.

"Yes, sir."

They had boarded the train at nine o'clock that night and were due to arrive in San Angelo at eleven o'clock the next day. Because they would only be on the train for one night, and to save money, Jesse had bought tickets in the day car.

At about eleven o'clock that night, the train came

to a sudden and unscheduled stop. Several in the car made comments about it, many complaining that the stop had been so rapid that they were nearly thrown from their seats.

"What do you think this is?" Billy asked.

"I don't have any idea," Jesse said. He tried to look through the window. "It's too dark to see anything outside."

"Ha!" Billy said. "Hey, Pa, wouldn't it be funny if someone was holdin' up *this* train?"

Jesse glared at him.

"I didn't mean nothin'," Billy said. "I was just makin' a joke is all."

"Jokes like that can be dangerous," Jesse said under his breath. "Billy, from now on, you have to think about everything you say. Do you understand that? You have to be on guard at all times."

"Yes, sir, I understand," a chastised Billy replied. "I'll be more careful from now on, I promise."

"See that you are."

"Folks!" the conductor said, coming through the car then and holding his hands up. "I'm sorry about the sudden stop, but there were some cows crossin' the track, 'n the engineer had to stop to keep from hitting them."

"He shoulda hit one of them," a man in the car said, "if the cows don't have any more sense than to wander out onto the right of way. We coulda had us steak for breakfast."

There were a few weak laughs at the man's joke.

"Soon as the last one is gone, we'll . . ." the conductor said, but even as he was explaining the condition, the train started up again, ". . . get under way," he said, completing the sentence.

"Here's another lesson for you," Jesse said as he folded his arms across his chest, then leaned back in his seat. "Anytime you have an opportunity to get some sleep, you'd better take it."

"Yes, sir," Billy said, following his father's lead as he, too, crossed his arms, leaned back in the seat, and lowered his head.

CHAPTER THIRTEEN

When they reached San Angelo the next day, Jesse bought a newspaper and took it with him as they had dinner at one of the local restaurants. He began reading it during the meal.

"That's a funny way of reading the paper," Billy said. "You haven't even looked at the front page."

"That's because I'm not interested in the front page," Jesse said. "This is what I'm interested in."

Jesse turned the paper around, then tapped one of the stories, inside.

Business News

First Trust Bank of San Angelo will be transferring sufficient funds to the San Francisco Bank and Savings to cover checks drawn against it when Emerson Williams arranged for the shipping of his beef to Japan. The money transfer will go out on Friday next, so that it will be there for deposit on Monday morning. The amount, to be handled by Texas Pacific Express, is said to be in excess of five thousand dollars.

"You asked how much money?" Jesse said. "How does this sound to you?"

"How did you know to look for this in the paper?" Billy asked.

"I've seen such announcements before," Jesse said.

"When are we going?"

"Tomorrow is Thursday. I want to be there in plenty of time. For now, after we eat, I want to go over to the depot and time the trains for a while."

"Pa, after that, could we find us a saloon and maybe have a couple of beers?"

"Yeah, we can do that. But don't get drunk. When people get drunk they start talking. And sometimes when they start talking, they say things they shouldn't. We have to be very careful."

"I'll have a beer," Billy said, stepping up to the bar of the Brown Dirt Cowboy Saloon a few hours later.

"Honey, if you'll buy me a drink, I'll sit and talk with you for a while," a pretty, heavily painted, and scantily dressed young woman said, stepping up to him.

Billy smiled. "And a drink for the lady," he added.

With drinks in hand, the two started toward a table that was near the vacant piano.

"My name is Rose," the woman said as they sat at the table. "What's yours?"

"Bil—" Billy started, then paused. "Billings," he said. "Seth Billings."

"Well, Seth, you are a handsome man in that suit.

You aren't dressed like most of the cowboys who come in here."

"That's because I'm not a cowboy," Billy said. "I'm a cattle buyer. My pa and I are here to look at cattle."

Rose laughed. "What's there to look at? They all look the same to me."

Billy laughed, too.

"Tomorrow," someone said from the next table over. "They're goin' to hang both of 'em tomorrow."

"I hate to see that. Both of 'em have been in here several times. They both seemed to be good ole' boys, as far as I was concerned."

"Yeah, but when they robbed the stage, they kilt Emmett Drew. He was the shotgun guard, 'n don't forget, Emmett had hisself a wife 'n two kids."

"I'm not sayin' that Lou 'n Harry don't deserve to get hung. I'm just sayin' I hate that it come to this."

"You goin' to watch?"

"I don't know. I reckon I prob'ly will watch."

"There's goin' to be a hangin' here, tomorrow?" Billy asked Rose.

The smile left Rose's face. "Yes," she said.

"Do you know the two they're talkin' about?"

"Like the man said, they used to come in here. Yes, I know both of them. I never thought they'd do anything like holdin' up a stage and killin' Mr. Drew, though." Rose forced a smile. "Let's not talk about them anymore. Let's talk about you. Where are you from?"

"Colorado. Denver, Colorado."

"I've heard there are mountains in Colorado," Rose said. "It must be very pretty there."

"It is."

* * *

The next morning, there were at least three hundred people gathered at the corner of North Main and Pulliam streets. The scaffold stood at the junction of the two streets, with two nooses dangling from the crossbeam. A few minutes earlier, filled sandbags had been placed on the two trapdoors, and the handle pulled to test the operation. Billy had jumped at the sound.

"Pa, why are we here?" Billy asked. "I don't think I'm goin' to like watchin' a couple of men get their necks stretched."

"Let's just say it's part of your education," Jesse replied.

"But what kind of lesson is this?" Billy asked.

"Let's just say that it will make you aware of what could happen if you aren't careful." Jesse saw someone close by and realized that his comment might have sounded a little suspect.

"You need to always walk the straight and narrow," he added.

Apparently, his added comment satisfied the curiosity of the man because the man turned his attention back to the empty gallows.

"When are you goin' to do it?" someone shouted. "We're gettin' tired 'a standin' out here all mornin'."

As they waited, Jesse, subconsciously, put his fingers to his neck where he could feel the slight puffy welt of the scar.

"Where's your brother Frank at?" Union soldiers asked the sixteen-year-old Jesse James.

"I don't know. He's gone."

"He's with the Bushwhackers, ain't he?"

"He didn't tell me where he was goin'."

"String the little whelp up," a sergeant said. "If he ain't goin' to talk, he ain't no good to us. We may as well hang 'im."

A rope was looped around Jesse's neck, then the end tossed over the limb of a big oak tree. Two soldiers pulled on the rope, hoisting Jesse, by his neck, from the ground. He began to choke.

"Sergeant! What are you doing?" a lieutenant called.

"The little bastard ain't tellin' us nothin', so I figured to hang 'im," the sergeant replied.

"Let him down! We aren't here to hang kids."

The soldiers let go of the rope, and Jesse fell, collapsing to the ground. His neck was on fire from the rope burn.

"Let's go. Frank James isn't here, and we're just wasting time."

Jesse heard the soldiers riding off and as he lay there, recovering his breath, he made the decision to find Frank. He was going to join him, and the group he was riding with, which he knew, but didn't tell the soldiers, was Todd's Guerillas. He would show the Yankees who was a kid.

A shout from someone in the crowd jerked Jesse back from his reverie. "Here they come!"

Looking back toward the jail, Jesse could see the two condemned men being led to the gallows. Their legs weren't hobbled, but their hands were handcuffed behind their backs. Apparently, one of them had been given a chew of tobacco earlier, because just as he reached the foot of the gallows he stopped to squirt out a stream.

"Go on up there now, Lou," the sheriff said. "You

don't want to keep these folks standin' out in the hot sun any longer than they already have, do you?"

"Sheriff, I'm just all broke out with pity for 'em," Lou answered. There was a smattering of nervous laughter in the crowd at his remark.

"Come on, boys, the longer you wait, the more time you have to worry about it. If it was me, I'd be wantin' to just get it over with."

"I'd be happy to trade places with you," the other prisoner said.

Again, there was a scattering of nervous laughter.

"You boys are both just full of laughs," the sheriff said.

The two men moved onto the scaffold, then both were positioned on the trapdoors, under the noose. A clergyman, who had been standing silently in one corner of the gallows, moved over to them.

"Lou Clayton and Harry Foster, since you both are soon to pass into an endless and unchangeable state, and your future happiness or misery depends upon the few moments which are left you, I require you strictly to examine yourselves, and your estate, both toward God and towards man, and let no worldly consideration hinder you from making a true and full confession of your sins, and giving all the satisfaction which is in your power to everyone whom you have wronged or injured, that you may find mercy at your heavenly Father's hand and not be condemned in the dreadful day of judgment."

"How 'm I s'posed to do that?" Lou asked. "Hell, Parson, folks I've wronged is spread out all over the place."

"Make contrition in your soul," the parson said.

"And, as the soul of the good thief saved by our Lord, so, too, can your soul be saved."

"Ha! This is workin' out real good then," Lou said. "I've done near 'bout ever' sin can be done, 'n you're tellin' me all I got to do now is say I'm sorry, 'n I won't be goin' to hell?"

"That is exactly what I'm saying. I beg of you, sir. Repent. Repent now, before it is too late."

"I don't repent of nothin'."

"I do, Parson," Harry said. "I repent of ever'thing. I'm just real sorry for all the things I've done."

"Then you, sir, like the Good Thief, are saved," the parson said with a beneficent smile.

"When I get to heaven, I'm goin' to tell Emmett that I'm just real sorry we kilt him," Harry said.

"And when I get to hell, I'm goin' to kick the devil right in the ass 'n take the place over," Lou said with a loud cackle.

Now the crowd gasped.

"All right, Parson, step aside, please," the sheriff said. He slipped masks over the heads of each of the prisoners, then stepped to the edge of the gallows. The sheriff glanced down toward the hangman, who had his hands on the lever that would open the trapdoors.

The crowed grew silent, and neither of the prisoners said a word.

The sheriff nodded his hand, and the hangman pulled on the lever. The trapdoors opened with a bang, and the two men fell through them, waist-deep into the opening. Both were perfectly still.

* * *

"Pa, watchin' that hangin'," Billy said an hour later as the two men started west on their forty-mile ride, "I didn't like that."

"I didn't figure you would."

"Why did you say it was a lesson?"

"For two reasons. One reason is, there is a very real possibility that, given the business we're about to go into, that one or both of us could wind up in the same place. I thought you might need to know that."

"What was the other reason?"

"To show you how awful it is, so that we're careful enough to keep either of us from winding up in the same place."

"Well, if you wanted to get my attention, you sure as hell did," Billy said. "Because I really don't want to wind up bein' hung. I think if it came right down to it, I'd rather be shot."

"Gettin' shot isn't all that good, either."

"I'll tell you what really got my attention," Billy said. "And that's the way that fella, Lou, acted."

Jesse chuckled quietly. "He was a feisty bastard, wasn't he? All full of piss and vinegar."

"Yeah," Billy said, and he managed a chuckle as well. "You reckon he really done it?"

"What? Hold up the stagecoach and shoot the guard? I reckon so, seeing as the other fella much as admitted it just before the hangin' took place."

"No. I mean do you reckon he really did kick the devil in the ass when he got to hell?"

Jesse laughed out loud.

"Well now, I wouldn't put it past him."

"Pa, do you remember what Frank said when he

spoke over Ma's grave? I mean about her not havin'
to learn to be an angel and all that."

"Of course I remember," Jesse said. "I was real
proud of your brother that day. I think the words
he spoke were just fine."

"I think they were, too. Pa, his talk about Ma being
an angel and all. Do you reckon she is in heaven?"

"Yes, as sure as a gun is iron she is in heaven."

CHAPTER FOURTEEN

They spent that night down in an arroyo.

"Why are we throwing out our sleeping rolls down here?" Billy asked. "There ain't no breeze down here. Seems to me it would be a lot cooler up top."

"You want to eat your food raw?"

"No."

"Do you have any idea how far away you can see a campfire at night?"

"No, I don't know. I've never really given it any thought."

"If you are down on the ground, you can see it for three or four miles. If you're up on a high enough hill, so the world doesn't curve away from you, you could see a campfire from fifteen to twenty miles away. But down in the arroyo, can't nobody see it."

"Who thinks about things like that?"

"I do," Jesse said. "And you are going to have to start thinking about it. Billy, I may not always be here. But believe me when I say that if you want to stay out of jail, better yet, if you want to stay alive . . .

you absolutely must start thinking about things like that."

"I will, Pa," Billy promised. "I will."

As Jesse and Billy stretched out that night, Jesse looked over at the low-burning fire and let his thoughts drift back more than thirty years ago. That was when he held up his first train.

Near Adair, Iowa—July 21, 1873

"One hundred thousand dollars in gold," Frank said. "That's what this train is carrying."

"If we wreck the train, someone could be hurt," Bob Younger said. "Someone could even be killed."

"Do you think the train would just stop if we held up our hand?" Jesse asked.

"No, but if someone gets killed, wouldn't your conscience bother you?"

"Whatever conscience I had, I left back in the war," Jesse said.

"Conscience is but a word that cowards use, devised at first to keep the strong in awe," Frank said.

"That don't make no sense at all," Cole Younger said.

"It's probably from one of those books Frank is always reading," Jesse said.

"You're right, Dingus. It is from King Richard the Third. Shakespeare."

"The third? You mean there was three kings named Richard?" Bob asked.

"There were."

"How did they tell them apart?"

"Get ready," Jesse said. "Here comes the train."

"One hunnert thousand dollars," Bob said. "Woowee. I didn't know there was that much money in the whole world."

Earlier, the men had loosened a length of the rail that was just beyond a blind curve, choosing the location so that by the time the engineer saw it, he wouldn't be able to stop.

Just as the train came around the curve, they pulled on the rope that was tied to the track. The locomotive hit the dislodged rail and turned over. The boiler burst with a loud noise and a gush of hot steam as the engine slid along the ground, throwing up rocks and dirt. Finally it stopped, and with guns drawn, Jesse and the others ran toward the train.

The first thing they saw was the engineer. He had been thrown from the cab when the engine overturned. They didn't have to examine his mutilated body too closely to see he was dead.

The tender, baggage car, and express car also left the track, though the express car had not overturned. The express agent, who was uninjured, opened the door to see what had happened.

"Throw down that money shipment," Jesse called up to him.

"Did you men do this?" the agent asked.

"The one hundred thousand dollars," Jesse repeated. "Throw it down now, if you want to live."

"Mister, you've made a big mistake," the agent said. "We aren't carrying that money shipment. They delayed it. It's going on another train."

"I'm coming onto the car to have a look for myself," Jesse said. "And if I find you're lying, I'm going to kill you."

"Come on, look for yourself. I'm not lying, I swear to you, I'm not lying!"

"Open the safe," Jesse ordered.

With shaking hands, the agent opened the safe and stepped back. Inside, there was a canvas bag marked, BANK OF DUBUQUE.

"What is this?" Jesse asked, holding up the bag.

"It's two thousand dollars," the nervous agent replied. "That's all the money we're carrying."

"Damn," Cole said. "All this for two thousand dollars?"

"Maybe we can get a donation from some of the passengers," Frank suggested.

A trapped gas bubble in one of the logs popped, sending up a shower of sparks and jerking Jesse back from his thoughts. Tomorrow he and Billy would hold up a train. He was leading his son into a life of crime.

No, that wasn't right. Billy had already taken up a life of crime. Jesse was just showing him how to survive.

The sign painted on the side of the water tank read: TANK NO. 27, TEXAS AND PACIFIC RAILROAD.

Jesse and Billy had come here an hour earlier, and they waited now behind some scrub brush that grew just high enough to keep them out of sight from the approaching train. They had ground-tethered their horses just on the other side of a tree line, which was about twenty yards behind where they were waiting.

"Pa, what are we going to do with the money?" Billy asked excitedly.

"Boy, haven't you ever heard the term, 'Don't count your chickens before they hatch'?"

"Well, yeah, sure, I've heard that."

"Then don't spend the money before we've got it in our pocket."

"Yeah," Billy said. "Yeah, I see what you mean. I guess I'm just gettin' excited is all."

"Don't. Don't get excited; don't get scared. Just stay calm. That way you won't make mistakes."

"Pa, how do you know about all this, anyhow?"

They heard a distant whistle.

"There's the train," Jesse said, not answering Billy's question. "All right, get ready. And Billy?"

"Yeah, Pa?"

"Remember when I told you that anytime you pull your gun, you must be ready to kill if you have to?"

"I remember."

"The other side of that is, don't shoot anyone unless you absolutely have to."

"All right," Billy replied.

The train rumbled to a stop by the water tank.

"Wait until the fireman swings the spout over," Jesse said quietly.

The fireman climbed onto the tender, then opened the hatch.

"Damn, Hank, this tank is as dry as a bone. Whatever steam we got in the pipes is all that's left. Don't think we coulda gone another mile," the fireman called down to the engineer.

If the engineer answered, neither Jesse nor Billy heard the reply.

The fireman pulled the spout down from the tower. A moment later, there was the loud rush of water pouring into the tank.

"Now," Jesse said.

Jesse and Billy closed the distance between them

and the train. The engineer was on the other side of the cab, looking out the window, so he didn't see Billy climb onto the locomotive deck.

"Mr. Engineer, I would like for you to step down onto the ground, if you would, please," Billy said.

"What? You can't be up here! Where did you come from? Get back down," the engineer said, surprised by Billy's unexpected appearance.

"My pa and I are the ones giving the orders now. Just do as we say." Billy cocked his pistol.

"No, no! Don't shoot! I'm gettin' down!"

"Hank? What are you doin' out of the cab?" the fireman called from the top of the tender. Because he was busy monitoring the water transfer, he had not seen Billy climb onto the locomotive.

Jesse stepped out where the fireman could see him. "Stop the water," he said.

"What? I can't do that. This tank is nigh empty."

Jesse pointed the pistol at him. "I said, stop the water. Return the spout to the tank."

The fireman did as he was ordered.

"Now, climb down into the cab and extinguish your fire, then let off all the steam."

"Mister, if I do that, it'll take near an hour to get the steam back up. We'll have to clear the track before then 'cause there'll be another train comin' along."

"You'll just have to signal the train to wait until you can get yourself going again," Jesse said. "Now, do what I tell you."

"Yes, sir," the fireman replied.

The fireman climbed back down into the cab, then under Billy's watch opened the steam pressure relief valve. Steam began gushing from the drive cylinders on both sides of the engine.

"There," the fireman said. "The pressure is at zero."

"All right, now put out the fire."

"How am I goin' to do that?"

"If it was me puttin' out the fire, I'd be usin' that fire extinguisher," Billy said, pointing to the copper instrument in the corner.

The fireman extinguished the fire.

"Now, climb down to join your friend on the ground," Billy ordered.

"What is this?" the engineer asked as Billy and the fireman stepped down from the cab. "Paul, why'd you vent the steam?"

"I had no choice," the fireman said. "This feller made me do it." He nodded toward Billy. "Not only that, he made me put out the fire."

"Good Lord, man, we have to reach the double track in San Martin in forty-five minutes, or we'll be head-to-head with the eastbound."

"There warn't nothin' I could do, Hank."

"What is all this about?" the engineer asked Jesse.

"Isn't it obvious? We're robbing the train," Jesse said.

"People don't rob trains anymore."

"Really? Well, I guess nobody ever told me that. Now, come with me, back to the express car."

Jesse motioned with his pistol, and the engineer complied.

"Knock on the door and tell the express man to open up," Jesse ordered.

"Don't know as he'll be able to hear me if I just knock with my fist. That door's pretty thick."

"Pick up a rock," Jesse suggested.

The engineer picked up a rock from the ballast

and knocked on the door. "Earl Ray?" he called. "Earl Ray, this is Hank. Open the door."

The door slid open. "What do you need, Hank?"

"Hello, Earl Ray," Jesse said, showing the express man his pistol.

"Who are you? What's going on?" Earl Ray asked.

"What's going on is a train robbery."

"Are you serious? Who robs trains anymore?"

Jesse looked at the engineer and chuckled. "Tell him, Hank. Who robs trains anymore?"

"This feller does," Hank said.

"Now, Earl Ray, this is what I'd like for you to do. I want you to drop down the money shipment bag."

"What makes you think we're carrying any money?"

"How else do banks pay off checks, other than by money exchange?" Jesse asked. "Every train carries a money shipment now. And I know that you are carrying at least five thousand dollars to the San Francisco Bank and Savings to cover the check written by my friend Emerson Williams. Now, toss it down here, like I asked."

"I can't do that."

"If you don't toss it down, I'm going to kill Hank. And if that doesn't get you to toss it down, then I'll kill Paul. And if you still won't toss it down, then I'll kill you, and just go find another train to rob where the express agent has more sense thàn you do."

"For God's sake, Earl Ray, give him the money," Hank said. "It's not like it's your money!"

"Hank does have a point, Earl Ray," Jesse said. "It isn't your money. Now, toss it down to the boy."

"All right, all right, I'll toss it down."

"Thank you, I appreciate that," Jesse said.

The express agent tossed a canvas bag down to Billy.

"It's got a lock," Billy said.

"Drop it onto the ground," Jesse said.

When Billy complied, Jesse shot the lock off. "Make sure there's money inside."

Billy glanced in, then, with a big smile, pulled out a bound packet of twenty-dollar bills.

"Look at this!" he said.

"All right, Paul, you can start the water going again, then get your fire going and the steam pressure built back up. I expect your passengers are anxious to get to where they're going," Jesse said.

"Yes, sir," the engineer said.

"What's going on here? What was that shot?" someone yelled several cars back.

The shout came from the conductor, who was on the steps of the car holding on to the assist rail and leaning out.

Jesse fired toward him, the bullet hitting the assist rail just above the conductor's hand. The expression on his face reflected his panic, and he disappeared quickly back into the car.

"I tell you what, Earl Ray, maybe you'd better go back there and keep ever'one in the train calm, while Hank and Paul are getting the pressure built back up," Jesse said. "Someone else is liable to get curious, and if I can't scare him back the way I did the conductor, then I'll have to kill him. And I know that neither one of us wants that, now, do we?"

"I'm going, I'm going," Earl Ray said, moving quickly toward the passenger cars of the train.

Jesse and Billy waited until the fireman was once again filling the tank with water, and both Hank and Earl Ray were back onto the train. Then, they ran away from the track, disappearing quickly into the line of trees so they couldn't be seen by anyone on the train.

"Let's put some distance between us and the track," Jesse said.

CHAPTER FIFTEEN

"How much did we get, Pa?"

Jesse and Billy were camped on the Brazos River, and it wasn't until then that Jesse counted the money.

"Five thousand seven hundred and fifteen dollars," Jesse said.

"Wow! That's quite a haul."

"It's more than we could get from a grocery store."

"Yeah, I guess it is," Billy said, chagrined by the reminder.

Jesse chuckled. "Don't feel bad about it. I've pulled jobs that brought in less money."

"I knew it!" Billy said. "I knew you had done this before! What are we going to do next?"

"What about a bank?" Jesse suggested.

"Do you have one picked out already?"

"Yes, in Culpepper."

"Culpepper?"

"It's a small town north of here. It isn't served by the railroad."

"If it's a small bank there won't be that much money in it, will there?"

"More than you think. Culpepper is a coal-mining town, so the mine will keep a reserve of money on hand. And because it's a small town and a small bank, the security won't be that high. That means the risks will be less."

"All right, that sounds good to me. Let's do it," Billy said. "What do we do first?"

"The first thing we do is scout out the bank and the town."

"Pa, what about this money?" Billy asked.

"What about it?"

"I mean, what are we going to do with it? We can't just carry it around with us, can we?"

"We'll put it in our saddlebags," Jesse said. "Have you ever heard of anyone robbing a saddlebag?"

Billy laughed. "No, I don't guess I have."

"We'll keep it in our saddlebags and just act normal. It'll be safe there."

"But can we spend any of it?"

"Spend it on what?"

"You said we were going into the town to scout it out, didn't you?"

"Yes."

"Well, won't there be a saloon there?"

"I'm sure there will be."

"And if there's a saloon there, there will also be . . . uh, you know."

"Yeah, I know. Billy, I've known men to get drunk and start trying to impress some doxie. Can I trust you not to do that?"

"I'll be careful, Pa, I promise. Uh, how much money can I spend?"

"We'll each have twenty dollars in our pocket when we go in."

"Twenty dollars? Is that all? That's not very much money. I mean, considering all this." He took in the money with a wave of his hand.

"Billy, that's more than a week's pay for most men. Anything more than twenty dollars is going to get some unwanted attention. By the time we get to town, word will already be there that two men robbed a train. And I'm pretty sure there will be a fairly good description of us."

"Yeah," Billy said. "Yeah, I see what you mean. I guess I've got a lot to learn, haven't I?"

"You're coming along," Jesse replied.

Culpepper, Texas

Jesse and Billy dismounted in front of the livery and were met by a thin, white-haired man with a prominent Adam's apple.

"Wantin' to put your horses up, are ya?"

"Yes. Probably, just for the night. Unsaddle them, but just leave the saddles in the stall with them."

"That'll be a dollar for the two of them."

As Jesse gave the man a dollar, he was startled by a woman screaming. The scream had come from the saloon across the street, and he looked toward it but the scream was quickly followed by an outbreak of laughter.

"Pay no attention to that," the stableman said with a dismissive wave of his hand. "That's more'n likely Screamin' Lily."

"Screamin' Lily?"

"She works over there at the Wet Mouse. She's

always screamin' and cacklin' 'n takin' on so that that's what she's called."

"Well I guess we'll have to check it out," Jesse said.

With their horses put up at the livery, Jesse and Billy walked across the street to the saloon known as the Wet Mouse. It was suppertime, which was peak business time for the saloon, so it was full. At the back of the room a man wearing a vertical striped shirt with sleeve garters, a bow tie, and a bowler hat was grinding away at a scarred piano. A beer mug sat on top of the piano, about one-third filled with coins.

There were seven or eight saloon girls working the customers, and when one of them suddenly cackled out loud, Jesse was able to identify Screaming Lily.

"Two beers," Jesse ordered, sliding a piece of silver across the bar. The man behind the bar drew two mugs and set them, with foaming heads, in front of Jesse and Billy. The long ride had made the men thirsty, and they drank the first one down without taking away the mug. Then they wiped the foam away from their lips and slid the empty mugs back toward the barkeep.

"That one was for thirst," Jesse said. "This will be for taste. Do it again."

Smiling, the bartender gave them a second round.

With the beer in his hand, Billy turned his back to the bar and looked out over the saloon. One of the girls pulled herself away from the table and sidled up to the two. She had bleached hair, was heavily painted, but behind her tired eyes was a suggestion of good humor. She smiled at Billy.

"What a handsome devil you are," she said. "I'll just bet you've broken many a poor girl's heart."

"I've bent them around a few times," Billy replied with a broad grin. "Don't know as I ever broke any."

"You aren't going to bend Dolly's heart, are you?" the girl asked.

"Dolly? That would be your name?"

"You guessed it, cowboy. What's your name?"

"Joe. My name is Joe," Billy said. Billy turned toward the bartender. "It looks to me like Dolly needs a drink."

"Coming right up," the bartender said, filling a glass from Dolly's special bottle.

As Billy was visiting with Dolly, another of the bar girls came to visit with Jesse.

"Hello. My name is Sheila."

"Hi, Sheila." Jesse hesitated for a moment, then called upon a name he had used in the past. "My name is Tom."

"I like you, Tom," Sheila said.

Jesse chuckled. "I don't have that effect on everyone. And, I'm a little old for you, aren't I?"

"No, not at all. I have a thing for mature men. Why, you're much more handsome than your little brother here."

"How do you know he's my brother?"

"Because you two look exactly alike."

Jesse laughed. "If we look alike, how can I be a lot more handsome?"

Sheila laughed as well. "Let's just say that when your brother gets to be your age, he'll be more handsome."

Jesse turned toward the bartender. "How about you give Miss Sheila here whatever it is she likes to drink. And tell me where might be a good place to eat around here?"

"I'd recommend Dewey Gimlin's place, right next door," the bartender answered.

"Joe, what do you say we go have some supper? I could eat a horse."

"Don't say that around Dewey," Dolly teased. "You never know but what he might take you up on it."

Those close enough to overhear laughed.

Billy looked at Dolly. "Will you be here when I come back?"

"Honey, in case you ain't noticed it, you've done got my comb red," Dolly said. "I'll be here waitin' for you, just anytime you're ready."

Dolly's directness caused Billy to take a quick breath.

"On second thought, Pa— uh, Tom, why don't you go on over there without me?" Billy suggested.

"I thought you were so all-fired ready to have supper?" Jesse said.

"Yeah, well, I've got somethin' else in mind right now."

"All right. I guess I can eat by myself."

"You don't have to eat by yourself, Tom," Sheila said. "I was about to go over to Gimlin's for supper my own self, and I would be glad to go with you. That is, unless you don't want company."

Jesse smiled. "Well now, how can I turn down an offer like that? I'll even buy your supper, if you will allow me."

"Well, that's just real sweet of you, Tom. Now you see why I prefer more mature men."

Billy watched the interplay between Sheila and his

father, then he turned his attention back to Dolly. "So, what do we do now?" he asked.

"I'm sure something will . . ."—Dolly paused and looked pointedly at the front of his pants—"come up," she said, emphasizing the last two words.

Billy laughed. "I'm sure it will."

Dolly turned and started walking away, glancing back over her shoulder to let Billy know that she intended for him to follow her. They went up the stairs and along the second-floor hallway.

"Sheila, I believe you said something about supper," Jesse said, turning his attention back to the young woman beside him.

"I did, indeed," she said.

Jesse offered her his arm.

The china, silver, and crystal gleamed softly in the reflected light of more than a dozen lanterns. Gimlin's Restaurant was an oasis of light in the darkness that had descended over the little town. Jesse led Sheila to a quiet table in the corner.

"What do people do for a living around here?" Jesse asked. "When I rode in I didn't see any cattle or anything under cultivation."

"You didn't see it, because there isn't any," Sheila said, and Jesse thought he detected some bitterness in her voice.

"Why is that?"

"Marcus Daniel Culpepper."

"Culpepper? You mean like the name of the town?"

"This town wasn't always called Culpepper. When

I was growing up, it was called Red Bluff. Isn't that a pretty name?"

"Why Red Bluff? I didn't see anything that looks like a red bluff."

"You wouldn't. Culpepper took that down long ago, with his coal mining. After he got control of everything, including the mayor and the city council, he decided to change the name of the town to Culpepper."

"You sound like you don't like Culpepper."

"How can I like him? His coal mine has poisoned the streams so there is no water for the livestock, and the ranchers can't make a living. I know this, because I grew up on Trailback Ranch."

"So your father is a rancher?"

"He was a rancher and so was my grandfather before him. When Culpepper took over Trailback, he got a ranch that had been thriving since Texas was part of Mexico."

"I don't understand. If the ranch was doing that well, why did your father sell out to Culpepper?"

Sheila looked up sharply. "My father didn't sell Trailback," she said. "He had it taken from him."

"How was that?"

"Culpepper got Trailback the same way he got all the other ranches and farms. He started a bank and gave crop and stock loans to the farmers and ranchers, just as they had taken out every year from other banks. Only they were so proud that Red Bluff had a bank, they wanted to keep the business in their hometown.

"What they didn't realize is that the coal mine was going to kill all the farming and ranching, and when the notes came due, Culpepper foreclosed on them.

After my father lost his ranch he was a broken man. I . . ." Sheila stopped talking for a moment and her eyes filled with tears.

"We had no way of making a living, so I took this job. But my father couldn't face what had happened to us and he . . . he put a gun to his head and he . . ." Again, Sheila paused in midsentence.

Jesse reached across the table and put his hand on hers. "You don't have to go on," he said.

"I'm sorry," Sheila said. She forced a smile through her tears. "Here I was supposed to be pleasant company for you while you ate."

"While *we* eat," Jesse said, and at that moment the food was delivered to the table.

"So," he said a few minutes later, "Culpepper owns the bank, does he?"

"Yes. There was an investigation a while back, something about how he was using the bank to finance improvements in the mine, making loans to the mine, then collecting on the interest. It's all very confusing, but it eventually came to nothing. And as far as improvements on the mine, the miners who come into the Wet Mouse are always talking about how dangerous it is, because he cuts corners on safety."

"And the law does nothing about it?"

"Are you kidding?" Sheila said. "Marcus Culpepper is the law."

Jesse and Sheila had just finished eating and were about to leave the restaurant, when Billy came in.

"So, how was supper?" Billy asked. His words were jaunty and his mood was ebullient.

"Well now . . . Joe," Jesse had to pause for a moment to remember what name Billy had used, "you sure look all full of vinegar."

"Do I? Well, a little lady named Dolly might have something to do with that."

"So it appears. I'm glad to see that you decided to take the time to eat," Jesse teased.

"Believe me, after what I've just been through, I need to eat," he said. "I have to get my strength back."

Sheila laughed, and Billy suddenly realized that he was being a bit ribald. He smiled, sheepishly, and put his hand to the brim of his hat. "I beg your pardon, ma'am," he said. "I sure don't mean to say anything out of line, I mean, being as you are a lady 'n all."

"For heaven's sake, Joe, you certainly don't have to apologize to me," Sheila said. "From what I have heard, Dolly can be a most energetic woman."

"Yes, ma'am, I'll vouch for that," Billy said. Then, to Jesse he asked, "Are you leaving?"

"Yes, I'm going to walk Sheila back, then I'll get us a room at the hotel."

"How will I know which room? Or, are you goin' to wait in the lobby?"

"Just ask for Tom Howard," Jesse said. It had to be over twenty years since he last used that name, so he was sure it was safe to use now.

CHAPTER SIXTEEN

"If there was ever a bank that needed to be robbed, it's this one," Jesse said to Billy that night, after he told him the story Sheila had recounted over supper.

"How are we going to do it?"

"We're just going to go in there and ask, politely, that they give us the money."

"We're going to ask politely?"

"Well, as politely as you can ask, when you are holding a gun in your hand," Jesse said.

Billy laughed.

"Whoever chose the location for the bank wasn't very smart," Jesse said.

"Why do you say that?"

"Think about it, Billy. It's the last building at the edge of town. Most of the time, they are right in the middle of town."

"What difference does that—" Billy started, then stopped midsentence and smiled. "If it's at the end of town, we can make our getaway easier."

"You're beginning to catch on," Jesse said.

* * *

"Good mornin'," the stable hand said the next morning when Jesse and Billy retrieved their horses. It was the same white-haired man who had taken their horses the day before.

"You're here awfully early," Jesse said pleasantly. "You must have slept here."

"Yes, sir, as a matter of fact, I did. One of the things Mr. Culpepper does is he lets me sleep in one of the empty stalls."

"Culpepper owns this livery?"

The old man chuckled. "Mister, Culpepper owns ever'thing you see in this town."

"Culpepper must be quite a man."

For just a moment there was a flash of something in the man's eyes, an expression that Jesse couldn't quite make out. He didn't think it was an expression of admiration.

"Yes, sir, I reckon you could say that," the old man said. He led them back to the two adjacent stalls where the horses were, then reached for one of the saddles.

"No need for you to do that, we can saddle them. You go on back up front in case you get another customer."

"All right, thank you, I will."

"Billy," Jesse said quietly after the stable man left. "Check your saddlebags."

Even as Jesse was speaking to Billy, he was checking his own. He moved his spare shirt aside and saw the money from the train robbery exactly as he had left it.

"It's all here, Pa," Billy said.

A few minutes later they said good-bye to the stable hand and led their horses across the street and tied them off in front of Gimlin's Restaurant, then went inside for breakfast.

"Where are all your customers, Mr. Gimlin?" Jesse asked.

"They're all down in the mine, working."

"Already? It's not even eight o'clock yet."

"The first mine shift starts at five a.m. and goes to five p.m. The second shift goes from five p.m. to five a.m."

"You mean they have to work all night?" Billy asked.

Gimlin chuckled. "Sonny, night or day, it's all the same down in the mine."

"Yes, I suppose it would be," Jesse said. "Are there many who work in the mine?"

"Almost everyone in town," Gimlin replied. "I made fresh biscuits this morning."

"Sounds good. Could we have that with bacon and eggs?"

"You got it," Gimlin replied.

After breakfast Jesse and Billy stepped out front to untie their horses.

"You think the bank is open yet, Pa?"

"I looked at the clock inside the restaurant; it said ten minutes until eight. I expect the bank will be open by then. What do you say we take a ride up and down the street first, just to get our bearings."

"All right. What are we looking for?"

"You take the left side. Count everybody you see carrying a gun. I'll take the right."

The two men rode slowly down the entire length of the town, then they turned their horses and rode back.

"I saw three that was wearin' guns," Billy said.

"I only seen one on my side," Jesse added.

"Any of them look like they knew how to use them? More important, did anyone look like they would use them?"

"No, I don't think so," Billy answered. "They didn't any of 'em look like they knew much more'n which end of the gun the bullet come out."

"It looked pretty clear on my side as well," Jesse said. "All right, I expect the bank is open by now. Let's ride on down there."

The two rode down to the bank, which, as Jesse had pointed out the night before, was at the far end of the town. Not only was this bank different from most, in that it was at the far end of town, it also wasn't of brick construction. Instead, it was a rather flimsy-looking building, thrown together from rip-sawed lumber and leaning so that it looked as if a good, stiff wind would knock it over. Billy chuckled when he saw it.

"Hell, we don't have to rob this bank, Pa. We can just kick it down," he said.

"Keep your attention on the job," Jesse said.

"All right, Pa, I'm ready."

As soon as Jesse and Billy were inside, they pulled their pistols.

"This is a holdup!" Jesse shouted. "You, teller, empty out your bank drawer and put all the money in a bag!"

Nervously, the teller began to reply, emptying his drawer in just a few seconds.

"How much is there?" Jesse asked.

"Fifteen hundred dollars," the teller replied nervously.

"Fifteen hundred dollars? You expect me to believe you are operating a bank on just fifteen hundred dollars?"

"That's all there is," the teller insisted. "Mr. Culpepper will never let me have more than that at any given time. If I need more money, I'm supposed to call him, and he will bring me some from the mine office."

"What about the safe?" Jesse asked.

The teller pointed to the safe. "As you can see, it's standing wide open. I just got all the money out a few minutes ago. That's why I knew exactly how much there was."

"You expect us to believe that?" Billy asked.

"I believe it," Jesse said. "Based on what I've heard about Culpepper, he is the kind of son of a bitch who would do something just like that."

At that moment a customer stepped in through the front door of the bank, and, seeing two men with drawn pistols, turned and ran back outside.

"The bank!" he shouted. "They're robbin' the bank!"

"Let's go," Jesse said.

Clutching the bank bag in his hand, Jesse, along with Billy, started out of the bank. Just before they left, Jesse turned and fired shots at all the windows of the bank, bringing them all down with a crash.

"Let's go!" Jesse shouted as he and Billy swung into the saddle. They rode south, out of town, holding their horses at a gallop for at least two miles before they slowed them to a walk.

"How long do you think before they'll be comin' after us?" Billy asked.

"It'll take them at least ten more minutes to get a posse put together. Maybe longer," Jesse said. "Then they'll be coming south after us, but we won't be here. We're going to circle back around north, then be on our way."

"Where are we going?" Billy asked.

"Missouri."

"Missouri? I've never been to Missouri. What's it like?"

"It's like Missouri," Jesse said.

The cabin on the Brazos—March 2, 1942

"You didn't take long putting into action some of what you had taught Billy, did you?" Faust asked.

"What's the sense of teaching him all that, if we weren't going to put it to use?" Jesse replied.

"Yes, well, I guess you have a point there. It's funny."

"What's funny?"

"I've written about this, I mean, train robberies, bank robberies, and the like. In my books and in my short stories, I've probably robbed a dozen trains, a dozen banks, and as many stagecoaches. But I've only written about it. Now, I'm writing about it again, but this time I'm writing about it from the perspective of someone who has actually done it, many times. It's just a rather unreal feeling, that's all. Tell me, Jesse, what is it like?"

"What do you mean what is it like? Damn, Fred, haven't I been telling you what it's like?"

"No, not really. Oh, don't get me wrong, you've given me some very vivid detail, detail that I hope I'm doing justice to, as far as enabling my readers to visualize the scene.

"But I want to know what it feels like here, and here." Faust put his hand first to his head, then over his heart.

"Yeah," Jesse said. "All right, I guess I can see what you mean. I'll try and tell you, but I'm not sure that I can.

Jesse thought a moment. "First, you are scared."

"Really? I wouldn't have thought that. I mean, you're the one holding the gun; you are the one dictating what's going to happen. Why would you be scared?"

"Because you don't always know what's going to happen," Jesse replied. "The disaster, and that's the only way I can refer to it, the disaster at Northfield is a perfect example of you not knowing what's going to happen. I mean, who would have thought that the entire town would turn out with every kind of gun you can imagine, pistols, rifles, and shotguns like they did?"

"Yes, but Northfield was an anomaly, wasn't it?"

"A what?"

"It was unusual. They didn't normally happen like that."

"No, the robberies weren't normally like that, but there was always a chance that something like that could happen again. And you are always at a disadvantage when you are pulling a robbery."

"Why do you say that?"

"If some citizen is killed, even if you didn't intend to do it, you are guilty of murder. But if some citizen kills you, he is a hero."

"I see what you mean."

"I never let on to Frank, or to anyone else, and I especially never let on to Billy, how I felt. But the truth was, that before every job, I could feel my heart pounding a mile a minute. My mouth would get so dry I couldn't even work up a spit, and it was all I could do to keep my hands from shaking. If any of the people I was stealing from ever knew what I was really going through, it could have been all over right then."

"Do you think everyone feels like that? I mean, people who are about to rob a bank, or a train, or something?"

"I really don't know. This isn't anything I ever shared with anyone." Jesse chuckled. "Never until this moment, that is. And I don't expect the average person would have shared it with me.

"There are some people, though, I knew them during the war, who actually enjoyed doing things like this. Hell, Anderson enjoyed killing. Why do you think they called him Bloody Bill Anderson?"

"Thanks," Faust said. "I always try and put myself into the mind-set and point of view of my characters when I write a book or a short story, or even when I work on a screenplay. But most of the time I can do that by recalling situations I have been through that are very similar. But having never committed a holdup, that has been very hard for me to do. This may give me some insight.

"But, back to your story. You rode south out of

town, but you circled back around to the north, you said?"

"Yes."

"Were you careful to cover your tracks so that the posse couldn't follow you?"

Jesse chuckled. "Oh, yes, we did everything that I had taught Billy to do. In fact, he insisted on it, though to tell the truth, I doubt that they were able to raise much of a posse, not the way that town was run. I mean when you think about it, the men who weren't down in the mine were in bed asleep."

"And the name of the town you say is Culpepper?"

"Yes. But it's like Wild Horse, I doubt there's anything left there now but a few tumbledown buildings and a caved-in mine shaft."

"Caved in?"

"They had a terrible mine cave in back in twenty-eight or twenty-nine, I'm not exactly sure. There were a lot of miners killed, and when they found out that Culpepper was cheating—he had only about half of the supports he was supposed to have—he wound up goin' to jail. After that, the town just sort of dried up and went away."

"I'm sorry about the miners. Mining is a dangerous job as it is, and even more so when you have some unscrupulous bastard like Culpepper. So, you went to Missouri did you? Was that the first time you had been back since you left?"

"Yes."

"Where did you go?"

"Kansas City."

CHAPTER SEVENTEEN

Kansas City, Missouri—August 1904

It took them two weeks to reach Joplin, and there they sold their horses and tack, and bought new clothes. Both had grown beards, but here they shaved them off so that it was unlikely that even if the teller of the bank in Joplin was standing three feet in front of them, he would be able to make a positive identification. Here, too, they bought leather valises in which to carry their money, though, to the casual observer they could have been businessmen, carrying the papers of their profession.

From Joplin they caught a train to Kansas City. There were several tracks here, with brick-paved walkways between them. At least half a dozen trains were standing in the station, and as they walked from the tracks into the building they were assailed by the sounds of trains leaving and arriving. Inside the depot more than two hundred people crowded the ticket counters, the food vendors, the information booth, or just lounged on the many benches.

Outside the building they saw trolley cars arriving and departing.

"Which one do we take?" Billy asked.

"I don't think it matters much," Jesse replied. "All we want to do is get down town. Once we're there, it won't be hard to find a hotel."

They stepped onto one of the trolleys, dropped a nickel in the coin box, then took a seat halfway back in the car.

"Pa, look at that!" Billy said excitedly, pointing through the window. "You know what that is? That's an automobile! There's another one. There's another one! Damn, they're all over the place."

Billy counted the automobiles during their trip, and got to twenty before they reached their destination.

"There's a hotel," Jesse said. "Let's get off here."

Stepping down from the trolley, they waited for it to pass, then started toward the hotel when they heard a strange honking sound. Looking toward the sound, they saw an automobile coming quickly toward them, and they had to jump back quickly to avoid being hit.

"Get out of the way!" the driver shouted as the car whizzed past them.

"That's twenty-one," Billy said.

Looking both ways, they hurried across the street. As they approached the hotel, the doorman opened it for them.

"Good afternoon, gentlemen," the doorman said, greeting them with professional courtesy.

Inside they learned that each room of the hotel had its own bathroom, which included a flush toilet and a porcelain bathtub with hot and cold running water.

"There is also an elevator to take you to your floor," the desk clerk told them proudly.

"What are we going to do with our money?" Billy asked when they reached their room. "Where are we going to keep it?"

"What do you mean, where are we going to keep it? You've got a leather case for it."

"I mean when we go out. I want to take a look around."

"You'll take the money with you," Jesse said.

"You mean I have to carry it around all day?"

Jesse laughed. "Listen to you. You're bitching because you have to carry a lot of money with you."

Billy laughed as well. "Yeah, I guess that's right. All right, I'll take it with me. I'm really looking forward to wandering around this afternoon. I've never been in any town that was this big before."

"Enjoy yourself, but just be careful and hang on to your bag. Also, don't get drunk and careless."

"I won't."

"We'll meet here for supper tonight," Jesse suggested.

The painted sign on the window read KANSAS CITY STAR. Jesse stood on the sidewalk in front of the building for a moment, then he pushed the door open and stepped inside. He could hear the clacking of half a dozen typewriters and smell ink from the pressroom. There was a counter across the front that denied access of the rest of the office to anyone not specifically invited. Someone was on one of the telephones, even as the other phone began to ring.

"Yes, sir," a smiling man said, stepping up to the counter. "You wish to place an ad?"

"Place an ad?"

"Do you wish to place an advertisement in our paper? A classified announcement, perhaps."

"No."

"Buy a subscription, perhaps?"

"No, I don't want to do that, either. I would like some information about someone who used to live here."

"Sir, there are over one hundred and sixty thousand people who live in Kansas City. Surely you don't think you can just come into a newspaper office and ask about someone and expect us to tell you how to find them, do you?"

"Well, this person is rather well known. That is, her husband was well known. I know for a fact that her husband's name appeared in many newspapers throughout the state. At least it did back in the 1860s and 1870s."

"Just a minute, let me get Josh up here. He's been here since the paper started, and if there is anyone who can answer your question, it would be him. He knows everything there is to know about Kansas City history. Josh?" he called.

A gray-haired man who was sitting at one of the typewriters, pecking with two fingers on the keys, looked up.

"This fella has a question that you might be able to answer."

Josh stood up, reached for his pipe, and clamped

it between his teeth as he came up to the counter. "Yes, sir, what can I do for you?"

"I'm trying to find someone that I think lives here. Her name, that is, unless she has gotten married again, is James. Zerelda Mimms James."

"Zerelda Mimms James. Well now, you would be talking about the wife of Jesse James, wouldn't you?"

"Yes."

"Well, Jesse James was quite a well-known figure in Missouri. I guess he is one of the best known Missourians of the last fifty years."

"I'm looking for his wife. Does she live here?"

"Well, sir, she did live here. That is, until she died."

"She died?" Jesse felt a quick surge of unexpected emotion. "When did she die?"

"Two years ago."

"How did she die? I mean, she wasn't all that old. She would only have been fifty-five then."

"You must have known her fairly well," Josh said, his eyes narrowing in curiosity. "You look very familiar to me. Have we ever met before?"

"No. That is, I wouldn't think we have met. This is my first time in Missouri. And I didn't know Mrs. James, either. But I've heard about her and I just wanted to meet her, to ask her some questions about her famous husband."

"You're a writer, wanting to write a story about her, aren't you?"

"Yeah, that's it." Jesse figured that letting the man think he was a writer was an easy enough way to keep him from asking any more questions.

"Well, I can tell you right now, it wouldn't have done you any good if you had met her. There were just a whole lot of people who wanted to write her story, and they kept pestering her. Some even offered her a lot of money if she would give them her story, but she wouldn't do it."

"Well, I can see how she might not want to do that. I'm sure she was well enough fixed that the money didn't really mean anything to her."

"Well fixed? Are you kidding? You really didn't know her, did you? From the time Jesse James was killed, she became destitute. Nobody would hire her because of who she was, and she wound up moving in with her sister because she couldn't support herself and her kids. You asked how she died? I'll tell you how she died. She died of a broken heart and humiliation. That's how she died."

The emotion Jesse had felt when he first heard she had died intensified now to a sense of hurt, guilt, and anger. He clenched his hands into fists to keep from showing it.

"Do you have any idea where she is buried?" Jesse asked.

"Yeah, I know exactly where she is buried. She is at Mount Olivet Cemetery in Kearney. Kearney's about—"

"I know where Kearney is," Jesse said. "Thank you."

"How is it that you know where Kearney is? I thought you said you had never been in Missouri before."

"When I got interested in this, I read about Kearney, and I looked it up on the map."

Satisfied with the answer, Josh nodded. "Yes, I can see how you might have done that. Are you going to visit the grave?"

"I thought I might," Jesse said.

"Lots of people do," Josh said. "Jesse James was sort of a folk hero to people around here. All over Missouri, I suppose."

"How did you feel about him?"

"I don't know as I can say. He was an outlaw, that's for sure. But the Civil War and the next twenty years or so were tumultuous times. I don't think you can judge anyone unless you walk in his shoes for a while."

"Well, I thank you, sir, for the information you've given me."

"My pleasure," Josh said, turning to walk back to his desk.

Jesse walked back outside, feeling an intense emotion of sadness and loss, equal to that last moment he ever saw Zee in the park back in St. Joseph, twenty-two years ago.

"Pa, I've been walking around this place all day," Billy said that night. "This is the biggest town I've ever been in, in my whole life."

"It has over a hundred and sixty thousand people," Jesse said.

Billy laughed. "You know the damndest things."

"Let's take a ride tomorrow. There's a little town just north of here that I want to visit."

"Are we going to scout another job?" Billy asked.

"Not in Kearney," Jesse replied.

"How are we going to get there?"

"Like you said, Kansas City is a big place. We'll find a livery and rent a couple of horses."

"Pa, I've got a better idea."

"We're going to Kearney," Jesse insisted.

"I mean I have a better idea than renting horses."

Jesse shook his head. "I don't want to go by stagecoach or train. I want some way of getting around while we're there, so we're going to have to have horses."

"That's not the only way of getting around," Billy said with a broad smile.

"Do you have another idea in mind?"

"Yeah. You remember I told you that I was walkin' all around Kansas City?"

"Yes."

"Well, here's the thing. Pa, you saw it when we was in the trolley car comin' to the hotel. This town is just full of automobiles. Why, there's nigh as many automobiles as there is horse and wagons. You should see them."

"I did see them," Jesse said. "Like you said, you can't walk around in this town without seein' them."

"Well, what I would like to do is go to one of them places where people buy automobiles and look at one of them up real close."

"Why do you want to see one real close?"

"Why, if we're goin' to buy one, don't you think we ought to look at it real close?"

"Buy one? Who said we're goin' to buy one?"

"Why not, Pa? Horses are on their way out. Why, I bet you there will come a time when the only place you can see a horse is in a zoo somewhere."

"If that time ever comes, I don't want to be here," Jesse said.

"Let's buy an automobile, Pa," Billy said. "It's not like we can't afford one."

"What in the world has put an idea like this in your craw?"

"This is the twentieth century, Pa. I think automobiles are the thing of the future."

"All right, we may as well go have a look," Jesse agreed.

"Ha! I knew you would come around!"

"If we're going to get one, I say we get this one," Jesse said, pointing to a red automobile with yellow wheels. It had front and rear black leather seats.

"Why this one, Pa?" Billy asked. "This one looks a bit more snazzy." He pointed to a smaller, racier looking model, which had only two seats.

"Because this one has a top in case it rains. And it's got enough room for us to carry our things."

A salesman who had been standing by, listening to their conversation, chose this moment to step in.

"Your father has made a wise choice, young man. This is the Oldsmobile Brougham. It not only has a roof, as you can see, but it also has these isinglass curtains that you can roll down." He stopped to demonstrate. "This will keep you perfectly dry even in the hardest downpour. And, the engine develops ten horsepower."

"Wait a minute," Billy challenged. "Are you tellin' me that this engine here would be the same thing as hookin' up ten horses to this carriage?"

"Oh, no, it wouldn't be like that at all," the salesman said.

Billy smirked. "I didn't think so."

"Even with ten horses, the fastest you could go would be about twenty miles an hour, and that would only be for a short distance. In this automobile you can go forty miles an hour for as long as you have road to drive on, and gasoline to operate your engine. When we say ten horsepower, we are talking about how strong the engine is. If you hooked ten horses up to a dead weight and pulled it, you could pull that same weight with this machine."

"How much is it?" Jesse asked.

"Six hundred and fifty dollars."

"Oh, I don't know. That's a lot of money," Jesse said.

"But, Pa, if it will go that fast, think of it. It will outrun the fastest horse. It will, won't it, mister?" Billy asked the salesman.

"Oh, indeed it will."

"There is one problem," Jesse said. "We don't either one of us know how to operate this machine."

The salesman smiled. "Oh, that's no problem at all, sir. Mister Stallings, who is on our staff, will teach you how to become an excellent motorist."

"An excellent what?"

"Motorist. That's what one calls the operator of an automobile."

"See, Pa? That's not a problem."

"All right," Jesse said, acquiescing to Billy's petitions.

CHAPTER EIGHTEEN

"Twenty-four miles in only forty-five minutes!" Billy said, examining his pocket watch as they passed the sign welcoming them to Kearney. "Ha! You know how long it would have taken us to get here if we had rented horses like you wanted to?"

"It would have taken us a little longer," Jesse agreed.

"A little longer? It would have taken us at least three hours. Three hours, and we got here in forty-five minutes!" Billy, who was driving, reached up to pat the windshield. "Pa, buyin' this car was the best idea you ever had."

Jesse laughed. "It was a good one, all right. The drive over here made me thirsty. Why don't we stop in front of this store and get us a soda pop?"

"All right."

Going into the store Jesse lifted the lid of a red box, and sticking his hand down into the ice water, pulled out a Dr Pepper. Billy got a Coca-Cola.

"That's a fine-looking machine you folks drove up

in," the proprietor said as Jesse paid for the two drinks.

"Thanks. I'm looking for the cemetery. Where is it from here?"

"Go north about seven blocks until you get to Sixth Street, then turn left. It's right there on Sixth, between Jefferson and the railroad tracks. You can't miss it."

"Thank you."

"We got us someone real famous buried here, you know."

"Really? And who would that be?"

"Why, Jesse James hisself is buried here. Yes, sir, after Jesse's wife died, well they dug him up from where he was buried, 'n they moved him here to lie alongside her. I reckon you've heard of Jesse James."

"I've heard of him," Jesse said.

"Jesse was from around here, you know."

"Was he?"

"Yes, sir, he was. Me 'n him was just real good friends. I don't like to tell folks this, I mean it was a long time ago, but still they might not understand 'n hold it ag'in me. You see, the truth is that me 'n Jesse rode together. That is, until my wife made me quit. You shoulda seen Jesse's face when I told him I was goin' to quit. He was awful put out with me when I told 'im I wasn't goin' to ride with him no more, 'n he just begged me to stay with him. I hated to let him down like that, I mean what with him dependin' on me as much as did 'n all. But I reckon if a man's wife has strong feelin's about it, then you purt' nigh have to do whatever it is she's a' wantin you to do. Don't you think?"

"Oh, absolutely. I'm sure Jesse got over it. And I can understand why you don't like to talk about it."

"No, sir, I don't like to talk about it all that much. Truth to tell, I hardly never mention it at all that I was purt' nigh Jesse's right-hand man."

"I thought his brother, Frank, was his right-hand man," Jesse said.

"No, sir. Now, that's another thing there don't most folks know. But the truth is that Frank, well, he was sort of a weak sister. I mean, he warn't nothin' without Jesse. You can see that, by what he done after Jesse got hisself kilt. Nothin' that's what he's done."

"Being as you were such a friend of Jesse James, I guess you took it really hard when he was killed."

"Yes, sir, I did indeed. 'N that's another thing. I wish now that I had told him not to trust that Bob Ford fella. I had a feelin' about him. He never did seem quite right by me. You know how it is when you have these feelin's about people? Like sometimes you can just know when a fella ain't tellin' you the truth."

Jesse chuckled. "Yes, I know." Finishing their soft drinks, Jesse and Billy put the empty bottles in one of the boxes.

"Enjoy your stay in our little town," the grocer called to them.

Two more blocks down the road, Jesse pointed to a weathered, two-story building. A sign in front identified it as the Morning Star Hotel.

"Let's check in there."

"All right," Billy agreed. "Pa, do you think that man really knew Jesse James?"

"I don't know whether he did or not. Remember, he said he doesn't like to talk about it."

Billy laughed. "Yeah, he doesn't like to talk about it. Wonder where I should leave the auto?"

"We'll ask the clerk when we check in."

"You can just leave it alongside the hotel," the desk clerk said, responding to the query a few minutes later when they checked in. "From time to time we get folks here with autos, so we've marked off a place alongside the building. It's best to keep the autos and the horses separate, 'cause the horses sometimes get spooked."

"Thanks."

"Come walk down to the cemetery with me," Jesse said after they checked into their room.

"Are we goin' to see Jesse James's grave?"

"I thought we might."

"Why?"

"Why not? The folks here seem real proud of the fact that he's buried here. Wouldn't you like to see the grave?"

"I reckon so," Billy replied.

"Let's stop in here for a minute, shall we?" He pointed toward a florist shop.

"A flower store? You want to stop in a flower store?"

"Yeah."

"Why?"

"Because I want to," Jesse said without any further explanation.

A heavyset, gray-haired woman greeted them when they stepped inside.

"Yes, sir, what can I do for you gentlemen?"

"Do you have any roses?"

"Yes, sir, we certainly do. I do believe that our red

roses are more beautiful this year than they have ever been before."

Jesse shook his head. "I don't want red roses, I want yellow."

"Yellow?"

"Yes, do you have any yellow roses?"

"I have a few. But I don't know that I could even make up a dozen for you. We don't get many calls for yellow roses. And besides, they aren't nearly as pretty as the red roses. Are you sure you don't want red?"

"No, ma'am. It has to be yellow. And don't worry about how many you have. I only need one."

The woman chuckled and shook her head. "All right if one is all you want." She went into the back, then returned a moment later clutching one yellow rose.

"I found you the prettiest one I could," she said. "That'll cost you a nickel."

"Here's a dime, for being nice enough to find the best one," Jesse said.

A broad smile spread across her face. "Well, I thank you, sir. And I do hope she appreciates the yellow rose."

"I'm sure she will," Jesse said.

"She?" Billy said after they left the flower shop. "Pa, do you know some woman in this town?"

"No."

"Then why did you say 'she' would appreciate it?"

"Boy, you ask too many questions."

When they reached the cemetery, they looked around for a moment until they found what Jesse was looking for. There was one obelisk, then a flat stone. The obelisk read:

JESSE W JAMES

Taylor's SQ

Todd's CO

Quantrill's

Regt

CSA

The flat stone on the ground read:

Jesse W.	Zerelda
Born	Born
Sep 5 1847	July 21 1845
Assassinated	Died
April 3 1882*	Nov 13 1900

"Pa, look, here's Jesse James's grave," Billy said. "And this must be his wife. Oh, she was older than he was."

"I don't think that made any difference to them," Jesse said. He stood there looking down at Zee's grave. He was quiet for a long moment, then he bent down and lay the yellow rose on her side of the slab. "I'm sorry, Zee," he said. "I'm really sorry." He spoke the words so quietly that Billy couldn't understand him.

*Jesse James's first tombstone read: Devoted husband and father, Jesse Woodson James, Sep 5, 1847 murdered April 3, 1882, by a traitor and a coward whose name is not worthy to appear here.

"What did you say?" Billy asked.

"Nothing," Jesse said. "I didn't say anything."

"I thought I heard you say something."

"I was just mumbling, that's all."

"Pa, why did you put that rose on her grave?"

"Well, now, it would have looked really ridiculous for me to put this rose on his grave now, wouldn't it?"

Billy laughed. "Yeah, I reckon so."

They stayed there for some time with Jesse standing over Zee's grave just looking down at it.

"Pa, how long are we goin' to stay here?" Billy asked.

"I'm about ready to go back to the hotel," Jesse said.

"I don't mean to rush you none," Billy said. "We can stay here as long as you want. I was just wonderin', is all."

Jesse smiled at Billy. "Well, you don't have to wonder anymore," he said. "Let's go back."

They walked without speaking for a few blocks until, finally, Billy broke the silence.

"Pa, can I ask you a question?"

"Go ahead."

"What was all that about? I mean, why did you stand there over those graves for as long as you did? And why did you put a yellow rose on Jesse James's wife's grave?"

"I just thought it would be a nice thing to do," Jesse said.

"Well, if you ask me, it's mighty peculiar."

Jesse laughed. "What do you mean, if I ask you? You are the one asking all the questions."

"I'm just curious, that's all."

"Boy, haven't you ever heard the saying that curiosity killed the cat?"

"Yeah, I've heard it. It never made much sense to me, but I've heard it."

"Here's the hotel," Jesse said, pointing out the obvious to change the conversation.

"Gentlemen," the desk clerk called to them as they walked through the lobby. "Here is a copy of the *Kansas City Star*. It is a courtesy that we provide our guests."

"Thank you," Jesse said, taking the proffered newspaper.

CHAPTER NINETEEN

The cabin on the Brazos—March 5, 1942

Frederick Faust poured himself a cup of coffee, then offered to do the same for Jesse, who declined.

"When you went to Kansas City, did you actually intend to look up Zee?" Faust asked.

"Yes. I had no idea she had died. Though I guess we had died to each other a long time ago."

"What if she had been alive, and you found her? What would you have done?"

"I'm not sure."

"Would you have tried to get together again?"

Jesse was quiet for a long moment before he responded. "Yeah, I think I would have. We had lived together as Mr. and Mrs. Thomas Howard, we could have lived together as Mr. and Mrs. Frank Alexander."

"Do you think she would have taken you back? I mean, parting had to be hard for her."

"It was hard for both of us," Jesse said.

"You don't think you could have held out some

hope to her that she could have joined you after six months, or a year?"

"Damn you, Fred, you aren't making this any easier, are you? The truth is, I've thought about it many times over the last sixty years. I should have gone on to California and then let her join me after about six months. As I think back on it now, I'm sure we could have lived out the rest of our lives together without any trouble at all."

"I'm sorry. I'm just trying to get the story here. The whole story. If I ask anything that's too uncomfortable for you to deal with, you don't have to answer if you don't want to."

"Ask anything you want. I'll answer. The truth is, just real soon after I left Zee, I met Molly. I'm sure I'm not the only man on the run who has ever taken up with another woman. The only thing I can say for myself is that I didn't use Molly. I married her, and we had a good life together."

"Did you love Molly?"

"Yes."

"Did you think about Zee?"

"There wasn't hardly a day that went by that I didn't think of her. I know it isn't right, but I still loved Zee, too, just as much as I loved Molly. But I figured Zee had made a new life for herself, and who was I to interfere with that? Besides which, I took comfort in knowing that she had enough money to look after herself and the children."

"But you told me she didn't. You told me that Bob Ford hadn't shared any of the reward with her. When you learned of her state of deprivation from the *Kansas City Star* journalist, was that the first you realized that Ford had not shared the reward as he had promised?"

"Yes," Jesse said. "Like I said, if I had known earlier what Bob Ford did, I would have killed the son of a bitch myself."

"I'm curious about the yellow rose. You told the florist that it couldn't be a red rose, it had to be a yellow rose."

"Yeah. Zee really liked yellow roses, and one day I picked one to give to her. She took on so much about having a single yellow rose, saying as how that was more romantic than getting a whole bouquet of flowers, that from time to time I'd just give her one yellow rose. She always liked that, so it just seemed like the thing to do, to get a yellow rose and put it on her grave."

"You said it confused Billy."

Jesse laughed. "Yeah, he was some surprised by it, all right."

"You had not yet told Billy who you really were?" Faust asked.

Jesse chuckled. "Thank you."

"Thank me?" Faust replied with a puzzled expression on his face. "Why are you thanking me?"

"You asked if I had told Billy who I really was. That means you believe that I am who I say I am."

Now it was Faust's turn to chuckle. "Well, I must say this. If you aren't Jesse James, you are certainly spinning a convincing yarn. Convincing enough to keep me here for weeks, listening to you, and taking notes."

"When are you going to write the book?"

"I'm writing it now. Every night, I transcribe my notes to the typewriter. Even this," he added.

"Even this? What do you mean, even this?"

"If this book is going to have any validity, it has to include our contemporary conversations as well, not just your reminisces of the years between the time the world thought you had been killed, and now."

"I reckon so."

"Jesse, do you mind if we take a break and listen to some news?"

"No, I don't mind at all," Jesse replied, walking over to turn on the radio. After a few squeals and whistles, the announcer's voice came through.

". . . *Pure Oil Company. And now, here is H.V. Kaltenborn.*"

Kaltenborn's clipped, precise voice followed.

"*This is H.V. Kaltenborn. The Fifth Navy District announced today, that two more U.S merchantmen of medium size were sunk off our Atlantic coast last week, with the probable loss of twenty lives.*

"*German aircraft roared over Southern England yesterday, and some bombs were dropped. It is not believed that any lives were lost.*

"*The Japanese have reinforced their already numerically superior forces on the island of Luzon. This is believed to be in preparation for their intention to wipe out the American and Philippine force on Bataan.*"

Jesse turned the radio off. "Why can't they have any good news?" he asked.

"Wouldn't you rather hear the truth, even if the news is bad?" Faust replied.

"Oh, yes, I do want the truth," Jesse said. He chuckled. "I just want the truth to be good news."

"I'm sure that time will come. Before this war, America had not been building up its military the way all the countries were doing in Europe and

Asia," Faust said. "I think we just thought that we were far enough away from the rest of the world, separated from both Europe and Asia by vast oceans, that the war wouldn't come to us. But it did. I do believe though, that with our industrial base, we will soon become the most powerful nation in the entire world."

"Aren't we already?" Jesse replied.

"If you count the potential, yes, we certainly are," Faust answered.

As Jesse lay in bed that night, the tree just outside his window cast moon shadows on the wall. The shadows were so sharply delineated that he could make out the individual leaves and branches as if they had been put there by a movie projector.

Getting out of bed, he padded over to the window to look out at the cottonwood tree. One of the leaves caught a flash from the moon and sent a sliver of silver slashing into the night.

Was he doing the right thing in telling his story now? Was it really, as he had stated, a need to purge his soul of all the evil deeds he had done in his life? Or was he just guilty of vanity? That was a charge that Frank had made first, then it had been picked up by newspapers around the country. "The persona of Jesse James is much larger than the man, Jesse James," one newspaper article stated. "He is a man consumed by the need to be famous."

Was that true? And if so, is that what he was doing now?

"No," he said aloud. "I've brought up too many painful memories for it to be something like that.

I'm doing what I must do. It has nothing to do with a need to be famous."

Jesse turned away from the window and got back into bed. He lay there, staring up into the darkness for nearly an hour before sleep finally arrived.

Kearney, Missouri—August 1904

"Hey, Pa," Billy said, looking up from the newspaper the hotel desk clerk had given them. "You know where I think we should go with our new automobile next?"

"Back to Kansas City?"

"No, sir. I think we should go to Saint Louis."

"Saint Louis? Why?"

"Because that's where they are having a World's Fair. Listen to this: *'The greatest gathering of mechanical wonders, scientific discoveries, and human oddities ever assembled are on display at the Saint Louis World's Fair. An entire village has been moved from the Philippines and reconstructed on the fairgrounds and the villagers go about their lives, with little attention being paid to the million or more visitors who have come to view them.*

The largest assemblage of automobiles ever to be in one place will be in Saint Louis for the world's fair.'"

"You want to drive all the way to Saint Louis in this machine?"

"Sure, why not? I think it would be fun."

"I don't know; it seems like a folly to me."

"Well here, just take a look at the paper and see for yourself," Billy said, passing the newspaper over to him.

"I still think it's—" Jesse started, then something

in the newspaper caught his attention and he read it with great interest.

"See what I mean?" Billy said.

"What?"

"The story about the World's Fair in Saint Louis. Don't you think we ought to go?"

"Yes," Jesse said. "I think we ought to go."

There was one item in the article about the World's Fair that particularly caught his interest. But he didn't mention it to Billy.

It took them two and a half days to go from Kearney to St. Louis. On at least five occasions the road ran right through someone's farm, and they had to pay tolls for passage, ranging from a nickel to a dollar. When they reached St. Louis the dirt road turned to a paved street. A sign identified it as Skinker Avenue, and although they had encountered a few motorized vehicles on their trip from Kearney, here they saw literally dozens of other automobiles, even though it was quite early in the morning. Many of the drivers honked and waved at them, as if all motorists were members of some exclusive club.

They were passing through an affluent residential area of the city where large, attractive, brick homes sat on well-manicured lawns. Uncollected newspapers lay on the front sidewalks.

"Billy, hop out and pick up one of those papers, then get back in. I'll go slow enough for you to catch up," Jesse said.

Billy did so.

"What does it say about the fair?"

"Wow," Billy said. "It's talkin' about all the automobiles."

"Read it."

"It says, 'At least ten thousand motorists and their passengers have arrived for the fair in more than twenty-five hundred automobiles worth an estimated five million dollars.' That's a lot of money," Billy added.

"It sure is."

"It also says," Billy started, then he stopped. "Pa, we made the newspaper."

"What?" Jesse asked sharply. "Our names are in the paper?"

"No, sir, it ain't our names, but it's talkin' about us."

"What do you mean? Read the article you're talking about."

"It says, 'No new lead on the bold robbery of the Texas and Pacific train near San Angelo, Texas, two months ago. The robbers, two men, believed possibly to be father and son, accosted the engineer and fireman when the train stopped for water. The robbery must have been well planned, for they forced the fireman to divest the engine of all steam pressure, then extinguish the fire before they left. That put the train more than an hour behind schedule, and it was only by sheer luck that no head-on collision ensued with the next east-bound train on the same line. A spokesman for the railroad said that not even Jesse James could have pulled off a more clever train robbery.

"'Within a few days after the bold robbery, two men robbed the bank in Culpepper, Texas, and as the description generally matched that of the train robbers, it is believed it may have been the same father and son team.'

"Ha! What do you think of that? Not even Jesse James could have done better," Billy said with a big smile.

"How could they have possibly known that we were father and son?" Jesse asked.

"Uh, Pa, that might have been my fault," Billy said. "I sort of let it slip to the engineer."

"Damn it, boy, you have to be careful about such things," Jesse said.

"I'm sorry."

"Well, what's done is done, and mistakes aren't all that bad if you learn from them. But think, next time."

"I will, Pa. I promise."

CHAPTER TWENTY

When they reached the fairground entrance, a police-man was standing at the gate, holding up his hand.

"Pa!" Billy gasped. "What do you think he wants?"

"Relax," Jesse said. "He's not holding a gun in his hand, so he damn sure isn't planning on arrest-ing us."

Jesse approached the gate, then put his foot on the clutch to disengage the transmission. The engine continued to pop and growl.

"There's a special lot for parking the automo-biles," the policeman said, pointing. "It's down at the south end of the park. Don't go into the same lot as the horses, because these infernal machines frighten them."

"All right," Jesse said, following the policeman's instructions.

After parking the car, they walked toward the Hall of Festivals, which was the largest and most iconic symbol of the entire fair. The dome, a pamphlet said, was larger than that of St. Peter's in Rome. A flow of water, fifty feet wide, gushed from the north side of the hall and splashed down ninety-five feet through a series of cascades, bottoming out at the grand basin, then splitting into three waterways. These waterways were filled with graceful gondolas, which carried hundreds of visitors to lagoons in various parts of the fairgrounds. Punctuating the system of lagoons, and placed for dramatic effect, were a series of gushing fountains.

ICE CREAM CONES a sign nearby read.

"Hey, Pa, what do you think an 'ice cream cone' is?" Billy asked.

"I don't know. Why don't we find out?"

A few minutes later Jesse and Billy were walking down 'The Pike' eating a scoop of ice cream in a rolled-up waffle.* The Pike was a solid stream of humanity, moving from one part of the fairgrounds to another. The newspaper article Jesse had read said that, already, three million visitors had passed through the fair, and they expected at least two million more.

"Look at that!" Billy said, pointing to a giant wheel. He read from the pamphlet they had picked up earlier. "The giant wheel is two hundred fifty feet high, and each of the cars can hold sixty people. It takes twenty minutes for the Ferris Wheel to make one revolution.'"†

---

*The ice cream cone was born at the 1904 World's Fair in St. Louis. George Bang, owner of the Bannery Creamery, apparently ran out of bowls in which to serve his ice cream at the fair, so he started using rolled-up waffles. They proved to be so popular that he stopped serving in bowls and served the ice cream only in the rolled-up waffles. That was direct precursor of the ice cream cone.

†It is believed, though it has never been definitely established, that the remains of the giant Ferris Wheel are buried under Skinker Blvd., near Forrest Park.

The first place they visited was the Palace of Machinery.

"Damn, Pa, look at this," Billy said, pointing to one of the displays. "It says here that this gasoline engine has the power of three thousand horses. Ha! What if we had that engine in our auto? I'll bet we could go one hundred miles per hour."

"I don't know, it's so big it seems to me like it would weigh so much it would hold the auto back," Jesse said.

From the Palace of Machinery they went to Transportation Hall, which boasted a network of railroad tracks carrying an array of full-scale models of the earliest engines to the latest and most powerful locomotives. They also had luxurious passenger cars, one of which had been the private car of President Abraham Lincoln. There was even a refrigerated freight car in which a sign proudly proclaimed PERISHABLE PRODUCTS MAY BE SENT WITHOUT RISK OF SPOILAGE.

Next, they visited something called the Magic Whirlpool. The water, according to the pamphlet, was drawn from the Mississippi River, and the effect of a giant whirlpool was created by using centrifugal pumps the draw forty-nine thousand gallons of water a minute.

"Now, I've got someplace that I want to go," Jesse said.

"Where?"

"Over there," Jesse said, pointing to a low, flat-roofed, white building. "When we passed by it awhile ago, I heard the barker out front announcing that some of the most feared and celebrated outlaws of the Old West are inside."

"Pa, are you serious? I mean who could possibly be there? The real ones are either dead or are old men still in prison. You know there won't be anyone worth seeing in there."

"Let's take a look anyway," Jesse said.

"Who's in there?" Billy asked.

"I'll read what it says," Jesse replied.

"'John Wilson Vermillion, alias "Texas Jack" and "Shoot Your Eyes Out" Vermillion, was a famous shootist of the Old West who rode with Wyatt Earp during his vendetta ride.'"

"I've never heard of him," Billy said. "Who else is there?"

"'David Anderson, better known under the alias Billy Wilson. He rode with Billy the Kid,'" Jesse read.

"I've never heard of him, either, but I have heard of Billy the Kid. Hey, Pa, what do you think? I believe I'll start calling myself Billy the Kid," Billy said with a chuckle.

"Not while you're with me, you won't," Jesse replied.

"John Vermillion and David Anderson. I have no idea why you want to see them, but if that's what you want, I'll go along with you."

"Come with me or not, it makes no difference. I'm going to go see them," Jesse said. What he didn't say was that there was one more outlaw listed in the pamphlet, and though he didn't read that name aloud, that was the person he really had come to see. It was the same name he had seen in the paper back in Kearney when he agreed with Billy to come to the World's Fair in St. Louis. It was, in fact, the only reason he had agreed to come.

"Let's go in here and have a look around," Jesse suggested.

"All right," Billy agreed. "But I tell you the truth, if it wasn't for you wantin' to come in here, I don't think I'd walk across the street to see 'em."

Jesse led a reluctant Billy into the building and looked onto the raised platform where there were three Old West characters sitting in chairs by the signs that identified them. There were the two that Jesse had read about, and the one that he didn't mention. All three were wearing jeans, boots, denim shirts, and a holster and pistol.

"Ha! What do you bet that there isn't a bullet in a one of them guns?" Billy said.

"I'm sure you're right," Jesse said.

"Folks," a barker said to those who were gathered in the hall. "This desperate character is Texas Jack Vermillion. While in Dodge City, Kansas, he became very good friends with such people as Wyatt and Virgil Earp, and Doc Holliday. When those men went to Tombstone, Texas Jack went with them, working there as a special deputy. After the shootout at the O.K. Corral, and the murder of Morgan Earp, Texas Jack rode with Deputy U.S. Marshal Wyatt Earp on the famous Vendetta ride where both Frank Stilwell and Curly Bill Brocius were killed. Texas Jack was one of the deadliest gunfighters in the Old West, and he picked up the sobriquet, 'Shoot Your Eye Out' Vermillion because in one of his gunfights, he did shoot out the eye of his adversary."

"How come he isn't in prison now?" someone asked from the crowd.

"He isn't in prison because every gunfight in

which he participated was a fair fight and, in every case, he was also representing the law."

"Our second desperado," the barker said to the crowd, is David Anderson who, during his time as a gunfighter in the Old West, was known as Billy Wilson. Mr. Wilson, if you would, give the crowd a greeting."

Wilson stood up and, drawing his gun quickly, fired it at the crowd; the muzzle flash was bright, and the sound of the shot ear-splitting.

Many in the crowd screamed and some started to run, until they realized he had fired a blank round. Then the crowd laughed, and, feeling a twinge of excitement over having been so frightened, they came back to the raised platform where Wilson twirled the pistol around his trigger finger before putting the gun back in its holster.

"Dave Anderson, or Billy Wilson, began his outlaw career by riding with a gang of rustlers, led by Billy the Kid," the barker continued. "There he met up with an old friend, Dave Rudabaugh, with whom he had outlawed a bit back in Las Vegas. The gang raised havoc throughout New Mexico. Soon after, Mr. Wilson was involved, with Billy the Kid and Rudabaugh, in the killing of Deputy James Carlyle at the ranch of Jim Greathouse. Then, on the nineteenth of December, 1880, six members of the gang were riding into Fort Sumner, when Pat Garrett and his posse opened fire on them from ambush. One of the rustlers, Tom O'Folliard, was killed, but the rest escaped. But just a few days later, on the twenty-third of December, that same year, at a rock house at Stinking Springs, Wilson, Billy the Kid, Dave Rudabaugh, and Tom Pickett of the Rustlers were captured by Garrett's posse. Rustler Charlie Bowdre was killed in that fight. Wilson went to trial, was convicted, and sentenced to serve seven years in prison. However, he managed to escape in September 1882.

"Ten years ago he turned himself in, and at that time was given a full and complete pardon."

The third man on the podium was almost totally bald, and with a full mustache. He was sitting by a sign that identified him as Frank James.

"It seems to me like that barker is tryin' to make these outlaw fellas more famous than they really are, 'cause I haven't heard of anyone in this—" Billy paused in midsentence, and pointed.

"Pa, look," he said in an awe-struck voice. "Look over there! There's somebody I *have* heard of. That sign says he is Frank James."

"Yes," Jesse said.

"I know why you wanted to come in here now. You seen his name in that pamphlet, didn't you?"

"Yes."

"Well, why didn't you tell me that Frank James was here? You know I would have come to see him."

"You're here now."

"Let's go over there to him."

"Not yet," Jesse replied.

"Not yet? Why not yet?"

"Just wait," Jesse said somewhat cryptically.

Jesse waited until after the barker had given his spiel about Frank James, connecting him frequently with his even more famous brother. Then, when the barker's little talk was over, and the crowd drifted away, there was no one remaining around the man identified as Frank James.

That was when Jesse and Billy walked up to him. Jesse stood there for a while, just staring. Frank had changed so much that at first he didn't believe it was him, but upon closer scrutiny, he saw that it really was.

"Pa, what are we doin' just standin' here like this?" Billy asked.

"Son. I want you to say hello to your uncle Frank," Jesse said.

"What?"

Frank James was so used to people gazing at him that he had learned how to not pay any attention to someone, no matter how intensely they might be staring. Because of that he had taken no more notice of the two who had just approached him than he had of any of the other hundreds of thousands of gawkers who had come through while he was on display.

Then he heard Jesse speak. And it wasn't the words that got his attention as much as it was the familiar voice. He looked down first in surprise, then in absolute shock, unable to believe what he was seeing.

"Dingus?" he said, the word barely audible. "My God! Are you a ghost? No, you can't be! Ghosts don't get any older, do they?"

"Hello, Lexy," Jesse replied. Those were the private names the two brothers had used with each other for their entire lives. Lexy from Frank James's first name, Alexander. Jesse never swore when he was a young man, and he had made up the word "dingus" as a substitute curse word. As a way of teasing him, Frank had pinned that on him as a nickname.

"I'm not a ghost."

"But . . . I don't understand," Frank said. "How can this be?" He shook his head. "No." He held his hand out toward Jesse. "No, this isn't real. Get away! Get away from me."

"It's real, Lexy. I swear to you, I'm really here, talking to you."

"But, how? How?"

"I guess you and I have some talking to do, don't we?" Jesse asked.

"Talking? You've been dead for twenty-two years, then you suddenly show up and say we've got talking to do?" Now Frank's voice was more agitated than shocked.

"Please, Frank," Jesse said.

Frank reached over and turned his sign around so that, instead of reading FRANK JAMES, it read WILL BE BACK SOON.

"You won't actually be back soon," Jesse said. "Not if you let me tell you the whole story."

"I'm getting paid to do this," Frank said. "I have to be here until six o'clock tonight."

"All right. We'll come back at six."

Frank ran his hand over the top of his head, then sighed and shook his head.

"No, hold on for a minute. There's no way I can wait until six o'clock to find out what this is all about," he said. "I'll go see the display manager and tell him I'm not feeling well and I want to take the rest of the day off. If he wants to dock my pay, so be it."

"All right, we'll meet you just outside the door," Jesse said.

"Pa?" Billy asked. His voice was as shocked as Frank's voice had been. "Pa, what is this? Why did you tell me to say hello to my uncle Frank?"

"I know you've got questions, son, but so does Frank. And he's had questions for a lot longer than you have. Just wait, it'll be easier for me to talk to both of you at the same time. I'll answer all the questions either of you have then."

"You promise?"

"I promise," Jesse said. "You have no idea how long I've been wanting to tell someone the truth."

A few minutes later, Frank came out of the building.

"All right, let's hear it," Frank said.

The building was just off the Pike, and the fair was alive with sound—thousands of voices, motorized machines, and music.

"Not here," Jesse said. "Isn't there somewhere we can go where it will be quiet enough that a fella can hear himself think?"

"I know a place down by the river. We can go get our supper there. It might be hard to hire a cab, though, what with all the people in town."

"I have an automobile," Jesse said.

Frank smiled, for the first time, and shook his head.

"You would, Dingus. You would."

CHAPTER TWENTY-ONE

The Riverboat Café sat on the west side of Broadway, which was the brick-paved road that separated the café from the cobblestone riverbank. At least half a dozen steamboats were tied up at the landing, the twin, fluted chimneys of the wedding cake craft rising high into the air. Jesse, Billy, and Frank were sitting in the single booth located at the rear of the café. They had chosen this location because it was far enough away from any of the other diners that it would allow them to speak without being overheard.

"You can't beat the fried catfish and hush puppies here," Frank said.

"I always have liked catfish," Jesse said.

Frank sighed. "Jesse, I don't know how it's possible that I'm sittin' across the table from you. But I know this is you. What are you doing here?"

"I came back to Missouri, hoping to look up Zee and make amends with her. I didn't know she had died."

"How could you know? You never bothered to check, did you?"

"Ma is still alive, isn't she?" Jesse asked without responding directly to Frank's challenging comment. "I figure she is, because when I visited the cemetery, I didn't see any tombstones with her name."

"She's still alive."

"That's good to know."

"How could you have done this to Zee? How could you have done this to Ma? How could you have done this to me? All these years, you've been alive, when every one of us thought you were dead. Did you never give us a second thought, Jesse?"

"Of course I did."

"Pa?" Billy asked, his face contorted by confusion. "Pa, why is Frank James callin' you Jesse?"

"You mean even the boy doesn't know? He just called you Pa. I know this isn't Jesse Junior. Who is he?"

"Don't talk about me like I'm not even here, mister," Billy said. "My name is William Anderson Alexander. And this is my pa."

"Alexander? Is that what you're callin' yourself now?"

"Yes. My name is James Frank Alexander," Jesse replied.

"Pa, what is goin' on here? What are you all talkin' about?"

"Your pa is Jesse James," Frank said.

"What?" Billy gasped. "You're . . . you're Jesse James?" Billy was as shocked now as Frank James had been earlier.

"Yes, son. My real name is Jesse James."

"Pa, I don't understand. I thought Jesse James

was dead. I thought he was killed. The whole world thought he was killed."

"That was the way I planned it," Jesse said.

"You mean that, through all these years, you've been lyin'? You've lied to me and Frank?"

"He hasn't been lying to me all these years, boy. I hadn't laid eyes on him until this afternoon."

"When I said Frank, I wasn't talking about you. I was talking about my brother."

"Sorry, son, it was an easy mistake for me to make," Frank said.

"What about Ma? Did she know?"

Jesse shook his head. "No, Billy, your mother never knew. I thought it best that she not know."

"So, you took a second wife, and you weren't honest with her, either," Frank said accusingly.

"I wanted to be honest with her, but the time never came where I could tell her without just making things worse."

"Oh, what a tangled web we weave, when first we practice to deceive," Frank said.

"Still quoting Shakespeare, I see," Jesse said.

"That's not Shakespeare. That's Sir Walter Scott."

"You always were one for reading. You used to carry books in your saddlebags, even when we were on the run."

"What about Zee?" Frank asked. "Apparently, when you married this boy's mother, it didn't bother you that you were still married to Zee. But I guess you figured if Zee thought you were dead, it wouldn't matter all that much."

"Zee knew I wasn't dead. She not only knew, she helped set it up so that the rest of the world would believe I was dead," Jesse explained. "She knew it was probably the only way to keep me from being hung."

"Did she know you had another family?"

Jesse shook his head. "I never got in touch with her again after I left. I thought it would be safer for her."

"And easier for you. Would you mind telling me who that is that's lying in the grave beside her?"

"Then that means Zee kept the secret even into her grave. I can see that she would do that. She was a good woman, Frank. A better woman than you ever knew, and a better woman than I deserved. Especially after what I did to her." Jesse sighed, then ran his hand through his hair. "I expect the person beside her is Charlie Bigelow."

"Charlie Bigelow. Hmm, I remember everyone wondering whatever happened to him. Jesse, you and I both have done our share of killin'. Please don't tell me you murdered Charlie just to set this up. I never liked the squirrelly little bastard, but I wouldn't like to think of you killin' him in cold blood."

"I didn't kill him, Frank. Bob Ford did it, just like everyone thought. Only it wasn't me he killed, it was Charlie Bigelow. And at the time, Bigelow was goin' for his gun to kill me."

"Here it is, gentlemen," a waiter said then, arriving with a large tray bearing three empty plates in addition to a platter of fried catfish, another of hush puppies, and a third of fried potatoes.

"The fish you're sending down to your liver spent last night in the Mississippi River," he said, laughing at his own joke.

Frank drummed his fingers on the table until the waiter left.

"What are you goin' to do now, Jesse?" Frank asked. "Are you goin' to come out of hiding? Because I don't think that would be such a good idea."

"Why not? You did it."

"It's not the same."

"How is it that you can sit back there at the fair in front of Lord knows how many people, telling God and everyone who you are and not have the law comin' for you?" Jesse asked.

"You might remember, Jesse, that right after Northfield I told you that I had had enough. Do you also remember how much money we got for that raid? We got twenty-six dollars. Everyone in our gang but you and I were either killed or captured, all for twenty-six dollars. We never should have gone. You might remember that I was against it."

"You might have been against it, but you went. When I told you how much money we could have gotten . . . should have gotten, you went along easily enough."

"It turned into a slaughter pen."

"You were the one who killed Heywood," Jesse reminded him.

"He had a gun, Jesse, and he was pointing it straight at you. If I hadn't killed him, he would have killed you. I had no choice."

"I thanked you for that before, and I thank you again," Jesse said.

Frank was silent for a moment. "I tell you the truth, Jesse, by God if I had known then what I know now, I would have let the son of a bitch kill you."

"No, you wouldn't," Jesse said. "You wouldn't

because we are still brothers. Despite everything, we are still brothers."

"When we got back home from Northfield, I was ready to quit," Frank said.

"You didn't quit, though, did you? You haven't forgotten the Blue Cut train robbery, have you?"

"That was another fizzle," Frank said. "We only got three thousand dollars."

"Three thousand? Pa, that's—" Billy started to say, but at a stern glance from his father, he altered what he was going to say in midsentence, "not a lot of money for a train robbery, is it?"

"No, it wasn't," Frank said. "And half of that we took off the passengers. The passengers, Jesse. We had never stolen from the ordinary people before. We had only stolen from institutions. Banks, trains, but never from the common people. And that wasn't bad enough. You had to walk through the cars, without a mask, bragging to everybody that you were the famous Jesse James."

"I was a lot younger then."

"You were thirty-two years old, Jesse. You were a long way from being the kid you were right after the war."

"You took your share of the money, didn't you?"

"Yes, I had to. I was sick of the whole thing, and I needed that money to get away. I left Missouri and went to Tennessee."

"I knew you had gone to Tennessee," Jesse said. "And I knew you had no wish to ride with me anymore. And I figured it would be better for you, and for Annie, if I stayed away from you."

"You figured right."

"How did you avoid the law down there?"

I took the name Ben J. Woodson."

Jesse chuckled. "We took each other's names. I am James Frank Alexander, which is your whole name, but just backward, and you are using my middle name for your last name. What was the J. for? Jesse, or James?"

"I've never actually had to use anything other than the initial, 'J.' If you want to think so, I guess you could say it's Jesse."

"Tell me, how are Annie and little Bobby getting along?"

"Annie is fine, and 'little' Bobby, as you call him, is twenty-six years old. He is home, managing the farm."

"What did you do in Tennessee? How did you make a living?"

"I worked some as a teamster; I raised hogs. Frank smiled. "I even joined the Methodist church. And Annie got a job teaching school."

"I remember that Annie was a real smart lady, well educated."

"Yes, she graduated from college. I made it a point to make friends with prominent citizens and officers of the law. I figured it might be good to have their favorable opinion of me, if ever the time came when my true identity might be exposed."

"I can understand that. I've made a few friends of the law myself," Jesse said. He thought of his friendship with Sheriff Larry Wallace, and even the fact that he had acted as a deputy and posse member. He recalled having killed Pete Arnold when he was riding with a posse, and he wondered how Frank would take that. He didn't tell him.

"I have to tell you, Jesse, my old life grew more detestable the further I got away from it."

"But now you are in the open about who you are. How come you aren't in prison?"

"You're getting ahead of the story," Frank said. "I'm coming to that."

Jesse smiled. "You always did like to draw a story out. All right, go ahead."

"I was in Tennessee when I heard you had been shot. I had been out for a walk, and when I came back, Anne told me you had been killed. That did it for me. Up until then, I had been keeping my identity a secret, in part to protect you. But with you dead . . . that is . . . at least I thought you were dead, I decided to see what I could do about starting over. I sent Annie back to Missouri to meet with Governor Tom Crittenden about my surrendering. I hoped I could get a pardon from him, but he said he couldn't do that. He did offer me a fair trial and promised not to extradite me to Minnesota. And, I'm sure you know that if I had gone up there, I would have been hanged for sure, not just because of Heywood, but with all the killing that took place during our failed attempt to rob the bank there. I was tried in Clay County, Missouri, which was the best place I could possibly be tried. General Joe Shelby was there, and he testified for me, then came over to shake my hand after his testimony." Frank chuckled. "Neither the judge nor the prosecutor liked that one bit. As it turns out, the jury was almost entirely made up of former Confederate soldiers, or Confederate sympathizers, and after they retired for the deliberations, they came back within fifteen minutes with a verdict of not guilty."

"I thought it must be something like that. You said it wouldn't be good for me to come out of hiding now and tell everyone who I am. Why not? I mean, it worked for you."

"I never was anything more than second banana to you, Jesse, and you knew that. Knew it? Hell, you reveled in it. It didn't bother me any that you were the one all the newspapers wrote about, but if you were to try and come out now, believe me, that would come back and bite you. The war was too long ago, attitudes have changed, and I promise you, Jesse, you would not get a sympathetic jury. Not at this late date, and especially after everyone found out what a . . . trick you had played on people. Including your own family," he added.

"All right, maybe I'll just be quiet about it so that only you and Ma know. I would love to see her again."

"No, you can't see her, and she can never know."

"What do you mean, I can't see her?"

"Jesse, you are my brother, and I love you. But I'm going to have to ask you never to see me again. Or our mother."

"Frank, I—"

Frank held out his hand. "Jesse, after what you put Ma through, if you would show up now, the shock would kill her. And I can't let that happen. I won't let it happen. As far as the world is concerned, you are dead. As far as Ma is concerned you are dead. As far as your two children are concerned, you are dead. And as far as I am concerned from now on, you are dead. Don't ever come to see me again; don't ever write to me. And for your own safety, don't ever let anyone know you are still alive because, Jesse, sure as a gun is iron, they will hang you."

"I'm sorry you feel that way, Frank. After all this time, I thought, that is, I was hoping, that maybe we could—"

"You thought after all this time you could just come back like the Prodigal Son, as if the last twenty-two years had not happened?" Frank shook his head. "No, Jesse. It doesn't work that way."

Frank stood and looked down at Jesse, and at Billy. "Boy, if you care about your pa at all, you'll keep just real quiet about what you've heard here today. Don't ever say a word about it, because they'll hang him sure."

"I won't ever say anything," Billy said quietly.

"Frank, you don't have to leave yet, do you? You haven't eaten any of your fish. I mean, if we are never going to see each other again, the least we can do is have one last meal together. For old time's sake."

"There's nothing about old times that I want to remember," Frank said as he turned and walked away.

CHAPTER TWENTY-TWO

The cabin on the Brazos—March 5, 1942

After repeating his brother's last line, Jesse got up from the table and walked over to the porch railing to look out over the river.

Faust gave him a long beat of silence before he spoke.

"Did you ever see Frank again, Jesse?" Faust asked.

"After the Fair closed Frank went back to his farm in Excelsior Springs, Missouri, where he charged fifty cents apiece for people to come tour the farm, and he sold pistols with his and my initials carved in the handle, claiming that they were the very pistols we had carried during our life of crime."

The tone of Jesse's voice was bitter. "The son of a bitch said that his old life grew more detestable the further he got away from it. But that didn't keep him from showing himself off like some fool at the fair, or from charging people to tour his farm.

"He died in 1915. Ma died in 1911. And to answer

your question, I never saw either one of them again. Ma never even learned that I was still alive."

"When you learned that your brother had surrendered himself, was tried, and found not guilty, weren't you just a little envious of him?"

"Was I envious of him? No, why would you ask such a thing?"

"Well, after all, he was able to start a new life for himself, just as you did. The only difference is, he lived out the rest of his life with his wife and son, and with your mother. You had to give everything up to accomplish that same thing. He kept his family; you lost yours."

"I lost one family, that's true," Jesse said. "But I had another family, a wonderful family."

"Now comes the big question. Once Billy learned that you were Jesse James, how did he take it?"

St. Louis, Missouri—August 1904

Billy had not said one word during the drive back to the hotel. Not until they were in the hotel room did he speak about it.

"Pa, it's true? You really are Jesse James?"

"Yes, Billy. It's true. I'm sorry I never told you, or Frank, or Molly about it. But I thought it would be better if none of you knew. By the way, if it will make you feel better, I never told Jesse Junior or Mary who I was. Jesse Junior didn't even know what his real name was. He thought his name was Timmy Howard."

"But your wife knew who you were. Your real wife."

"Billy, do you think your ma wasn't my real wife?"

"How could she be, if you were already married?"

"Technically, I wasn't married. The state of Missouri thought I was dead, so my marriage to Zee was no longer valid. It was the same as if we had gotten a divorce."

Billy was quiet for a moment, then he smiled. "Yeah, I guess that's true, isn't it? Ma really was your wife. And that's good, because that means I'm not a bastard."

Jesse chuckled. "Oh, now, hold on there. Your ma and I might have been married, but that doesn't mean you aren't a bastard. In fact, I do believe I've heard your brother call you that more than once."

Billy laughed, too.

"How do you feel about this, Billy? I mean, knowing that I'm Jesse James."

"Damn," Billy said, but the smile on his face showed that it wasn't an angry 'damn.' "Damn, you're Jesse James. And that means that I'm the son of Jesse James. Ha! I think that's great!"

"So, you aren't upset by it." It was a statement, not a question.

"Are you kiddin', Pa? I'm not upset at all. Like I told you, I think it's great! Wait until Frank finds out."

"No!" Jesse said sharply, holding up his finger in admonishment.

"What?"

"Billy, you must never tell Frank. He's not like you, you know that. He's got Ethel Marie and young James to look after. I'm afraid that knowing who I really am would only cause him trouble."

"All right, Pa, if you say so. I won't say anything to him."

"We probably won't be seeing much of him from now on, anyway. Not on the path we'll be taking. I hope you understand that. It's one of the costs of riding the outlaw trail."

"Hot damn, that means we're going to do more jobs, doesn't it?" Billy asked excitedly.

"We have no choice. We've started down this trail; that means we are going to have to ride it to wherever it takes us. We have to make a living, don't we?"

Commerce, Missouri—Spring 1905

Jesse and Billy left St. Louis shortly after the meeting with Frank. They drove south along *El Camino Real*, a road that ran from St. Louis to the Missouri Arkansas state line at the bottom of the boot heel. They didn't go all the way to the state line but rented a house in Commerce, a small town in southeast Missouri on the Mississippi River. There, Jesse got a job as a bartender, and Billy worked down on the river landing, loading and unloading the boats that called at Commerce.

"Pa, why are we doing this?" Billy asked one night after a particularly hard day. "We've got enough money that we don't really need to work."

"This is a small town, Billy. If we didn't have some visible source of income, it would cause a lot of questions. People are already curious as to how we can afford an automobile. There are only five in the entire town; three are owned by riverboat owners, one is owned by the bank president, and one is owned by the grain elevator operator."

"I know, but we've got to find something else to

do. This job is killing me. And this isn't what I meant when I said I wanted us to do some more jobs."

"Stay with it a little longer," Jesse said. "It's not going to last forever."

"That's good, because I'm not going to last forever. Hell, at this rate, I'm not going to last much longer," Billy complained.

The name of the tavern where Jesse worked was the Boatman's Bar. He didn't have to worry about serving mixed drinks, because there was no market for them. The customers were either farmers or boatmen, and their drink of choice was either beer or whiskey. There was very little wine served.

". . . Jesse James," someone said.

At the moment, Jesse was pouring whiskey into a glass, and hearing his name he turned around quickly to see who was addressing him.

Jesse needn't have been worried, because no one was addressing him. His name had come up in conversation among two of the customers who were standing at the bar. They were regulars, both of them boatmen, and Jesse knew them.

"The hell you say," Gib Crabtree said.

"Well, that's what they're saying," Dago Wyatt replied. "I haven't heard it from the fella his own self, but folks are sayin' that he used to ride with Jesse James."

"What's his name?" Crabtree asked.

"Cummings, or Cummins, somethin' like that. His first name is Jim."

"I thought ever'one that ever rode with Jesse James was either dead or in jail," Crabtree said.

"Apparently not. That is, if this feller really did ride with Jesse James like folks is sayin' he did. I heard 'em talkin' about it last time we put in at Osceola."

"This fella you're talkin' about," Jesse said, "he lives in Osceola, does he?"

"No, from what they was talkin' there, he actually lives in Blytheville. Leastwise they say he has a farm just north of Blytheville."

"You wouldn't know where that farm is, would you?" Jesse asked.

Crabtree laughed. "What are you wantin' to know for, Frank? Are you thinkin' maybe he's still wanted 'n you can go down there like a bounty hunter 'n get a reward?"

Jesse laughed as well. "Is he?" he asked. "I hadn't thought about that."

"I can see Frank doin' that. I can see him takin' that hog leg he has under the bar here and goin' down to Blytheville to take that Cummings fella in," Wyatt said.

"You still got that hog leg, ain't you, Frank?" Crabtree asked.

Jesse reached under the bar and pulled out a Colt .44. "Right here," he said. "Just in case someone wants to come in and rob the place."

"Hell, Frank, ever'one on the river knows you've got that piece, and there's enough folks who have seen you shoot that it ain't likely anyone's goin' to try you."

The reason they knew that Jesse could shoot well was because shortly after Jesse and Billy arrived in Commerce there was a shooting contest, and Jesse won the first prize of one hundred dollars.

"I'm not a bounty hunter," Jesse said. "But I've read a lot about Jesse and Frank James, so I'm just curious is all. I saw Frank James up at the World's Fair in Saint Louis last fall."

"Yeah, I heard he was up there, showing himself at the fair, along with the fat lady, the man who swallowed swords, and those little Igorots from the Philippines who ate all the dogs that fella from over in Dexter rounded up for 'em," Crabtree said.

"I tell you what, if that son of a bitch had rounded up my dog, I would have shot his ass," Wyatt said.

"What dog? Hell, Dago, you ain't got no damn dog."

"Well, if I had one I would'a shot him if he took it. Frank, are you really wonderin' about this Cummings feller?"

"I was just curious about him, is all."

"Well they say he's got him a farm just off the road about halfway between the state line and Blytheville. I'm told there's a red and green barn that's right next to each other, and those two barns are just before you get to his farm."

"If I bring him in and I get a reward for him, I'll split it with you," Jesse teased.

Jesse had a supper of chicken and dumplings when Billy got home from work that night.

"Wow," Billy said. "You haven't made this in a long time."

"This is sort of a celebration," Jesse said.

"What are we celebratin'?"

"I told my boss today that I quit," Jesse said. "You can tell your boss tomorrow."

"You've got something in mind, haven't you?" Billy asked excitedly.

"Yes, but it's going to take more than just the two of us."

"Oh? Where are we going to get someone else?"

"In Blytheville."

"Blytheville? Where's that?"

"It's in Arkansas, just across the state line, about eighty miles south of here. And, I'm told that Kings Highway is a good, smooth road all the way there. We can drive it in half a day."

"Do you know someone in Blytheville?"

"It turns out that I do," Jesse replied without being specific.

Blytheville, Arkansas

Jesse was correct in his assessment of the time it would take to make the drive down. Four hours after leaving Commerce, they stopped on the side of the road, just south of the Missouri state line, and just beyond two barns, one of which was red, and the other green. A ditch ran parallel with the road, and on the other side of the ditch was a fence. On the other side of the fence was a field, half plowed. In the middle of the field, and coming toward them, was a man, sitting on a riding plow that was being pulled by a team of mules. Jesse and Billy stood at the fence until the plow reached their end of the field.

"Jim!" Jesse called.

"Whoa, there," the man riding on the plow called to the mules.

"Jim, I'd like to talk to you for a moment."

The farmer looped the reins around the plow-lift handle, then climbed down and walked back to the fence.

"Do you know me?" he asked, his face registering curiosity.

"Yeah, I know you," Jesse said with a smile. "You are James Robert Cummins; you rode with Quantrill during the war. And you took part in a train robbery at Blue Cut, Missouri."*

"Mister, I don't know who you are, but you got the wrong man. I never done none o' them things."

"Yes you did, Windy Jim."

"Who are you? Do I know you?"

Jesse smiled. "Yeah, you know me. Look close, Jim. I know I've changed, but then we all have. After all, it's been more than twenty years since we last saw each other."

Cummins studied Jesse, then he gasped, took a step back, and held out his hand.

"You're a ghost!" he said. "Get away! Get away!"

Jesse chuckled. "That's funny, that's exactly what Frank said when he saw me. Tell me, Jim, have you ever seen a ghost drive an automobile?"

"You . . . you *have* to be a ghost!"

---

*James Cummins lived near Kearney, Missouri, and, like Jesse James, rode with Quantrill. He joined the James-Younger gang after the war and took part in train robberies at Winston and Blue Cut, Missouri. He was suspected of being involved in the plot to kill Jesse James because his sister, Artella, married Robert Ford. After the breakup of the James Gang, he became a farmer in Arkansas. He died in the Old Soldiers Home at Higginsville, Missouri, on July 9, 1929.

"Come over here and shake hands with me," Jesse said. "You've never heard of a ghost who could shake hands, have you? If I'm a ghost, you won't be able to feel me."

Cummins, with his anxiety showing, approached the fence slowly and cautiously. He held out his hand but waited for a long moment."

"Oh, for heaven's sake, Jim, grab my hand," Jesse said.

With one last surge of courage, Cummins reached out his hand. When he felt that the flesh was real, he smiled.

"Jesse James," he said. "It's good to see you aga—" He paused in the middle of the word and cocked his head. "Wait a minute. How is this possible? You're supposed to be dead!"

"Let's just say it was a case of mistaken identity," Jesse said. "And I took advantage of it. I'm calling myself Frank Alexander these days."

"Yeah, well, who can blame you? Does anyone else know you're still alive?"

"Just you, and my boy here. And now, Frank. Billy, meet Jim Cummins. Jim and I rode together with Quantrill, and afterwards he was part of my outfit."

Cummins chuckled. "That's how you knew I took part in the Blue Cut train robbery. Tell me, Jesse, what brings you to Arkansas?"

"You."

"You mean you came here just to look me up?"

"Yes."

Cummins, with an anxious look on his face, took a step back. "Why for are you looking me up? Bob

Ford was my brother-in-law that's true. But it was him that kilt you. I didn't have nothin' to do with it, I swear!"

Jesse laughed. "I know you didn't, Jim, and as you can see, Bob Ford didn't kill me. By the way, my name isn't Jesse anymore. Now my name is Frank. J. Frank Alexander. I swear, you're actin' as skittish as a long-tailed cat in a room full of rocking chairs. All I want to do is ask you a question. And whatever you answer will be up to you. Do you like being a farmer, working an entire year for . . . well, how much do you make in a year?"

"About five hundred dollars," Cummins answered.

"How would you like to make ten times that in one day?"

"You're puttin' your gang together again?"

"Yes. Are you in?"

Cummins smiled. "You're damn right, I am."

CHAPTER TWENTY-THREE

"Jim, do you have a wife or kids to worry about?" Jesse asked after Cummins agreed to be a part of Jesse's new gang.

"No, I ain't got nobody dependin' on me but this team of mules. But I can sell them and buy a horse."

"You don't need a horse," Jesse said. He pointed to the Oldsmobile. "We've got ten horses," he said with a smile.

"How many men do you have?" Cummins asked.

"For now, just the three of us."

"Do you want anyone else?"

"Only if it's someone dependable. Why, do you have a suggestion?"

"I do. He rode with Billy the Kid for a while, but he's a Missouri boy, like us. Right now he lives in Texarkana."

"What's his name?"

Cummins chuckled. "You'll like this. His name is Jesse. Jesse Evans."

* * *

It took them two days to reach Texarkana.

"Stop here," Cummins said, leaning over the seat to point to a building that had a large mug of beer painted on one of the front windows. "Jesse works here, only there don't nobody know him by that name. Here, he is called John Tucker."

"How is it that you know him?" Jesse asked.

"Me 'n him done a few things together," Cummins replied without being more specific.

"You think you can get him to come talk to us? Without telling him who I am, I mean."

"Well if we are goin' to work together, don't you think he ought to at least know who you are? I mean, I done told you who he is."

"If you tell him who I am, I'll have to kill both of you," Jesse said, and the almost nonchalant way he spoke the words had a more chilling effect than if he had said them more menacingly.

"I won't say a word," Cummins promised.

"Frank, this here is John Tucker," Cummins said. "He's workin' as a bartender down at the Arktex Saloon."

Jesse extended his hand. "It's good to meet you, John. This is my boy, Billy." Jesse glanced over at Cummins. "Does John know why I wanted to talk to him?"

"He knows. When I asked him if he might be interested in something a bit more excitin', and something that might pay a little more, he said he was ready to listen."

"This is more than just talk, ain't it?" Evans asked.

"I mean, I got me a job now, so I'm not interested in just talk."

"How much do you make a week?"

"Fifteen dollars."

Jesse reached into a sack and drew out two hundred dollars. "Here's a hundred dollars for each of you," he said. "If you throw in with me, there will be a lot more where that came from. Are you in?"

The two men smiled as they took the money.

"Yeah," Evans said. "You can count me in."

"This is our plan," Jesse said. He showed them a newspaper, tapping an ad.

HATHAWAY RANCH
Linden, Texas

Angus Cattle for Sale
Cattle Dealers Welcome

"We're goin' to steal cattle?" Evans asked. "I've done that, and to tell the truth, stealin' cattle is almost like workin'. You got to drive the critters somewhere to sell after you get 'em stoled. Then you don't hardly get nothin' for 'em, 'cause most of the time whoever you're sellin' 'em to knows they was stoled."

"We're not going to steal cattle. That is just our excuse for being there," Jesse said. "What we're going to do is rob a bank."

"All right!" Evans said with a big smile. "Now, that's more like it."

"When are we goin' to do it?" Cummins asked.

"Not until the end of the month," Jesse said. "The bank will have more money then because all the ranchers and businesses will be paying their workers."

"What do we do until then?"

Jesse indicated the money he had just given them. "Well, you've got enough money not to have to do anything if you don't want to."

"Where will you be?" Jim asked.

"Billy and I will stay here in the hotel until the time comes. We'll meet here for breakfast on the morning of the thirtieth, then we'll take the automobile down to Daingerfield."

"Daingerfield? I thought we was goin' to Linden."

"We are. We just aren't going to go all the way in the auto."

"Hey, Pa," Billy said later that afternoon. "What are we goin' to do while we're waitin' here?"

"I hadn't thought much beyond just waiting," Jesse said. "Why do you ask?"

"I want to go to a moving picture show."

"What? Why would you want to do something like that?"

"Listen to this," he said, reading from the newspaper.

"'*The Great Train Robbery* is a moving picture show that is a faithful duplication of the genuine holdups made famous by various outlaw bands in the far West. This motion picture is based upon a true event, that being the robbery that occurred on August twenty-nine, 1900, when four members of Butch Cassidy's Hole in the Wall gang halted the Number three train on the Union Pacific Railroad tracks toward Table Rock, Wyoming. The bandits forced the conductor to uncouple the passenger cars from the rest of the train and then blew up the safe in the mail car to escape with about five thousand dollars in cash.'"

"You actually want to see that?" Jesse asked.

"Yeah, Pa." Billy chuckled. "You could call it professional curiosity. If we watch how other people do it, we might learn a thing or two."

"Son, every train robbery there's ever been was copied from me," Jesse said. "But if you want to go see it, we will."

The cabin on the Brazos—March 5, 1942

"So, did you go see the movie?" Faust asked.

"Yes, we did." Jesse chuckled. "It wasn't like the movies today. I don't mean just because it doesn't have sound. It was only about ten minutes long."

"I know, but I owe much of my career to Mr. Porter."

"Who?"

"Edwin Porter. He's the one who wrote the story to *The Great Train Robbery*. It was not only the first Western movie; it was the first film that actually told a story. I've made a good living working on films, not only my own but others as well. And people like Gary Cooper, Tom Mix, John Wayne, Roy Rogers, all of us owe a debt of thanks, not only to Edwin Porter, but also to 'Broncho Billy' Anderson, who starred in that picture, at a time when the actors' names were never even mentioned."

"Tyrone Power," Jesse said.

"Yes, him, too."

"Especially Tyrone Power. He played me in the movies."

"That's right, he did, didn't he?"

"He's not the only one who ever played me in a movie. I've got a story I'll tell you about the movies when I come to it," Jesse said. "But the only way I can tell a story is from the beginning to the end, so if you don't mind, I'll just keep on the way I'm going."

"I don't mind at all," Faust said. "I believe you said you were going to rob a bank."

"I said I was goin' to, and that's just what I did," Jesse said, continuing with the story.

Daingerfield, Texas

The drive from Texarkana to Daingerfield took less than an hour. Although automobiles were not all that common, neither were they so rare as to cause a great deal of attention anymore. And some towns and cities even had special parking lots for them. Daingerfield was such a place.

"You wait here with the auto," Jesse said to Billy. "The rest of us will go into Linden and take care of business. When that's done, we'll come back here. That way nobody in Linden will be able to connect us to this machine."

"Pa, why does anyone have to stay with the car?" Billy asked. "Wouldn't it be better if we all went to Linden together?"

"There is no way I am going to leave this thing with nobody to watch over it," Jesse said. "They draw too much curiosity. There's no telling what might happen to it if we just left it here."

"I don't like it that I don't get to do anything," Billy complained.

"You are doing something. You are making sure that when we come back with the money, we have a way out of here."

"All right, all right, I'll watch over the damn automobile."

"Good," Jesse said. "John, Jim, we've got a stagecoach to catch."

When Jesse, Evans, and Cummins stepped down from the stagecoach in Linden, they walked from the coach depot to the livery stable. There was, about the stable, a familiar odor of horseflesh, hay, and, though it was kept relatively clean, even horse droppings. Jesse found something comfortable about the smell for it was an aroma that had been a part of his life for as long as he could remember.

"Yes, sir, something I can do for you folks?" The question came from a boy of about fourteen.

"Yes, my associates and I just arrived on the morning stagecoach," Jesse said. "We are cattle buyers, and we need to go out to the Hathaway Ranch to look over his stock. We'll need to rent some horses to ride out there."

"I'll have to get Mr. Heckemeyer," the boy said. "He owns the stable, 'n he's the only one that can rent out horses."

Heckemeyer came out to greet Jesse a moment later. He was a big man, baldheaded, with a round face and full cheeks. "So, you're goin' out to Irv Hathaway's place, are you?"

"Yes. I've been told that he has fine cattle for sale.

Is that true? Or will we just be wasting our time riding out there?"

"No sir, you won't be wasting your time at all, and you won't be disappointed," Heckemeyer said. "If you ask me, Irv has some of the best stock in the entire state of Texas. The boy said you wanted to rent some horses, but wouldn't you rather rent a surrey? I think it would be a lot more comfortable for refined businessmen like you three."

"No, thank you. We're all three quite comfortable in the saddle, and if we're going to go out to look at the herd, I think it would be better to be mounted."

"I guess you do have a point there. How long will you be a' wantin' 'em?"

"Just long enough to ride out to the ranch, look over Mr. Hathaway's stock, then ride back. What time will you close this afternoon?"

"I'll be here until six," Heckemeyer said.

"Oh, I'm sure we'll have your mounts returned by then."

"That'll be fine. Come far, did you?"

"Far enough. We're from Bowling Green, Kentucky," Jesse said.

"Oh, my, that is a long way. Well, come on out back and we can pick out the horses for you."

Half an hour later Heckemeyer walked back out front with the three men, each of whom was leading a saddled horse.

"Now, which way would we go to find the Hathaway place?" Jesse asked.

Heckemeyer laughed. "Yes, sir, I guess you would be needin' to know that, wouldn't you? Well, it's straight west down that road, for about six miles.

Irv's got hisself a big fancy arched gate just over the drive and it has his name, Hathaway, wrote out in steel letters. You can't miss it."

"You've been very helpful Mr. Heckemeyer. I appreciate it," Jesse said.

"Yes, sir, well, it's always good doin' business with gentlemen," Heckemeyer replied. "You good folks take care now and you tell Irv that Tony Heckemeyer said hello."

"We'll do that, Mr. Heckemeyer."

The three men rode out of town, heading west. Not until they were around a curve, and hidden from observation by anyone in the town, did they leave the road. Then they made a wide loop back around town, coming in this time from the north. They rode up the alley, then dismounted behind the furniture store that was next door to the bank.

Evans stayed with the horses, while Jesse and Cummins walked down the end of the block to Graham Street, then back up Main Street, entering the bank through the front door.

There was one teller behind the window and another man behind the desk over to one side. At the moment, there were no customers in the bank.

"Are you the bank president?" Jesse asked.

"I am Joel Dempster. I own this bank," the man replied with a rather smug smile. "I suppose that makes me anything I want to be."

"I suppose it does," Jesse agreed. "This is for you." Jesse handed him a folded over sheet of paper.

"What is this?" Dempster asked.

"I guess you'll just have to read it to find out."

Dempster unfolded the paper and read it.

*This is a bank robbery. Go to the vault and empty it
of all paper money. Do not give an alarm, for if you
do, you will be shot dead.*

"You can't be serious, sir!"

"Oh, I'm quite serious," Jesse said, pointing his
pistol. "Mr. Jones, would you pull down the shades,
then put the little clock sign out that says the bank
will reopen," Jesse glanced up at the clock, "at ten
fifteen? Then lock the front door, if you would,
please," he said to Cummins.

"Yes, Mr. Smith, I will."

"You can't do that. The bank is supposed to be
open now," Dempster said. "When the people see that
they can't do their business, they will be suspicious."

"Not too suspicious," Jesse said. "Banks often
close in the middle of the day when they have some
special business to attend to. And I know you have
some payrolls to get ready."

Dempster gasped. "How did you know that?"

Jesse smiled. Dempster had just verified what he
had suspected.

"Who are you people?"

"I'm Mr. Jones, and he is Mr. Smith," Jesse said.

"You called him Jones, and he called you Smith."

"Well, sometimes we get each other mixed up.
Now, open the vault and take out the money, like I
told you to."

Nervously, the bank president started toward the
vault, which was behind the counter. Jesse went
with him.

"Mister, you can't come back here; you have to
stay on the other side of the counter," the teller said.

"Tell him it's all right, Mr. Dempster," Jesse said.

"It's all right, Homer, he's with me," Dempster said.

"Yes, sir. Mr. Dempster, why are the shades pulled? Have we closed the bank?"

"Just for a few minutes, Homer," Jesse said. "My associate and I are bank examiners."

It was obvious by Homer's expression and demeanor that he didn't believe Jesse.

"Mr. Jones, perhaps you had better keep an eye on the teller," Jesse suggested.

"Bank teller, would you come out here on this side of the counter, please?" Cummins ordered.

"I see no reason why I should do so," the bank teller said.

Cummins raised his pistol, pointed it toward the teller, and pulled the hammer back.

"Is this reason enough?"

"Oh, my God! Are you men robbing the bank?" the teller asked.

"Well now, he ain't quite as dumb as he looks, is he, Mr. Smith?" Cummins asked with a little chuckle.

CHAPTER TWENTY-FOUR

All the time the conversation was going on with the teller, Dempster, under Jesse's watchful eye, was putting bound stacks of bills into one of the bank bags. He reached for some of the coins.

"Don't bother with any of the silver," Jesse said. "Your paper money is good enough for me."

"This is all of it," Dempster said. "We are a very small bank, in a very small town. And the town isn't very wealthy."

"I'll bet you are just real wealthy though, aren't you?" Jesse asked.

"I earned my money. I haven't stolen it."

"By loaning money to poor folks, I suppose?"

"They have to have some place to get their money. Without banks, how else would people buy houses, or put in their crops?"

"You hold mortgages on quite a few houses, do you?"

"I am proud to say that I do."

"Let me have them."

"What?"

"You heard me. Let me have all the mortgages you hold on the houses in this town."

"Why would you want that? They are of no possible use to you. What are you going to do with them?"

"I'm going into the banking business."

More angry now than afraid, Dempster reached back into the vault and took out a small metal box. "They're in there," he said.

"All of them?"

"Yes, damn you. All of them!"

Jesse took the mortgages from the box, then dropped them down into the bag of money.

"Mr. Jones?" Jesse said.

"Yes, Mr. Smith?" Cummins answered.

"I believe it is time to go. Mr. Dempster, do you have a back entrance to this bank?"

Dempster didn't answer, and Jesse raised his pistol and cocked it, the sound of the sear engaging the cylinder, making an ominous click.

"It's back there, in the corner," Dempster said, the pitch of his voice raised by fear. "Behind the stove," he added.

"Thank you, you have been most helpful," Jesse said.

As Jesse and Cummins started out the back door, the teller managed to get hold of a pistol, and he fired at them. The bullet hit the iron stove, then ricocheted through a side window. Instinctively, Jesse whirled and returned fire. He saw the teller clutch his stomach, then go down.

"Damn!" Jesse shouted. "What did you make me do that for?"

* * *

Evans, having heard the gunshot, mounted his horse and rode to the back of the bank, leading the other two horses. When all three were mounted, they rode up in the gap between the bank and the furniture store, then pulling their guns began firing them into the air and shouting as they rode down Main Street. Jesse, in the meantime, had pulled the mortgages from the box and was scattering them in the street as they galloped away.

At first the people who were out on the street, walking up and down the sidewalks, hurried inside, or got behind the corners of the buildings, not comprehending what was going on.

"Stop them! Stop those riders!" Dempster shouted, running out into the street then. "Stop them! Get the sheriff! They have just robbed the bank!"

By then, some of the more courageous of the townspeople had come out from where they had taken cover and began gathering up the scattered paper.

"I'll be damn!" one of the men said. "Tom, this here is the mortgage to your house."

"Give that to me!" Dempster shouted angrily. "Those belong to the bank. They are all the town's mortgages!"

At that bit of news everyone within hearing ran out into the street picking up mortgages, looking at them, then passing them around.

"You can't do that!" Dempster said. "Those are mine! Give them back to me! Sheriff! Sheriff! Where is the sheriff?"

"I'm here, Mr. Dempster. Did you say the bank has been robbed?"

"Yes, but never mind that now! These are my mortgages! Get them back!"

"Help!" a woman screamed. "Homer has been shot!"

The sheriff, hearing the woman's cry, turned back toward Dempster. "What is she saying? Was your teller shot?"

"What? Yes, but never mind that. Sheriff, you must get these documents back for me! I'll be ruined!"

"Carl," the sheriff yelled to one of his deputies. "Get the doc down to look at Homer. Pete, start rounding up a posse. We're goin' after them."

"What about my mortgages?"

The sheriff fired his pistol into the air. It had the effect of getting everyone's attention and they all looked toward him.

"You people, leave these documents where they are. All of you, get out of the street now."

Nobody moved.

"Anyone who doesn't get out of the street right now will be thrown in jail!"

As the men and women walked away, the sheriff called out to them. "Men, any of you who will volunteer for a posse, go get a gun and get saddled. Most of you have money in the bank, and you'll be wanting to get it back."

Jesse, Cummins, and Evans rode at a full gallop for the first two miles, then they alternated between a trot and a walk. They reached Daingerfield within half an hour. There, after dismounting, they let the horses go with a swat on the rump. The horses started back toward Linden.

"They'll be back to the livery before it closes tonight," Jesse said. "Robbing banks is one thing, but I'll be damn if I'll ever let anyone call me a horse thief."

The others laughed as they got into the car.

"All right, Billy, you're driving. Let's go."

"Where?"

"John, you want to go back to Texarkana?"

"Not particularly. I didn't leave anything behind."

"Jim, think you could put us all up on your farm for a while?"

"I reckon I could."

"All right, Billy. Let's go back to Blytheville."

"Pa, if we do that, we'll have to go back through Linden," Billy said.

"That's right," Jesse said.

"Well, if they've sent a posse out, we're liable to run into 'em."

"Billy, they're looking for two roans and a black horse. They aren't looking for a red Oldsmobile."

Billy laughed. "You're right!" he said.

Starting the car, they left Daingerfield, going north. Five miles north of Daingerfield they saw a group of about ten horsemen, riding toward them.

"Stop the car, Billy," Jesse said.

"But, Pa, we can outrun them if we have to. You know we can."

"Stop the car; pull over to the side and give them the road."

"All right, if you say so."

The riders came by at a rapid trot. Jesse gave a friendly wave to them, and the lead rider, who was wearing a star, nodded as they rode by.

"Ha!" Billy laughed as they continued on. "They never even gave us a second look!"

"That's because nobody paid any attention to us as we rode out. They just saw the horses we were riding."

A short while later they drove right through Linden. There was a blacksmith shop and a garage on the corner, with a gasoline pump in front.

"Stop here for gas," Jesse asked.

"Pa, we got enough to get all the way to Texarkana," Billy said. "You really think it's a good idea to stop here?"

"Stop here," Jesse repeated.

Billy pulled up to the pump, and a man came out to meet them. "Gasoline?"

"Yes," Billy said.

The man turned and called back into the small building. "Eddie, gas!"

A much younger man came out to the pump, then moved the handle back and forth, which had the effect of filling the large graduated cylinder on top of the pump with gasoline. Then, sticking the hose into the car's gas tank, he began dispensing the fuel.

The man who had come out first was now washing the windshield. "You folks just missed it," he said.

"What did we miss?" Jesse asked.

"We had some excitement here in town today," he said.

"Oh? What kind of excitement would that be?"

"Why, we had the bank robbed, that's what happened. There were three of 'em. Say, you might have seen 'em as you was comin' into town."

"What did they look like?" Jesse asked.

"What did they look like?" The man stroked his chin. "Well now, I don't rightly know. He smiled. "But I can tell you this. They was ridin' two roans and a black. And they was shootin' up into the air and shoutin' bloody hell when they galloped out of town."

"Shooting you say. Was anyone killed?" Jesse asked, thinking of the man he had shot.

"No, nobody was kilt. Homer, he's the teller, he was shot in the stomach, but the doc said it was mostly in the side 'n more'n likely didn't hit none of his vitals. But that ain't the most excitin' thing."

"You mean there was something happened that was more exciting than a bank robbery?" Jesse asked.

"Yes, sir. It seems that the bank robbers," the man laughed, "the bank robbers also took all the mortgages from the bank, 'n they scattered them all up 'n down Main Street as they was ridin' out."

"Ha!" Jesse said. "I'll bet that bothered the banker more than getting his bank robbed."

"Yes, sir, you better believe it did. You see, gettin' the bank robbed, well, that weren't hardly none of Dempster's own money. But the mortgages now, that's how he makes his money, so he was fit to be tied."

"You mean he didn't get them back."

"Oh, he got most of 'em back, I reckon. But there was quite a lot of 'em that he didn't get back." The man pulled the cloth away from the windshield, then looked around to make certain no one overheard him. "He didn't get mine back," he added with a conspiratorial smile. "Want me to check the oil?"

"Yes, please."

Eddie finished putting gas into the car, and he pulled the hose out of the tank, screwed on the cap, then squinted up at the graduated glass on top of the pump. "Looks like you used about three and a half gallons," he said. "That'll be twenty-one cents."

Billy paid him, then drove away.

Blytheville

"I got a cured ham," Cummins said. "And some eggs. I can make us some ham 'n eggs if that's all right with ever'one."

"Fine with me," Jesse said.

"When are we goin' to count the money, Pa?"

Jesse laughed. "You're gettin' a little anxious, aren't you there, boy?"

"I reckon I am," Billy admitted.

Jesse dumped the contents of the sack out onto the table.

"Woowee!" Evans said. "Have you ever seen so much money?"

Jesse began counting, and the total came to forty-five thousand five hundred and twenty dollars.

"This sure beats farmin'," Cummins said.

"Do you plan to stay here in Blytheville?" Jesse asked.

"I reckon so. I don't have any place else in mind to go to."

"What about you, John? You goin' to stay in Texarkana?"

"I don't know," John said. "Why are you askin'?"

"Well, if something else comes up where I can use you boys, I might want to know how to get hold of you," Jesse said. "But if you're going to stay where you've been for the last few years, don't suddenly start spending a lot of money. That would be the surest way of drawing attention to yourselves, and that, you don't want to do."

"Yeah, don't worry," Cummins said. "I know better 'n to do that."

"I do, too," Evans agreed.

"Pa, look out!" Billy shouted.

Jesse was driving, and they were passing through the town of Sikeston, Missouri, when a car pulled out in front of them. The two cars collided with a loud crash. The radiator of the Oldsmobile was split open, and steam began gushing forth.

"Are you two all right?" the driver of the other car asked, getting out quickly and coming back to check on them.

"Yeah, we're fine," Jesse said. "What did you do that for? Pull out in front of us like that?"

"Mister, I'm sorry," the driver said. "I just didn't expect to see another car. There are only three cars in Sikeston, and I know where the other two are, right now."

"Well now there are four cars," Jesse said. "Two that can be driven and two that can't."

"Like I said, I'm awfully sorry," the other driver said. "My name is McMullen. C.F. McMullen. "I fully admit that this accident was my fault, and I'll be glad to pay to replace your automobile."

"I don't suppose there's a place I can buy another automobile in this town, is there?"

"No, sir, I'm afraid not. Saint Louis is the nearest place you can buy one."

"Is there train service to Saint Louis?"

McMullen smiled. "Yes, sir, that we do have. If you'll come to the bank with me, I'll draw out the money to pay you for your car, then I'll have someone take you both down to the depot." McMullen looked at the car. "Would you say three hundred dollars is a fair price?"

"Yes, three hundred dollars seems fair."

CHAPTER TWENTY-FIVE

The cabin on the Brazos—March 10, 1942

Faust chuckled. "Three cars in town, and two of you run into each other."

"Ah but there were four cars, counting us," Jesse said.

"Four cars? Why, there must have been a veritable traffic jam. So, you took the train to Saint Louis. Did you buy a new car there?"

"No. From there, we took a train to Chicago, and from Chicago we went to New York. It was the first time I'd ever been in either one of those places, and the only time I ever went." Jesse made a dismissive wave with his hand. "You can keep them both. They're too damn big for me. Why, there are so many people there I don't know how a person can even get his breath."

"I guess a big city like that can be a little intimidating."

"You might say that," Jesse said.

New York City—September 11, 1905

Jesse thought that riding on the elevated train in New York must be a little like flying. The train whizzed down the track at breakneck speed, and looking out of the car he could see that he was level with the second-, and sometimes the third-story windows of the adjacent buildings. Looking down to the street below, he saw the much slower pace of traffic, electric trolleys, horse-drawn carriages, freight wagons, and a very large number of automobiles. But even the automobiles appeared to be crawling, limited as they were by law to a speed of no more than ten miles per hour. By contrast, the elevated train was moving at a very rapid clip of thirty miles per hour.

"Wow, this is something, isn't it?" Billy said, his eyes wide with excitement.

At that moment the car started around a curve, the centrifugal force throwing Jesse and Billy to one side.

"We seem to be going awfully fast to be taking this curve," Jesse said.

"You worry too much, Pa," Billy said. "Why, I'll bet the engineer of this train takes this curve ten times a day. I'm sure he knows how fast he can—"

Billy was interrupted in midsentence when the brakes were applied and they were thrown forward. Then there was a sickening lurch, and the front of the car shot off the track.

The women in the car screamed, and several of the men shouted as the car fell, front first, to the street below. It hit the ground hard, and when it did, everyone in the car was thrown to the front. The roof of the car was torn off, and it was standing on the front end, while the back end was still on the track.

The car behind it didn't leave the track, but its front truck did, and the heavy steel wheels came crashing down on the people who were all piled together.[*]

Jesse had been tossed through the window, and Billy had grabbed hold of the back of the seat, so that neither of them were caught up in the cluster of people who had been thrown to the front of the car.

The back of the car was across the third rail, which began emitting electrical sparks. That caused a fire to start.

[*]The only way to check on the validity of J. Frank Alexander's claim to be Jesse James is to, when possible, authenticate certain aspects of his story with historical fact. It seems unlikely that he would have an easy command of relatively obscure historical events, but this story is verifiable. During the morning rush hour on September 11, 1905, a train was mistakenly switched from the straightaway track, onto the curve. The train was traveling at 30 mph when it entered the sharp curve, for which 9 mph was the company-mandated limit. The motorman, realizing the error, braked quickly, but it was too late. The lead car remained on the tracks but the second was thrown off the trestle and down to the street, coming to rest with one end on the ground and the other across the third rail on the trestle, which sparked an electrical fire. The roof was torn off and some passengers were crushed under the car by a falling truck from the third car. The rest of the train also derailed but, fortunately, did not leave the trestle. The motorman, Paul Kelly, later went to prison for reckless endangerment which resulted in the death of 13 passengers, and 48 serious injuries.

Jesse reached back in to the window to grab Billy and pull him through to the outside.

"Billy, are you hurt?" Jesse asked anxiously.

"No, I'm all right. I'm not hurt."

"Help me get these people out before they burn to death."

Jesse and Billy worked to get the passengers out of the car, helping those who, though hurt, could still walk, and carrying those who couldn't. They worked alone for the first few minutes until others came to help. The whistles of policemen, and the clanging bell of approaching police and ambulance automobiles, soon added to the cacophony of the scene.

Finally all the dead were removed from the wreckage and laid out on the ground, covered quickly by tarpaulins, and the more seriously injured were put in ambulances and hauled away. The train motorman, who was in shock, walked away from the wreckage and sat down to lean against the brick front of the apartment building; he hung his head in shock and shame.

Jesse and Billy, now no longer needed, also sat down on the sidewalk and leaned against the wall, partly because they were tired from the effort expended, and partly because they, like the others, were in a condition of shock over what had just happened.

"There they are!" a woman said, pointing to Jesse and Billy. "It was those two!"

A uniformed police officer was with the woman, and he started to Jesse and Billy.

"Pa, what's this about?" Billy asked, his concern evident by the tone of his voice.

"Don't get all nervous on me, now," Jesse said. "We haven't done anything up here to be worried about."

There was a stern look on the policeman's face as he approached the two.

"Sure 'n 'twas a terrible thing what happened here," the police officer said in a thick, Irish brogue.

"Yes, it was," Jesse said as he started to stand.

"Here now, you two stay right where you are," the policeman said, holding his hand out. "This lady, and some of the others, too, told me what all you two did here. If there is anyone who deserves to sit and rest for a spell, it's you two. Some of the ladies in these apartments have made some cool lemonade. Would you two be for enjoying a glass?"

"Yes, sir, that would be mighty welcome," Jesse said.

The policeman turned, but he didn't have to say anything because two women, each carrying a large glass of iced lemonade, were coming toward them.

"Thank you, ma'am," Billy said as he accepted the glass.

"'Tis thankful the city is for what you two did this morning," the policeman said. "You were both heroes, that's for certain. Sure 'n it wouldn't be for surprising me if his honor Mayor McClellan hisself didn't want to personally come and thank you. Ah, 'n there he is. His pa was a general durin' the Civil War, you know."

"I remember General McClellan," Jesse said.

"Sure 'n you are of the age to have served with him, too, I'm thinkin'."

Jesse smiled. "Let's just say that we were in the same war."

A rather short, clean-shaven man, who looked too young to hold down such an important job as mayor of New York, came toward them, smiling. By now Jesse and Billy were standing.

"I understand we owe you two gentlemen our thanks for what you did here this morning."

"Anyone would have done it, Mayor," Jesse said.

"But nobody else did. At least, not in the beginning." The mayor handed Jesse a card. "If you would, please come to my office this afternoon. I want to thank you officially. And I'll have the newspapers there as well. Show this card to the receptionist; he will personally escort you to my office."

"We will, thanks," Jesse said.

"Mr. Mayor, could you come here for a moment, please?" someone called. "We've got a little problem."

"Pa, are we going to the mayor's office this afternoon?" Billy asked.

"With newspapers there? No. We aren't known up here now, and I have no intention of us being known. Come on, we're going back to the hotel, getting our things, then we're going to the depot and catch a train."

"Where are we going?"

"California," Jesse said. "I've always wanted to go there."

The cabin on the Brazos—March 15, 1942

Jesse had grown tired and asked if they could take a few days off from working on the book.

"How would you like to go into town to see a movie?" Faust asked. He smiled. "There's one playing in town that you might like. It's based on one of my books, *Destry Rides Again*. Would you like to see it?"

"Yes, I would. It's a Western?"

"It is."

"I'll tell you what I think about it, after we've seen it."

"I liked it," Jesse said as they drove back to his cabin on the river. "I like that actor, Jimmy Stewart."

"Jimmy Stewart is in the army air corps, you know," Faust said.

"Really? No, I didn't know that."

"He got a commission in January. The thing is, he already knew how to fly. We've known about his flying bug out in Hollywood for a long time now."

"Damn, everybody is getting into this war," Jesse said. "If they ever make another picture about me, I would like to see him in the role."

"You didn't like Tyrone Power?"

"Yeah, he did a good job. I don't have any complaints. I told you before that I had a story I'll tell you about the movies when I come to it; well, this seems as good a time as any. My son, Jesse, played me in two movies. Both were silent films."

"Yes, I'm aware of that," Faust said. "When Oran first told me about you, I started doing some research."

"You didn't contact him, did you?" Jesse asked anxiously.

"No, I didn't. And I take it that you've never contacted him, either."

"No. I think my brother Frank was right when he said it would be better if nobody knew."

"Like I said before, Jesse, when this book comes out, he's going to know. Either that, or he won't believe you and he'll sue you. He is a practicing attorney back in Los Angeles, you know."

"Yes, I know. I reckon I'll just cross that bridge when I come to it."

The next morning, the two men resumed working.

"Let's see," Faust said, checking his notes. "When we left off last week, you were about to leave New York and go to California. Did you go?"

"Oh, yes, we went. I met Wyatt Earp out there. Ha, him being the big lawman that he was, I wonder what he would have thought if he had known who I really was."

"What did you think of California?"

Jesse was quiet for a moment. "Like I told you, we were going to move there," he said. "If things had worked out the way I wanted. We were going to leave Missouri and go to California where nobody had ever heard of me."

Faust chuckled. "Jesse, they knew about you in California. You were one of the most famous people in America. There wasn't anyone between the age of ten and ninety, anywhere in the country, who hadn't heard of you."

"Well, they might have heard of me. But nobody actually knew me. That is, nobody knew me well enough that they could identify me."

"That's probably true, or you would have been recognized when you moved to Wild Horse," Faust said. "Why didn't you go?"

"We didn't have enough money. The last job I

pulled, the train robbery at Blue Cut, barely gave us enough money to get along. I wanted to do one more, big job. But Zee, she wouldn't hear of it. She wanted me to quit, like Frank did right after the Blue Cut job.

"I was already thinking we could move to California with enough money that we could buy a house, and perhaps a little business, or, maybe even a farm."

"Like you ended up doing with Molly," Faust said.

"Yeah, like I did with Molly."

"Did you ever think about that?" Faust asked. "I mean, while you were with Molly, did you ever think that you could have done that same thing with Zee that you did with her?"

"I have to confess that from time to time I did think about it. But, don't get me wrong, Fred. The truth is, I loved Molly. I reckon I loved her as much as I did Zee. I guess that's hard for some folks to understand, how a man can love two women just the same, but I did."

"That's not hard to understand at all," Faust said. After a quiet moment, he asked, "Were you active during that time?"

"By active, do you mean did we pull any more jobs?"

"Yes."

"Well, as a matter of fact, we did."

"In California?"

Jesse shook his head. "Before we got to California."

CHAPTER TWENTY-SIX

Emporia, Kansas—September 25, 1905

Jesse and Billy left the train in Emporia.

"How long are we going to stay here?" Billy asked.

"I don't know. A few days, a week maybe. Truth is, Billy, I'm just damn tired of riding that train."

The two, with their share of money from the bank job they had done in Texas stuck down behind the liners of the valises they were both carrying, checked in to a hotel. They had a little over ten thousand dollars apiece remaining from the bank robbery they had pulled in Texas.

They spent two weeks in Emporia, spending little, and keeping a low profile. Then, midway through the second week, Jesse saw an article in the *Emporia Gazette*.

> The Citizens Bank of Emporia announced that it will be opening a branch in Matfield, and is sending Mr. Chester Barnes to Matfield on Thursday's stage with sufficient funds to begin business there.

"How would you like to pull another job, just to keep our hand in it?" Jesse asked.

"Sure. What do you want to do?"

"I want to hold up this coach," Jesse said. "But we're going to need to buy a couple of horses and saddles."

On Thursday, Jesse, wearing boots, jeans, and a stained white shirt, bought a ticket on the stage-coach that was bound for Matfield. He was pleased to see that there was only the driver, and no shotgun guard.

There were two other passengers on board; one, a rather small man, was wearing a three-piece suit, tie, bowler hat, and *pince nez* glasses. Jesse would guess his age to be about forty. He was holding a cardboard accordion file on his lap, gripping it tightly with both hands. The file was secured by tied string.

The other passenger was dressed pretty much the same way as Jesse, with dirty boots, old jeans with holes in the knees, and a torn shirt. He was even older than Jesse, probably in his late sixties.

Those two men were sitting together on the seat directly across from Jesse's seat. Shortly after the coach left Emporia, Jesse smiled and stuck his hand out.

"Well, since we are going to be riding together, it seems to me like we should get acquainted," he said. "My name is Peacock. Alexander Peacock. Who might you boys be?"

The older man smiled and extended his hand. Jesse noticed, when he shook it, that the hand was heavily calloused, the result of a lifetime of hard work.

"Crawford is the name, Mr. Peacock. Roy Crawford."

"Call me Lexy, Roy," Jesse said, falling easily into the name by which he had often addressed Frank. "All my friends do. I hope you don't mind my callin' you Roy."

"No sir, not at all. I don't ever turn down the opportunity to be friendly with other folk."

"And, what might your handle be?" Jesse asked the well-dressed passenger who had not taken either hand away from the accordion file.

"I see no need to exchange names with people I'll never see again," he said rather primly.

Jesse smiled. Barnes was making it so easy.

"Well then, I'll just call you Mr. Pinch Nose, I mean, seeing as you've got those glasses pinched up on your nose like that."

Crawford laughed. "Pinch Nose, that's a good one, that is."

"What have you got in that package you're holdin' on to so tight?" Jesse asked. "It must be somethin' awful important if you can't even let go of it long enough to shake mine and Roy's hands. I mean, seein' as we're fellow passengers 'n all."

"It is nothing important," Barnes said.

"Oh? Then why won't you shake hands with us?"

"As I said, circumstances have placed us in this coach together. But it is circumstances only that have brought us together. I would never have anything to do with either one of you, I assure you of that."

"Well then, Mr. Pinch Nose, I'll just not have

anything to do with you, either," Jesse said, and turned to Crawford. "Roy, you live in Matfield, do you?"

"No, sir, I'll be going on to Thurman," Crawford said. "I used to work for a rancher there, and I'm sort of hoping he'll put me on for the winter. I don't know that he will, and if he won't, truth is, I'm not sure where I'll be heading next. Someplace where I can get some work."

"You look like a man who's worked hard all your life."

"Yes, sir, I reckon I have. About the only time I ever had it easy was durin' the war. Not that the war was all that easy, but I pretty much knew where my next meal was goin' to come from, 'n where I was goin' to lay my head that night." He chuckled. "Sure, many was the night I lay my head under the stars, but at least I wasn't alone then. I tried to join up again, whenever we fought ag'in the Spanish, but they wouldn't take me, 'cause they said I was too old."

"You'll excuse me for sayin' this, Roy, but you look too old for the hard life of a ranch hand."

"Well, sir, that may be so. But I'm tryin' to save me up five hunnert dollars. See, if I had five hunnert dollars, I know where there's a little café I could buy. I've cooked near 'bout as much as I've punched cows. I think I could make me a good livin' for the rest of my life if I could buy that café."

"Why don't you go to a bank and borrow the money?" Jesse asked.

"I've tried. The bank says I've got to have somethin' they call collateral, an' I ain't got none of that."

"I guess banks can be sort of coldhearted that way."

"Hmmph," Barnes said. "Banks are here to help productive people finance their businesses. Banks aren't for charity."

"I reckon not," Crawford said. "Anyhow, it ain't somethin' I like to talk about. What about you, Lexy? You look 'most as old as me. Was you in the war?"

"Yes, sir, I was."

"I won't even ask you which side it was you fought for. When you think about it now, it don't really make all that much difference who fought on which side. I reckon we all, Johnny Reb and Billy Yank, went through about the same thing."

"You've got that right, Roy. Yes, sir, you've got that right," Jesse agreed.

"If you two old soldiers want to regale each other with war stories, please do it more quietly," Barnes said. "I don't care to listen to exaggerated tales of glory all the way to Matfield."

"Well then, Mr. Pinch Nose, we'll keep quiet, just for you," Jesse said.

They spoke little for the next half hour, then the coach came to an unexpected stop.

"Driver why are you stopping?" Barnes shouted, sticking his head out the window. "I must get to Matfield on time."

"It won't make any difference," Jesse said.

"What do you mean it won't make any—" Barnes started to say, but he stopped in midsentence when he saw that Jesse was holding a gun on him. "What is the meaning of this?"

"Well, Mr. Pinch Nose, this is a robbery," Jesse said. "I would appreciate it if you would hand me that package that you've been holding on to so tight."

"I will not!" Barnes said.

"Billy, is the driver sitting on the right side of the box?" Jesse called through the window.

"Yes, he is."

"Tell him to move over to the left side, will you? I'm about to shoot this banker in here, and he's such a scrawny little fella that the bullet is likely to go all the way through him. And there's no need in the driver getting hurt."

"No, no! Don't shoot! Don't shoot!" Barnes said. "Here, here, take the money!" He thrust the package over to Jesse.

Jesse smiled, because until that moment, he had only his intuition that there was money in the package.

"Thank you. I'll be getting out here, and so will you, Roy."

"Me? Why am I gettin' out here? I don't have any money."

"No, but you're going to make certain that my partner and I get away."

"How is that?"

"We're going to hold you hostage for a while," Jesse said.

"Damn!" Crawford said. "And here, I thought you was a nice guy."

"Get out now."

Crawford climbed down from the coach, with Jesse behind him. Billy was mounted, still holding the pistol he had used to stop the driver of the stagecoach. He was holding the reins to Jesse's horse.

"Driver," Jesse called up to the box. "You keep on goin' all the way to Matfield. If you see anyone along the way, don't say a word about what happened here. I'm goin' to hold on to one of your passengers. If anyone comes after us in the next twenty-four hours, we're going to kill Mr. Crawford here. Do you understand that?"

"Yes, sir. What about when we get to Matfield? You know that banker's goin' to talk."

"I figure we'll be far enough away by then, that it won't matter none," Jesse said. "Now, get."

"Hyeah!" the driver shouted to his team, and with the reins slapping against the backs of the horses, they bolted forward. The coach started so quickly it jerked up and down.

"Ha! I hope that jarred the glasses off that little feller," Jesse said.

"What's goin' to happen now?" Crawford asked. "I don't have a horse. If you two ride off, I sure can't keep up with you."

"Wait," Jesse said, holding up his hand. "Wait till the coach goes around that bend up there so that it's out of sight."

"Pa, what was you talkin' about, holdin' this man hostage?" Billy asked. "We're not really goin' to do that, are we?"

"Nah," Jesse answered. "Roy, how much money did you say you needed to start that café you're wantin' to start?"

"Five hundred dollars," Crawford replied. "Why?"
Jesse opened the accordion file and looked down

inside. "Because you just took out a loan from the bank, and you don't have to pay it back," he said. Reaching down inside, he came up with a bound packet of twenty-dollar bills, then counted out twenty-five of them. "Here's your money."

"What?"

"I couldn't very well have given it to you in the coach now, could I? Old Pinch Nose would have seen it, told the sheriff, and you'd have to give it back. This way, they think I took you as hostage."

"Damn, Mr. Peacock, I don't know what to say?"

"You just sit here and wait, and someone will be along soon. When they do, you tell them which way we went."

Crawford smiled. "You mean tell them the opposite of which way you went, don't you?"

"No, if you do that, they'll see the tracks and know that you lied. You tell them exactly which way we went. Only, you'd better find some way to hide that money before anyone gets here."

"Yes, sir, Mr. Peacock. Yes, sir. Oh, and Lexy?"

"Yes?"

"I can tell from your accent that you most likely fought for the South durin' the war, while I fought for the North. But it's like I said. It sure don't make no never mind anymore, since we both had to go through the same kind of hell, even if we was seein' it from different sides. I want to wish you and your boy lots of luck. I don't want to be readin' whereas you two got caught."

"We'll try not to," Jesse said, swinging into the saddle.

"Good-bye!" Crawford called as the two galloped away. "Good-bye!"

The cabin on the Brazos—March 17, 1942

"Did Mr. Crawford buy his café?" Faust asked.

"I don't know, I never came back to check. I'd like to think so, and I'd be willing to bet that he did."

"How much money was there in that file the banker was carrying? I know there was at least five hundred dollars, because you gave that much to Crawford."

"There was an even ten thousand dollars," Jesse said.

"So, you had just over ten thousand when you left New York—"

"Ten thousand apiece," Jesse interrupted.

"And you added another five thousand. You know, Jesse, in 1905, the average yearly income was about six hundred dollars. That means that you and Billy each had twenty-five years of income there. Did that hold you for a while? Or did you start spending it wildly and living the high life?"

Jesse chuckled. "We spent it wildly, but it didn't have anything to do with living the high life."

"I don't understand. If you spent it wildly, and it had nothing to do with the high life, what did you spend it on?"

"Ostriches."

"*Ostriches?*"

"Yeah, ostriches."

"What in heaven's name were you doing spending it on ostriches?"

"I'll tell you that when we come to it," Jesse said. "You're getting me a little ahead of the story."

"I suppose I am," Faust said. "You'll have to excuse me, but I'm so taken by the story that I can hardly wait for what comes next. I'll tell you this, Jesse James, or J. Frank Alexander. If what you are telling me isn't true, then the world has been denied one hell of a Western novelist, because that yarn you're spinning is right up there with anything Zane Grey, Owen Wister, Clarence Mulford, or I could possibly come up with."

"Yeah, well, it's easy enough for me to tell, 'cause all I have to do is remember what happened," Jesse said.

"When I interrupted the story, you and Billy were riding away from Roy Crawford, who you left standing along the side of the road. Where did you go?"

"Well, for a few days, we just kept ridin'," Jesse said. "We stayed off the main roads, and we didn't go into any of the little towns, just in case old Pinch Nose gave a good enough description that someone might recognize us."

CHAPTER TWENTY-SEVEN

Near Matfield Green, Kansas—October 5, 1905

Jesse and Billy rode south from the road where they had stopped the stage, then turned west.

"Are we going to find a railroad?"

"We'll go on into Colorado and catch a train there," Jesse said. "I've sort of got a hankerin' to see what has become of Wild Horse. Also, I'd like to visit your ma's grave."

"Yeah," Billy said. "Yeah, I think I'd like that, too."

"We can ride for a while. We don't have any urgent need to be in California."

"Pa," Billy said. "If there's anybody still in Wild Horse, they'll know us."

"Sure they will. They'll know us as neighbors who used to live there. Billy, I do want you to be careful, and watch what you do and what you say, but you can't go through the rest of your life being afraid of every shadow. If you do, it just isn't worth it."

"All right," Billy replied.

They rode on in silence for about another hour.

"Pa?"

"Yeah?"

"I'm hungry."

"Well, what do you think we ought to do about it?"

Billy laughed. "That was part of my schoolin', wasn't it?"

"Yes, it was."

An hour later Jesse and Billy were stretched out on blankets near a fire. A rabbit, stretched across a circle of rocks, was browning in the flames.

"I wish we had some salt," Billy said.

"We do. I never travel without it."

Billy laughed. "You never taught me that before."

"I thought that was something you could figure out yourself."

Fifteen minutes later, Jesse reached over to move one of the rabbit's legs. "Oh, yeah," he said. "It's done."

It was another week before they reached Wild Horse. By now, even Dunnigan's Grocery Store was gone, and the structures that remained were boarded up. As they rode down the street the sound of the hoofbeats seemed louder than normal, echoing back from the front of the silent buildings.

"It seems kind of spooky, don't it, Pa?" Billy asked.

Jesse chuckled. "Maybe that's why they call them ghost towns."

The only living creature they saw in the entire town was a coyote who stared at them from between two of the boarded-up buildings.

"There's where I went to school," Billy said.

The windows of the schoolhouse had all been broken out, and the front door hung askew on a single hinge.

"Pa, can we look inside?"

"Ha!" Jesse said. "It was all I could do to keep you in school when you were young. Now you want to look inside?"

"Yeah."

"All right."

They angled their horses toward the small building, cut across the school yard, then tethered them to the railing that was still intact on the front porch. There was drift dirt on the floor inside, but all the desks, including the teacher's desk, were still there. The blackboard was there as well, and there was a chalk message faded, but still legible.

> *The record is not yet written of those who learned here.*
> *Have we produced an artist, a writer, a doctor,*
> *perhaps even a president?*
> *I am a part of each of my students,*
> *and each of them a part of me.*
> *This school is gone, but it shall never be forgotten.*
> *—Pauline Foley, last day of the Wild Horse School,*
> *June 12, 1903*

Billy laughed. "Mrs. Foley was always putting little things like that on the blackboard. I wonder where she is now."

"I'm sure she's teaching school somewhere," Jesse said. "Everyone said she was a real good teacher."

Billy looked around the school, then began pointing out desks, naming who sat at each of them.

"That's where Ann Woodward sat," he said. "I sure

pined over her, but she never would give me a second look."

Billy was quiet for a moment, then he turned and started toward the door. "Let's go, Pa. I don't want to be in here anymore."

From the school they rode out to the cemetery and were surprised to see it was remarkably well kept up. There was a sign erected at the edge of the cemetery.

STRANGER, *pause here to take a reverent bow:*
These graves you peruse in idle curiosity
Are of those who were once as you are now
And as is certain that someday, you will be!

Jesse and Billy walked over to look down at Molly's grave.

"Pa?"

"Yes?"

"When we was in Missouri, you put that flower on your first wife's grave. Do you miss Ma as much as you did her?"

"Billy, I was only married to Zee for eight years. I was married to Molly for nineteen years. If you want to know the truth, I miss your ma more than I miss Zee."

"I'm glad," Billy said. "I mean, I'm real sorry about your first wife, how it had to be and all. But I'm glad to know how you felt about Ma."

"Let's go to California," Jesse said, turning to leave the cemetery.

"How far is it to California?"

"I don't know; I've never been there. But all my

life I've heard about how far it is. And how pretty it's supposed to be."

"Are we going to ride horses all the way to California?"

"No, we'll sell our horses and tack in Mirage, then take the train. Only not right away."

"Why not right away?"

"Damn, boy, you want to get on the train looking and smelling like we do now? They would more'n likely make us ride on the car with the horses. We'll get us a hotel room in Mirage, spend a few days there, get cleaned up, and maybe buy some new clothes."

"You know what I want? I want me a hat like the one that was on the head of that little banker feller on the stage."

Jesse laughed. "Yeah, you'll look real fine in that hat."

They reached Mirage late that afternoon, checked in to a hotel, took a hot bath, and spent their first night in a bed for some time.

The next morning, Jesse inquired at the desk about some of his friends.

"Larry Wallace? Oh, yes, he's still here. He's a deputy sheriff. I imagine you'll find him down at the sheriff's office now; he mostly just stays there and watches over the place."

Wallace was sitting behind a desk, reading the paper, when Jesse stepped into the office a few minutes later.

"I thought you weren't going to do law work anymore," Jesse said.

Wallace looked up at the sound of a familiar

voice. "Frank!" he said. "My, oh my. It's been a coon's age. How are you doing? What brings you here?"

"Billy and I are on our way to California, so we decided to stop by the cemetery and visit Molly. I was surprised at how well the cemetery is being kept up."

"Yes, well, half the town of Mirage has folks buried there, so several of them go over there from time to time and work. I'm sure glad you stopped by. You said you and Billy. Where's young Frank?"

"He got himself married to the prettiest girl in Oklahoma," Jesse said. "Or at least that's what he says, and you'd better not argue with him."

"You know, folks are still talkin' about what a great job he did, speakin' those words over Molly's grave like he done. I'm sure glad you stopped by on your way."

"What are you doing wearing a badge? I thought you had sworn off that."

"Well, I guess I just got it in my blood. You know how it is, you sometimes get used to somethin', and you find that you just can't walk away from it as easy as you thought."

"Yes, I know how it is," Jesse said, thinking of his own return to the outlaw trail.

"Oh, by the way, we've got us a stagecoach robber to look out for now."

"Where? Here in the county?"

"No, it was back in Kansas, but what with automobiles, and trains all over the place, and telephones, robberies aren't all local anymore. Although these two were ridin' horses. At least one of 'em was, 'n he brought the horse for the other robber, who had started out as one of the passengers. He stole a money shipment from a bank messenger, then took the other passenger hostage."

"What happened to the hostage? Was he hurt?"

"No, he managed to escape from them when they weren't looking. Say, do you remember that time you rode on the posse with us and shot down all four of the bank robbers?"

"Yeah, I remember," Jesse said. "But I don't like to dwell on it. Killin' those four men didn't sit all that well with me."

Wallace shook his head. "No, I don't reckon it did. Killin' don't sit well with any decent man. So, you're going to California, are you? Well, how long are you going to be in town?"

"Not long, maybe a day or two to catch up with some friends. Gene Welch, Glen Dunnigan. Are they doing all right?"

"Yes, both of them are. Dunnigan's got hisself another store."

"I'm glad."

Wallace picked up the phone. "Let me call my wife. I'll have her round up the Dunnigans and the Welches. You and Billy will come for dinner tonight, won't you?"

"Sure, we'd be glad to."

"New York City is absolutely the biggest place you've ever seen in your life. I thought Kansas City, Saint Louis, and Chicago were big. But New York is so big I can't describe it," Billy said at dinner that evening. "They've got trains that run by electricity on tracks that are so high they are halfway up the sides of the buildings. And they're as fast as greased lightning. And one of 'em we was in ran off the track and fell to the ground below."

Billy also told about the St. Louis World's Fair, and all the "wonderments" they had seen.

"I don't see any need for you folks to go on to California," Dunnigan said. "We can always use good neighbors right here in Mirage."

"I appreciate the invitation, Glen," Jesse replied. "But I've always wanted to see California, and you know what they say, I'm not getting any younger."

"Oh, California is a pretty place, all right," Dunnigan said. "I've been there a few times. But it can't compare with Colorado."

"I've heard about San Francisco for nearly my whole life," Jesse said. "That's where we're headed."

San Francisco—April 18, 1906

Jesse and Billy had rented a row house on Steiner Street in the marina district of San Francisco. It was early in the morning and Jesse was still asleep, when suddenly his bed tilted, dumping him onto the floor. At first he thought Billy had done it, coming into the room to play some joke on him. But as he lay on the floor, still in a stupor, he realized that the entire house was shaking. From outside, he heard a loud roar.

The closest he had ever come to experiencing anything like this was being caught in an artillery barrage during the war, and for one irrational moment, he thought perhaps that was exactly what was happening. But no, that couldn't be. The shaking continued and seemed to get worse with each second. Suddenly one entire wall came crashing down, exposing the outside.

He was unable to get to his feet because of the violent tossing of the floor, then as suddenly as it had started, it stopped.

"Pa! Pa, are you all right?" Billy called from his room.

"Yes, I think so. Are you hurt?"

"No," Billy said. "But I can't get the door open. I'm trapped in my room."

"Let me see what I can do," Jesse said.

Jesse didn't have the problem with his door that Billy did, because Jesse's door was off the hinges. When he stepped out into the hallway, he saw why Billy couldn't get his door open. A pile of bricks and board, shaken loose from the house, was stacked up in front of the door. Jesse worked on it for nearly half an hour, until he got enough of it moved aside to allow Billy to come through.

"Get dressed, gather up the money, and let's get out of here," Jesse said.

Fifteen minutes later, they were dressed and outside, where they saw that the streets had cracked and opened, with chasms extending in all directions. Entire buildings had collapsed, and they saw dead people and animals, crushed under the debris. And though the sun had come up, the sky was black with smoke roiling up from hundreds, perhaps thousands, of fires.

"Pa, you think we can get back in the house?"

"Why would you want to go back in?"

"We left all our clothes in there."

"We'll buy new clothes," Jesse said. "We aren't like the others; they live here, they have to stay here. We don't. We're leaving."*

*The San Francisco earthquake of 1906 struck San Francisco at 5:12 in the morning on April 18, 1906. The quake was followed by a conflagration that burned, unabated, for three more days. Because the quake had destroyed the city water supply, there was not only no water to fight the fire, there was also very little water to drink. Over three thousand people died, and approximately 85 percent of the city was destroyed. The San Francisco earthquake and fire of 1906 remains one of the greatest natural disasters in U.S. history.

CHAPTER TWENTY-EIGHT

Long Beach, California—November 1908

Jesse and Billy had bought a house on the beach. Both of them got jobs, as much to have something to do as to demonstrate to neighbors that they had a sustainable source of income. Billy got a job as a trolley motorman, and Jesse took a job in a store called Walkers Spirits and Fine Wines.

The liquor store stayed open till nine o'clock, and one night, at about a quarter until nine, Jesse was waiting on Mrs. Prescott, a middle-aged widow who was a regular customer.

"Mr. Alexander, I do declare that wine you recommended the last time I was in here was such a success. I served it to the ladies at our book club."

"I'm glad you enjoyed it, Mrs. Prescott. I have to confess that I don't really know that much about wine, but Mr. Walker does, and he suggested it. He goes up to where they grow the grapes and make wine."

"Well, I'll just have another bottle if you don't—"

"Put your hands up!"

The shout came from the front door as two masked men came bursting into the store. Both were brandishing pistols.

"You, old man!" one of them said, pointing his pistol toward Jesse. "Empty the cash box. You, bitch, hand over your purse."

"Now, is that any way for you to talk to a lady?" Jesse asked calmly as he put the cash box on the counter.

"I'll talk to her anyway I want. And if I hear another word from you, I'll shoot you and her both."

"Leave now, or die," Jesse said.

"You don't listen good, do you?" The robber turned his pistol back toward Jesse, but before he could pull the trigger, Jesse took his pistol from inside of the cash box and fired twice, in less than a second. Both men went down.

Mrs. Prescott screamed, and Jesse, with the smoking gun still in his hand, stepped around the corner and put one arm around her shoulders.

"I'm sorry you had to be here for this," he said.

"Are they . . . are they dead?" Mrs. Prescott asked in a tight, frightened voice.

"I expect they are," Jesse said. Walking over to the wall-mounted telephone, he lifted the receiver, then moved the hook up and down a few times.

"Operator, get me the police department," he said. Then a moment later he spoke again. "Police, my name is J. Frank Alexander, and I just shot two men who tried to rob me at Walker's Spirits and Wine. Yes, I'll be here when you arrive. What? Oh, yes, they'll be here, too. They're both dead."

Because both men were still masked, both were holding pistols, and Mrs. Prescott substantiated

Jesse's account, there were no charges filed against him. And, Mr. Walker, who had been summoned by the police as soon as they received the call, rewarded Jesse with a ten-dollar bonus.

The cabin on the Brazos—March 18, 1942

"Jesse, did you feel a little strange about shooting those two men? I mean, put yourself in their shoes. What they were doing was no different from what you, by your own admission, had done many times before," Faust asked.

"I suppose looking at it from your viewpoint I can see where you might think that," Jesse said. "But I didn't put myself in their shoes then, and I don't now. At the time, I believe those two men fully intended to kill me, and probably Mrs. Prescott as well. I had no choice but to shoot them before they did that. And if they didn't intend to shoot me, they made me think they were. That's one of the risks you take when you go down that trail. I've taken many of those risks myself.

"Did I feel strange? No, and I didn't even feel bad about it. I have been in those kill-or-be-killed positions many times in my life. They are never pleasant while you are in the middle of the situation." Jesse smiled. "But I'll tell you this. Life is never sweeter than it is when you have almost lost it. There aren't any of us going to get out of this world alive, Fred. You are a lot younger than I am, but who knows, I might well outlive you."*

*J. Frank Alexander (Jesse James) did outlive Frederick Faust by seven years, Faust being killed in 1944, whereas Alexander didn't die until 1951.

"I suppose that's true. Tell me, how long did you stay in California?"

"Almost three years. We were in San Francisco for half a year, until the earthquake drove us out. And we left Los Angeles a few months after the incident I just told you about."

"Where did you go from there?"

We went to Phoenix. Well, not exactly Phoenix. We wound up in Maricopa County, Arizona."

"Did you go into ranching in Arizona?"

Jesse laughed. "Sort of."

"What do you mean, sort of?"

"You remember when I told you we spent money on ostriches?"

Long Beach—February 10, 1909

"Ostriches?" Jesse questioned, not sure he had heard Billy correctly.

"Yes, we'll start an ostrich ranch, and we'll make a ton of money," Billy said.

"Ostriches are those great big birds, right?"

"They're big all right. From the ground to the top of their head is over six feet tall for the female birds, and the male birds could be as tall as eight feet."

"And would you tell me just what in the world did you plan for us to do with them? Do people eat ostriches?"

"I don't know if you can eat them or not. But we won't be raisin' them to eat. We're raisin' them for feathers."

"Feathers?"

"Yeah, Pa. I've been readin' all about 'em. Why,

did you know there are rich society ladies that will give forty dollars for one feather?"

"If one feather cost that much, it isn't going to be cheap for us to buy ostriches, is it?"

"Four thousand dollars for a pair," Billy said.

"Four thousand dollars?" Jesse shouted. "Are you kidding? A prize bull doesn't cost that much."

"Pa, when you pull out a feather, it grows back. Why, these things are regular money trees!"

Maricopa County, Arizona—June 9, 1916

The ostrich ranch didn't work out the way Billy thought it would. Ostriches proved to be very difficult to raise. It took three years for the birds to mature to the point where the feathers could be plucked, but they lost more than half their birds in the interim. The birds would step into a hole and break a leg, in which case they had to be put down, or they would get hung up in a barbed wire fence, cut their throats, and bleed to death. They were also very aggressive birds, and during mating season, sometimes the male birds would kill each other.

Then, the first year that they had enough birds, and enough feathers to go to market, the fashion changed.

"What do you mean, the fashion changed?" an exasperated Jesse asked the broker in Phoenix.

"The fashion moguls in New York say that feathers are too ostentatious for the new style." He pointed to the sacks of feathers Jesse and Billy had brought in. "You may as well make a feather mattress out of these feathers. Right now, that's all they're good for."

One month later they sold their remaining birds

to a zoo for display. The creatures, which once cost four thousand dollars for a pair, sold for twenty-five dollars apiece. They had ten of them. The land sold only for enough to pay off the note the bank held.

They bought a Ford Model T and left Arizona with one hundred dollars cash between them.

"What are we going to do now?" Billy asked.

"We're going to do what I do best," Jesse said. "We're going to rob a bank."

"Pa, it's been a long time since we've done anything like that. Do you think you still have what it takes?"

Jesse's only answer to Billy's question was to glare at him.

Ft. Worth, Texas—July 3, 1916

"Pa, I know you are used to going into banks with guns drawn, ready to blaze away if you need to," Billy said. "But I've come up with another idea. That is, if you're willing to listen to it."

"I'm always willing to listen," Jesse replied.

"Tomorrow is the Fourth of July. There's going to be all kinds of noise, fireworks, probably a few people shootin' off their guns. Especially tomorrow night."

"There probably will be."

Billy smiled. "I've got some nitroglycerin. We'll be makin' our own noise tomorrow night."

"You're planning on blowing a bank vault, are you?"

"Yes, sir, I am."

Jesse shook his head. "These new vaults can't be blown open. Not unless you use enough explosive to take down the whole building.

"The Cattlemen and Merchant's bank vault is the old-fashioned kind, with a square door," Billy said. "It can be blown."

"You know this for a fact, do you?"

"Yes, sir. I've already checked it out."

"All right, Billy, I'll go along with it. What's your plan?"

"Most of the fireworks will be goin' off between ten o'clock and eleven tomorrow night. That's when we'll break into the bank."

Just as Billy had predicted, the town was alive with fireworks the following night. Rockets burst high in the air, sending out showers of brilliantly colored sparks, firecrackers popped on the ground, and repeating bombs boomed loudly overhead.

Jesse and Billy parked the car on the street about a block away from the bank, and because there were dozens of other cars already there, one more car didn't arouse any curiosity. Leaving the car, they walked, unobserved, into the alley until they came up behind the bank.

"Wait," Billy said, and, climbing up the telephone pole, he cut enough wires to render every telephone within a three-block area mute.

"Now," he said, after he climbed back down.

It wasn't hard to get through the back door; Billy was able to slip the lock with his knife. The security that the bank counted on was the vault itself. Once inside, Billy used the flashlight beam to locate the safe. "See, I told you. It's the old kind."

From very close by some aerial bombs burst, the

noise so loud as to cause the two men to jump. Billy laughed.

"I told you this would be a noisy night."

Billy forced nitroglycerin into the cracks in the square door. Then taping on a dynamite cap, he ran the detonating wire back from the safe to the marble base of the teller's cage.

"We should be all right behind here," Billy said as he and Jesse squatted down behind the base. He touched the two wires together. The explosion was so loud that it made their ears ring, and pieces of the safe door were scattered around the room, joined by pieces of plaster from the nearby walls.

"There it is!" Billy said as his flashlight beam caught beams fluttering down through the cloud of smoke that had been generated by the explosion. The explosion was messy and loud, but it had done the job. The money was now there to pick up.

Jesse and Billy had decided that they would pick up as much money as they could in thirty seconds. Thirty seconds, they believed, would leave them enough time to escape from the bank before anyone came to investigate the explosion.

Their plan worked. They were out of the bank and in the car, driving away, before they saw the flashing red lights of an approaching police car.

Once they were safely out of Ft. Worth, they counted their take. As it turned out, several of the bound stacks were of one-dollar bills. They wound up with only four thousand seven hundred dollars.

"Damn, where were the stacks of twenties, fifties,

and one hundreds?" Billy complained. "You know the bank had to have that kind of money."

"We were grabbing stacks in the dark, and we limited ourselves to thirty seconds," Jesse said. "If you ask me, we had a pretty good haul, considering. Besides, how much money did we have left when we went into that bank?"

"Forty-two dollars and seventeen cents," Billy said.

"Four thousand seven hundred is better," Jesse said.

Billy laughed. "Yeah, it is."

The car began wheezing and coughing.

"Oh, now, this is just what we need," Billy said. "The car is about to go out on us."

"Maybe it's time we got a new car," Jesse suggested.

"Yeah," Billy said, smiling broadly. "Yeah, that's a good idea. And I know we have enough money for it."

CHAPTER TWENTY-NINE

They stayed in the finest hotel in Denton for the next two days, not leaving the hotel room except to come downstairs for their meals. On the evening of the second day, Jesse saw the article in the paper he had been looking for.

"Listen to this," Jesse said, reading from the paper. "'The Cattlemen and Merchants' Bank of Fort Worth was robbed of nearly five thousand dollars on the night of July Fourth. The bank robber, or robbers, took advantage of the exploding fireworks to blast open the safe. The identity of the perpetrators is unknown, but according to Mr. Travelstead, the bank president, the effect could have been much worse, as more than fifty thousand dollars were left behind.'"

"Damn!" Billy said. "I knew there had to be more money than what we got."

Jesse chuckled. "You're only looking at the negative," he said. "The good thing is that they have no idea who did it. Or even if it was more than one person."

"Yeah," Billy said. "Yeah, you're right. There is that."

Jesse divided the paper into two sections, keeping one section for himself and giving the other to Billy. The room had twin beds, and the two lay on the beds, reading the paper, occasionally pointing out an article of interest to the other.

"Pa," Billy said. "Were you serious about getting a new car?"

"I think we need a new one, don't you?"

"Yes, I do think. And this is the one we need." With a broad smile, Billy passed the newspaper back over to Jesse, pointing out a half-page advertisement.

The ad was for a Packard Twin Six, and it had a line drawing of the car, driving along a high coast road.

In plain speech, that car is best which will start quickest, control easiest, rides smoothest, and run longest. To obtain this result, the Packard Motor Car Company created the 12 cylinder engine, and provided in the Packard twin six greater safety, smoother action, and longer wear—with the elegance of a really fine carriage. By its performance, Packard has made the 12 cylinder car the world's standard of value.

$2750.00
Ask The Man Who Owns One

"Are you serious, Billy? Do you see how much that car costs? It costs more than half of all the money we have."

"We can get more the same way we got this money," Billy replied.

Jesse chuckled. "I guess you're right at that," he agreed. He looked at the ad again. "And what else are we going to spend it on?" he asked. "We can only eat and drink so much."

There was, sitting on the floor in the show room of the Denton Packard Car dealer, a Twin Six, exactly like the one they had seen in the newspaper ad. The car was a deep green, and it glistened in the overhead electric lights. Billy opened the door on the driver's side, then closed it, rewarded with a solid sounding thud.

"Please, be careful," a man said, approaching them. He was wearing a brown-tweed three-piece suit and glasses. His hair was combed over to cover the bald spot on his head. "That is a most expensive piece of machinery. Should you do something to diminish its value, I'm sure Mr. Proxmire would hold you liable."

"We're in the market for a new car," Billy said. "I'm afraid that one has just about given up the ghost." He pointed to the Ford Model T that was parked just in front of the display window.

"Oh, dear," the car salesman said. "Perhaps you would do better to shop for a car that is . . . shall we say, more in keeping with your class?"

"Our class?" Jesse said. "Tell me, mister, just what is our class?"

"Oh, please, do not misunderstand me. I mean nothing demeaning by it. I was just trying to help you avoid embarrassment is all. After all, this car costs—"

"Two thousand seven hundred and fifty dollars," Jesse said, finishing the comment. He reached down into a valise he was carrying and counted out twenty-seven bound stacks of bills. "You'll find that each of these stacks is worth one hundred dollars. And here is an additional fifty dollars."

"That is . . . so much money in one-dollar bills. How is it that you have so much money in one-dollar bills?"

"We sold our farm to a man who runs a vending operation, and he deals almost entirely in dollar bills," Jesse explained. "You will take dollar bills, won't you?"

"Yes, sir, of course we will. But it will take a few minutes to count it, to verify that it is all there," the salesman said.

"Don't you have people who can do that while you tell us all about this car?" Jesse asked.

"Yes, indeed, we certainly do have such people in our employ," the salesman replied, now all smiles. "Did you know that this car is equipped with an electric self-starter?"

"You mean we don't have to crank it?" Billy asked.

"No, sir, you don't. Allow me to demonstrate."

The salesman made a show of putting his left foot on the starter button. The engine turned over and caught quickly.

"You'll not get that on a Model T Ford," he said proudly.

A few minutes later Jesse was given a bill of sale, and he and Billy drove away in a brand-new Packard.

Chandler—November 21, 1916

When they drove the Packard into the front yard of the farm house that neither Jesse nor Billy had seen for nearly thirteen years, they were met by a young, barefoot boy.

"Gee, this is certainly one fine car," he said, running his hand over the smooth finish of the fender. "It's a Packard, ain't it?"

"That's what it is, son. Now, tell me. Would your name be James William Alexander?"

The boy looked confused. "Yes. But people call me Jimmy. How do you know my name?"

Frank stepped out of the house then, and, with a big smile on his face, came to greet his father and his brother.

"He knows your name, Jimmy, because he is your grandpa," Frank said. "Hello, Pa. Hello, Billy. I was beginning to think I never would see either one of you again."

"Hello, Frank."

"This isn't my grandpa. I see Grandpa all the time," Jimmy said.

"The grandpa you know is your mom's pa. This is my pa, so he is your other grandpa. And this your uncle Billy."

"Hello, Jimmy," Billy said, sticking out his hand. Jimmy took it, and smiled up at him.

"How long are you going to stay?" Frank asked.

"Not too long. We wouldn't want to put you out any."

"You wouldn't be putting us out at all," Frank said. He took a closer look at the car, then let out a little whistle. "My, oh, my, you two must be doing mighty fine to be driving an automobile like this."

"We were doing all right for a while, until the feather market went bust," Jesse said.

Frank chuckled. "Yes, in one of your very infrequent letters, you said that you were growing ostriches for the feathers. So the market went bust, did it?"

"I'm afraid it did. So we sold out and figured we'd come here to visit you for a few days. How is Ethel Marie getting along?"

"Come on in and see for yourself," Frank invited.

Ethel Marie greeted them warmly, then told Frank to go out and kill a hen.

"Are you going to make chicken and dumplin's, Mom? Oh, good! That's my favorite!" Jimmy said.

"Dumplin's?" Jesse asked.

Frank told me how much you love dumplin's, and how you sometimes made them because his mother couldn't," Ethel Marie said. "So I learned how from my aunt Eunice. She lives in Jackson, Mississippi, and she says every woman in Mississippi must learn how to make dumplin's, or they will be run out of the state."

"I expect that's right," Jesse said with a little laugh.

For the rest of the afternoon the house was permeated with the aroma of baking chicken, broth, dumplings, and rolls. As Ethel Marie worked in the kitchen, Frank, Jesse, and Billy visited in the living room.

"One letter about every four months," Frank complained. "And from all over the country. You said in one of your letters that you had been in that big earthquake they had in California."

"Yes," Jesse said.

"That must have been quite an experience."

"Not one that I want to go through again," Jesse replied.

"Me, neither," Billy added.

"You should write more often," Frank said. "We are family."

"I apologize for that, Frank," Jesse said. "But, like you pointed out, we never seem to stay in the same place very long."

"I believe you said in one of your letters that you went to Wild Horse and you visited Ma's grave."

"Yes," Billy said. "The town is all gone now, and what buildings there are left are all boarded up. But the cemetery has been kept up real good."

"I'm glad you stopped by to see Ma," Frank said. "I know she was lookin' down from heaven and appreciated it."

"Gentlemen?" Ethel Marie called from the dining room. "Dinner is ready."

"Oh, my, Frank," Jessie said later as he pushed away from the table. "That's the best thing I've eaten in a long time. You are one lucky man to have a wife who can cook like this."

Ethel Marie beamed.

"Come on out with me, let me show you the farm," Frank said. "We're all modernized now. I've got two tractors to do all the plowing."

"Two tractors? You can only drive one at a time."

"I've got a hired man named Ben, and he's a real good worker."

Frank hooked a couple of mules to a wagon, then the three men climbed in and he began his tour.

"I didn't grow any corn this year. I just grew cotton and soybeans," Frank said.

"What do soybeans taste like?" Billy asked.

Frank laughed. "People don't eat soybeans. They're most used as forage."

"I never heard of any animals eating beans," Billy said.

"It's not like they are butter beans or anything. As you can see, I've got all my crops out, and this was my best year ever."

As Frank continued with his tour, proudly pointing to everything, Jesse glanced over at Billy and saw that he was almost falling asleep with boredom. He wondered how twins could be so different.

After supper that night, they all sat out on the front porch, watching the sun sink with a blaze of color in the west.

"You know, Pa, I don't mean to carp about it, but you and Billy could have come to visit once or twice before this. You can't blame Jimmy for not knowing who you were. He's never seen you, not for his entire life."

"Has he heard of me?" Jesse asked pointedly.

"Not that much," Frank admitted. "Pa, sometimes it would be so long between letters, we didn't know if you were alive or dead."

"Can I ask Grandpa a question?" Jimmy asked.

"Sure you can," Jesse said before Frank could reply.

"Grandpa, have you ever seen an airplane?"

"Yes, I've seen a few of them."

"Have you ever gone up in one?"

Jesse chuckled. "I never have, and I don't plan to ever go up in one."

"I've been up in one," Jimmy said.

"You have?" Jesse replied, surprised at the boy's words. "You've actually been up in an airplane? You aren't foolin' your old grandpa, are you?"

"He's tellin' the truth, Pa," Frank said. "There was a fella who came to the county fair here, back this past spring. He gave rides in his airplane for a dollar, and Jimmy wouldn't be denied."

"He begged so that Frank finally gave in," Ethel Marie said. "I'm not lying to you when I tell you I was so frightened that I scarcely drew a breath until he came back down."

"Well how was it, Jimmy?" Billy asked. "What did you think of it?"

"It was the most funnest thing I've ever did," Jimmy said. "When I grow up, I'm going to fly one. You know what they call someone who flies an airplane? They call them a pilot, and that's what I'm goin' to be. I'm going to be a airplane pilot."

"Well if you are, I'm sure you'll be a good one."

"Jimmy, go wash your face and hands and brush your teeth," Ethel Marie said. "It's time for you to go to bed."

"I want to talk to Grandpa and Uncle Billy some more," Jimmy complained.

"We're goin' to be around for a few days," Jesse said. "We'll have plenty of time to talk."

"You promise?"

"I promise."

Jimmy smiled, then said his good nights and left to go to bed.

CHAPTER THIRTY

"You've done real well for yourself, Frank," Jesse said after Jimmy went to bed. "I can't tell you how proud I am of you."

"We've had some tough times, especially when there's a long drought. But these last few years have been really good. Chris Dumey is talking about selling his farm, and it's right next to this one, so I think I might buy it."

"Ha. Dumey was one of the original land rushers, wasn't he? Like us?"

"Yes, sir."

"Why is he selling out?"

"He's not selling everything. He plans to keep his house, but he says that he's too old to be farming anymore."

"I can understand that. I was beginning to feel my age back with the ostriches."

"Pa, didn't you say once that you farmed back in Missouri?"

"Yes, before my pa died. It wasn't much of a farm; mostly we just grew rocks and weeds."

"You know, I really don't know much about you. Now, Ethel Marie's ma, she has a Bible that's got all the names of her pa's family in it, 'n she has another Bible that's got all her family in it. Why, if you ask Ethel Marie who any of her folks are, on either side, 'n she can go all the way back to the Revolutionary War. All I know about you is that you're from Missouri, but you lived some in Kentucky and you were in the Civil War."

Jesse laughed. "That's all I know about me, too," he said.

"But you at least know who your grandparents were, don't you, Pa?"

"My ma's last name was Mimms, before she married Ike Alexander, who was my pa. I never met any of my grandparents. My real pa died when I was very young, and my ma married again and we moved to Kentucky."

"Do you have any brothers or sisters?"

"I had a brother, but he was killed in the war."

Jesse glanced over toward Billy, measuring his reaction. Billy knew the truth, and Jesse was concerned that the expression on his face may give away the fact that almost everything he was saying now was a lie.

"What was his name?" Frank asked.

"Sam. His name was Samuel Alexander."

"Well, that's something at least. Do you know that, in my whole life, you have never even told me that?"

Jesse had wanted to leave earlier, but Ethel Marie begged him to stay until November 30, Thanksgiving Day. "My mother and father will be here for

Thanksgiving Day dinner," she said. I think it would be just wonderful for all of us to celebrate together. It has been such a long time since you saw them."

"Is Horace still running the feed and seed store in town?"

"No, my brother is running it now."

"Will your brother be here?"

"He and Martha are celebrating the holiday with her parents."

Horace McGill was two years older than Jesse, but he looked ten years older. They arrived in a Studebaker, and from the living room window, Jesse saw McGill admiring the Packard. Jesse had heard, indirectly, that McGill believed his daughter was "marrying down" when she and Frank were married, and though he had never called him on it, it had always irritated him. He was glad that Frank was doing as well as he was, if for no other reason than to show McGill that he was wrong.

"Hello, J. Frank," McGill greeted when they came into a house that was filled with the aroma of the Thanksgiving Day dinner. He used the 'J. Frank' to differentiate Jesse from his son, Frank. "I heard you were back. Are you going to stay around for a while?"

"Just through the day," Jesse replied. "Billy and I recently sold our ranch out in Arizona, and we're looking for some other business to get into."

"Aren't you old enough to retire?"

"Probably," Jesse agreed. "But I'm not looking to retire just yet."

There were a few other exchanges, but during the meal McGill monopolized the conversation. Jesse didn't challenge him. As far as he was concerned, the more time McGill took up talking, the less Jesse would have to.

After the meal, as Jesse sat in an easy chair in the living room, listening and watching the conversation and the interplay between everyone, he couldn't help but wonder about his other two children, Jesse and Mary. Where were they on this Thanksgiving Day? What were they doing, and if they were celebrating, who were they celebrating with?

He put that thought out of his mind. He had managed to live a life without them all these years, and he knew that they were much better off without him.

The cabin on the Brazos—March 21, 1942

"I know from your story, so far, that Molly never learned your true identity. Billy did, because he was with you when you and your brother met. But what about your son, Frank? Did Frank ever find out who his father really was?"

"No. I thought it best for Frank, I mean, being the kind of boy he was, and the kind of man he became, that he not know about me. I believe it would have been more than he could take, to know that he was the son of an outlaw. I swore Billy to secrecy, and Billy never broke his trust. Neither Frank, nor his wife, nor his boy ever found out."

"Where are they all now? Frank, Jimmy, and Ethel Marie? They are sure to find out when this book comes out. Or I guess, now that you are telling the story, you are resolved to everyone finding out."

"You're right, I don't care who knows now. In fact, I want everyone to know; that's why I'm doing this. But Frank and Jimmy won't find out. They're both dead."

"Oh, I'm sorry I brought it up."

"That's all right, it's been long enough."

"What happened? That is, if you don't mind my asking."

"Jimmy got his wish to become a pilot. He joined the army air corps and learned to fly. But in 1928, he crashed and was killed. Frank died two years after that. The doctors said it was a heart attack, but I think it was of a broken heart. He never got over losing his boy."

"What about Ethel Marie?"

"The last I heard, she had remarried and moved to California. I haven't heard from her since, and there's no reason she should keep in touch with me. I just want her to have a good life."

Faust, not knowing what to say, just nodded in sympathy.

"The thing that bothers me most was that after both of the boys were grown, I never was the father to Frank that I was to Billy. I mean, I just wasn't a part of Frank's life like I should have been. And I was, for sure, not a part of Jimmy's life."

"I think we all have personal regrets in our lives," Faust said.

"If you don't mind, let's pick this back up tomorrow."

"All right," Faust agreed.

* * *

When Jesse woke up the next morning, it was to the aroma of coffee and bacon. He went into the kitchen to see Faust beating up some batter in a bowl.

"I thought I would make some of my world-famous pancakes for breakfast this morning," he said.

"World-famous, are they? By whose account?"

"I'm just telling you what John Wayne said when I was on the set for the movie *Stagecoach*."

"You wrote that?"

"No, Ernest Haycox wrote it. The short story, that is, not the screenplay. But he was invited on the set; he invited me, and one morning I made pancakes."

"John Wayne was right," Jesse said half an hour later. "They are world-famous. Or, if they aren't, they should be."

"Are you ready to get back to the story now?" Faust asked.

"Yeah, I'm ready."

"The big question I have is, did you pull another job after you and Billy robbed that bank in the middle of the night?"

"Oh, yeah," Jesse said. "We were just getting started."

"How did it go?"

"As far as the money is concerned, it went very well. But for the first time since the Northfield Raid, I had one of my men get killed."

Chandler—December 1, 1916

Jesse and Billy left Chandler just after sunrise the next morning after Thanksgiving.

"Where are we going, Pa?" Billy asked. Billy was driving.

"How about heading for Blytheville, Arkansas?"

"Blytheville? You mean Mr. Cummins? Do you think he's still there?"

"He was two months ago," Jesse said. "I wrote him a letter and asked if he would be interested in getting involved in another adventure with us."

"Hot damn, you've got something else planned, don't you?"

"Yes."

"And what did Mr. Cummins say?"

"He said he would be very interested."

They reached Blytheville before nightfall that same day, and they drove right up to Jim Cummins's house. He came out to see who it was when they honked the horn.

"I tell you the truth, Jesse, until I got that letter from you a couple of months ago, I thought maybe you two were dead or something," Cummins said after he invited them in.

"The name is Frank," Jesse said.

"Heck yeah, I know that. But I figured since it's just us, that it wouldn't matter that much."

"If you get into a habit of calling me Jesse, you might slip sometime. It would be better if you called me Frank all the time."

"Yeah, I guess you're right."

"Tell me, Jim, do you have money left from our last job?" Jesse asked.

"Hell, I damn near had it all spent the first year," Cummins said. "I've just been livin' sort of hand to mouth since then, tryin' to scratch enough money out of the farm to keep body and soul together. That's why when you asked in your letter if I would be interested in another adventure, I said yes."

"I was glad to hear that. To be honest, Jim, I wasn't sure you were even still alive, or that you would answer the letter if you were," Jesse said. "I just took a chance on it."

"What is this adventure you're talking about? You didn't say nothin' about it in the letter. Have you got somethin' in mind?"

"I do have something in mind, but it's going to take more than the three of us. Are you still in contact with Jesse Evans, or John Tucker, or whatever he's calling himself these days?"

"Yeah, I still hear from him from time to time. He's up in Joplin now."

"Do you think he would be interested in another job?" Jesse asked.

"I don't know. He told me once that he was goin' to go straight. But he's been workin' at a warehouse, loadin' and unloadin' trucks, so I expect he's gettin' damn tired of that by now. I'm pretty sure that if the money is good he'll be all in with us. What you got in mind? Another bank? That last one was a sweet job, all right."

"Not a bank," Jesse said. "What I've got in mind is a money transfer car."

"Really? Why would you do that? There would be more money in a bank, wouldn't there? I mean, how much money could we get out of one transfer car?"

"I'd say half a million dollars," Jesse said.

"Half a million dollars?" Cummins replied with a gasp. "Are you serious?"

"I'm not going to say that it will be half a million, but it could be. I'm sure it will be more than we got the last time."

"All right then, I'm in for sure," Cummins said. "And I think I can speak for Evans. Once he hears how much money we can make, he'll join us in a heartbeat, there's not a doubt in my mind."

"I think for a job this big that we'll be wanting at least one more man besides Evans," Jesse said. "The problem is, I've been out of the business for a long time now, and all the people I know, or I once worked with, are either dead or in prison somewhere."

"I don't know of anyone personally, but I'd be willing to bet that Evans does. He gets around a lot more than I do."

"What you say we drive out to Joplin and look up Mr. Evans?" Jesse suggested.

Joplin, Missouri—December 6, 1916

"How much money did you say?" Evans asked.

"I told Jim it could be as much as half a million dollars," Jesse said. "I can't guarantee that, but I'm sure it will not be less than one hundred thousand."

"What makes you think there will be that much money in the truck?"

"I read this article in the *Police Gazette*," Jesse said, showing it to Evans.

> With the perfection and reliability of the automobile, there has been developed, in this twentieth century, a new and more secure way of transporting money from bank to bank. This new method of currency exchange is the armored car. The armored car is a closed vehicle with steel siding, so constructed as to provide protection for the driver and messenger against any attempt at robbery by outlaws. The steel plating will turn away bullets of any caliber, thus insuring the safe and efficient transfer of money. Because of this security, banks are entrusting larger and larger amounts of currency in such transfers, many times up to half a million dollars or more in one transfer. Rarely is less than one hundred thousand dollars transferred by such a mode.

"That's a lot of money," Evans said.

"It's enough to get you away from the loading docks for a while," Jesse said.

"Yes, sir, I would say that it sure is."

"Do you want to be part of it?"

"I sure do. When do we go?" Evans asked excitedly.

"Not so fast. We need at least one more man. Jim said he thought you might know of someone."

"Yeah," Evans said. "Yeah, I know just the man. His name is Trainor. Nick Trainor. He lives in Kansas City."

"We'll pick him up on the way," Jesse said.

"On the way where?"

"On the way to where we are going to pull the job," Jesse said without further explanation.

Kansas City—December 10, 1916

"Hey, you two!" someone yelled at Jesse and Evans when they walked back into the kitchen of Seabaugh's Café. "Get out of here! You can't be back here!"

"Are you Mr. Seabaugh?" Evans asked.

"I am."

"Well, Mr. Seabaugh, I need to talk to my friend," Evans said. "He's back there washin' dishes."

"If you want to talk to him, you wait until his shift is over. Do you understand me, mister? Now get out of here!"

"Nick," Evans called out to a man who was standing at a steel sink in the scullery, his arms elbow-deep in soapy and greasy water. Nick looked around and smiled.

"Jesse, what are you doing here?"

For just a second Jesse gasped, then he remembered that Evans first name was also Jesse, and this man was talking to him.

"I've come to offer you a job," Evans said. "If you want to walk away from here I've got something I believe you'll be interested in."

"What are you talking about?" Seabaugh asked. "This man already has a job! You can't just come in here and hire him away like that."

"What's the job?" Trainor asked.

"It's the kind of job you and I have spoken about a few times. It's a big score, Nick, and I mean a really big score."

Trainor pulled his arms out of the water, then began drying off.

"All right, I'm in."

"What? You can't quit now! Not right in the middle of your shift!" Seabaugh said angrily.

"You don't think I can quit, do you? Well I tell you what, Seabaugh. You just watch me walk out," Trainor said.

"You won't get any of the money that's comin' to you," Seabaugh shouted, his face getting red from anger. "Do you understand me, Trainor? If you walk out now, you won't get one red cent!"

"The hell I won't. You owe me damn near a full week's pay," Trainor challenged.

"Nick, don't worry about that week's pay. Believe me, you don't need it," Evans said.

"Are you tellin' me the truth, Evans?"

"He's telling you the truth, Mr. Trainor," Jesse said.

"Who's this?" Trainor asked, nodding his head toward Jesse.

"This is Frank Alexander. I've worked with him before. He's the one who found the job for us, and it's big time, my friend. It's very big time."

"All right, let's go," Nick said.

"Trainor! Trainor! You come back here, you hear me? You come back here!" Seabaugh shouted. "How am I going to get these dishes washed?"

"Do 'em yourself," Trainor shouted, and without turning around he flipped the 'the bird' to Seabaugh.

CHAPTER THIRTY-ONE

Cow Palace Hotel, Kansas City

"You met Frank Alexander a few minutes ago," Evans said to Trainor after Jesse invited them up to his hotel room. "This is his boy, Billy, and this is an old friend, Jim Cummins. I told you that Frank and I had worked together before. Frank had it planned out really well, and we got forty-five thousand dollars for it. Billy and Jim were in on it as well."

"When was that?" Nick asked.

"It was about ten years ago."

Trainor looked at Jesse. "You ain't done nothin' in ten years?"

"I haven't done anything with any of these men," Jesse replied without adding any more information.

"How much did you say you got for that job?"

"We got forty-five thousand dollars," Evans repeated.

"That's good money," Trainor said. "I ain't never got more'n two thousand dollars for any job I ever done." He looked directly at Jesse. "You think we can get that much from this job?"

"No," Jesse said. Then he smiled. "I think we will get more. A lot more."

"What kind of job is it?" Trainor asked.

Jesse explained again how armored cars were now carrying so much money and how he planned to rob one.

"But if they are all covered with steel like it says in this article, how are we going to do it?" Trainor asked.

"Simple. We'll catch them when they are in front of the bank with their doors open, actually transferring the money. We'll hit them hard, and we'll have a fast car. We'll have the money and be down the road before anyone can react."

"Wait until you see the car," Evans said. "It's a Packard. There won't be anything on the road that can catch it."

Jesse shook his head. "We won't be in the Packard when we pull the job. That car stands out too much. We'll be in a different car."

"You've got another car?" Evans asked.

"We will get another car before we do the job."

"If we buy another car and one of the guards at the armored car describes it, don't you think the man who sells us the car might recognize it and describe us?" Cummins asked.

"Who said we were going to buy the car?" Jesse replied with a broad smile.

* * *

Two nights later, at about two o'clock in the morning, Jesse, Billy, and the other three men were driving slowly through a quiet and dark residential area in the west part of Joplin. Jesse was driving, and Billy and Nick Trainor were both riding in the front seat with him.

"There, Pa, that Dodge Touring Car," Billy said. "It will be perfect. Let me 'n Nick out here, then you drive around the block and park. We'll walk back and get the car, then join you in a minute."

"How are you going to get the car started without a key?" Cummins asked.

"Simple," Trainor replied. "All we have to do is cross the ignition wires."

Billy and Trainor stepped out of the Packard, then walked back to the Dodge.

"Set the brake, and make certain the transmission is in neutral," Trainor said. "When I tell you, cross these two wires right here." Trainor shined a flashlight on the wires. "I'll crank."

Billy set the brake and put the gear in neutral, then retarded the spark, opened the throttle, adjusted the mixture, and pulled out the choke.

"Now," Trainor said from the front of the car, "cross those wires I showed you."

Billy crossed the wires, which turned the ignition on. That was when Trainor jerked the crank handle up. The engine started, and Billy advanced the spark about halfway up the quadrant, then adjusted the throttle as Trainor, carrying the hand crank, hurried back to jump into the car.

"Let's go!" Trainor said.

* * *

"There they are," Evans said from the Packard as the Dodge Touring Car approached.

Billy pulled up alongside the Packard. "Pa, since we don't know much about this car, maybe you'd better follow us just in case we have trouble."

"All right. You know where we're going."

"I just know it's in Denver," Billy said. "I'm not sure where in Denver."

"It doesn't matter. After we get to Denver, we'll all be in the same car, anyway."

U.S. Mint, Denver, Colorado—10:30 a.m., December 18, 1916

The marking on the side of the gray, steel-plated truck read U.S. FEDERAL RESERVE.

Jesse was driving the Dodge down West Colfax Avenue, and as they approached the armored car, they saw only two men behind the truck. One was in the back of the truck, and another was standing beside a cart on the street behind the truck. The one on the street was passing canvas bags up to the one in the back of the truck.

Jesse came to a stop right behind the truck, and Billy, Trainor, Cummins, and Evans jumped out of the car. Trainor and Evans both had shotguns.

"Step away from the truck!" Trainor called.

Both messengers were armed, but their weapons were pistols and they were in holsters strapped to their sides. Trainor and Evans were pointing their shotguns at the two men, who had no choice but to react to the order.

Billy jumped up into the back of the truck, then started tossing down the money bags that had already been loaded into the truck. They had transferred four of them into the car, when all of sudden several armed guards came rushing out of the mint.

"Billy! Get in the car!" Jesse shouted. "All you, get into the car!"

Gunshots rang out as the Mint police began firing. Jesse saw one of the Mint policemen raise his shotgun and take dead aim at Billy. Jesse's pistol was lying on the seat beside him, and he picked it up and fired, quickly, before the policeman was able to fire. The policeman went down.

"Hurry!" Jesse shouted. "We've got to get out of here!"

Some of the guards were using pistols, but many were using shotguns, and a load of buckshot slammed into the back door of the car, but none of the shot carried all the way through the door.

"Where the hell did they all come from?" Trainor shouted.

For just a moment, it wasn't December 18, 1916, it was September 7, 1876, and Jesse wasn't in Denver, he was in Northfield, Minnesota.

"Where the hell did they all come from?" Frank shouted as they ran from the front of the bank.

"No!" Jessie shouted aloud. "No, not again!"

The gunfire was as intense here on the streets of Denver as it had been that day in Northfield, or as it had been in any Civil War battle in which Jesse had ever participated. It might have been even more intense.

By now, everyone was in the car but Trainor, and just as he was about to get in, Jesse saw a spray of blood erupt from the side of his face.

"Grab hold of him!" Jesse called, and almost kinesthetically he could feel himself on a horse, and he leaned forward as if urging the mount into a gallop. But he wasn't on a horse, he was in a car, and he pushed the accelerator all the way to the floor.

The car leaped ahead, but Trainor wasn't yet inside. Billy was holding on to him by his arms, and Trainor's legs were being dragged along the pavement of West Colfax.

"Let 'im go!" Evans was shouting excitedly. "Let him go! He's slowin' us down."

"No, he isn't slowing us any," Billy said. "Help me pull him into the car."

Cummins reached over, and, with him grabbing one arm and Billy jerking on the other, they managed to finally get Trainor pulled the rest of the way into the car. Evans closed the door.

Jesse checked the mirror, but nobody was in pursuit. All of the Mint guards had been on foot, though he was sure that, by now, many of them had gone to their cars. He was equally sure that the Denver Police had been alerted as well.

"How is Trainor doing?" Jesse called.

Billy saw that there was a large wound in the side of his head, and that about half of Trainor's brains were pouring out. Trainor's eyes were open, but they were opaque.

"He's dead, Pa."

"Damn!"

Trainor was the first man to be killed in one of Jesse's operations since the failed Northfield Raid, when Clell Miller and Bill Chadwell were killed.

They had gotten twenty-six dollars from the Northfield Raid. Was this experience an equal failure?

Earlier, they had left the Packard in the garage of an empty house on Gilpin Street. The house was chosen not only because it was empty, but also because the driveway curved around the house, to the garage in back. Jesse checked the mirror as they turned onto Gilpin and saw no other traffic. The entire street was empty, as were the sidewalks on either side of the street. He pulled around back, then waited as Billy backed the Packard out.

"What are we going to do with Nick?" Evans asked.

"We'll leave him in the car," Jesse said.

"We can't do that. I mean, just leave him like that."

"You know him. Does he have any relatives that you know about?" Jesse asked.

"No, none that I know about."

"Then we'll leave him in the car. He'll be found, and he'll be buried."

The others agreed, and five minutes later, as the Packard drove back through Denver, they saw that West Colfax was blocked off, and a policeman was standing there, directing traffic.

"What happened here, officer?" Jesse asked.

"There was a robbery at the Mint," the policeman said.

"You don't say. Can we drive by and take a look?"

"There's nothing for you to see there," the officer said. He pointed toward the crossroad. "Be gone with you now, and let us be about our work."

"Yes, sir. I do hope you catch them," Jesse said.*

They stopped for the night in Bennett, Colorado. There they got two hotel rooms and, gathering in Jesse's room, dumped the contents of the canvas bags onto the bed.

"Woowee, look at all that money!" Cummins said. "I swear, I ain't never seen that much money in my entire life!"

"How much is it?" Evans asked.

Jesse began counting it, dividing it into four equal piles.

"We should be dividing it into three piles," Evans suggested.

"Why is that?" Jesse asked sharply.

"Well, you and Billy, bein' as you're family 'n all, it'll be almost like you're gettin' a double amount."

"He may be my son, but we are two people."

*No one ever connected Jesse James, or J. Frank Alexander, with this case, and none of the perpetrators were ever identified, with the exception of thirty-six-year-old Nicholas "Chaw Jimmie" Trainor who was killed during the shootout. The gang, which got away with $200,000.00, fled, taking the mortally wounded Trainor with them after one of the guards, Charles Linton, was killed. Not until January 14 was Trainor's body found in their getaway car after it had been dumped in a Gilpin Street garage. No one was ever charged with the Denver robbery, and the case was closed on December 1, 1934, still officially listed as unsolved.

"Frank's right, Jesse," Cummins said quickly. "Anyhow, why are you complainin'? Didn't you just say this is the most money you had ever seen in your entire life?"

"Yeah, I did say that," Evans agreed.

"And it wouldn't be here at all if it wasn't for Frank and his boy getting it all set up for us."

"Yeah, you're right," Evans said. "I'm sorry, Frank. Besides, what with Trainor gettin' kilt, why I reckon we'll be dividin' up his share. How much is it all a' comin' to?"

By now Jesse had finished the count and he looked up at the others.

"Boys, there's fifty thousand dollars apiece here," he said.

"Sumbitch!" Cummins said. "What am I goin' to do with all this money?"

"The first thing we're going to do is split up," Jesse said. "The law knows there were at least four of us, so I don't think it's a good idea for the four us to stay together. Tomorrow, Billy and I will go on alone."

"Alone? What are we supposed to do?" Evans asked.

"There is a train depot right across the street," Jesse said. "You've got enough money to go anywhere in the country. Hell, you've got enough money to go anywhere in the world. I suggest that the two of you take a train tomorrow. But don't both of you take the same train."

"Yeah," Evans said, smiling. "Yeah, I've got enough money to do anything I want to do. I don't know about the rest of you, but I'm goin' out to California. I've always wanted to see California."

"Why stop there?" Cummins asked. "Why not go on to Hawaii? I think I read someplace that the women don't wear any tops in Hawaii."

"Sumbitch!" Evans said excitedly. "Yeah, Hawaii! I'm goin' to Hawaii!"*

---

*Thought to have been born in either Missouri or Texas in 1853, Jesse Evans had his first brush with the law when he was arrested along with his parents on June 26, 1871, in Elk City, Kansas, for passing counterfeit money. In 1872 he drifted into New Mexico, where he worked on John Chisum's ranch. Evidently, he found cow handling too hard, as he soon became an outlaw, committing cattle rustling and armed robbery with the likes of Billy the Kid, Frank Baker, Pony Deal, Tom Hill, and others. Evans was sentenced to prison in Huntsville in 1908, was paroled in 1915, but failed to report to his parole officer in December of 1916 and was never heard from again. Was he, as J. Frank Alexander (Jesse James?), one of the unidentified perpetrators of the Great U.S. Mint holdup in Denver, as described in this narrative? And did he go to Hawaii? That would certainly explain why he was never heard from again.

CHAPTER THIRTY-TWO

The cabin on the Brazos—May 20, 1942

DOOLITLE RAID ON JAPAN
WITHOUT LOSS, U.S. REVEALS

FAMED FLYER ANNOUNCES NIPPONESE
FAILED TO BAG SINGLE AMERICAN PLANE

Reports hits on warship, a/c plant

WASHINGTON, MAY 19 (UP)—Brig. Gen. James H. (Jimmy) Doolittle, famed speed flyer who led 79 intrepid American volunteers in a highly destructive raid on the Japanese mainland April 18, revealed Tuesday night that not a single airplane was shot down in the audacious attack.

Numerous details of the spectacular raid were revealed for the first time after Doolittle and his comrades in glory were decorated for the historic achievement that represented a substantial return payment for Pearl Harbor.

Jesse was sitting on the front porch of his cabin on the river, reading the newspaper, when he saw a Cadillac convertible, its dark blue color flashing in the sun, pull up front. He didn't recognize the car, but he did recognize the driver when he got out. It was Frederic Faust.

"I had about given up on you," Jesse said. "It's been two months."

"I had agreed to do some work on a small film. There's not that much to the story; I don't know that it will actually go anywhere, but it stars Humphrey Bogart, and I do like him."

"What is the name of the movie?"

"*Casablanca.*"

"*Casa blanca?* White house?"

"I guess it does mean that, doesn't it? Actually, this is about a city, the largest city in Morocco. It's a French colony that is controlled by the Nazis. It's an interesting little film, but as I said, I don't believe it will go anywhere. Anyway, I decided to drive back from California, just to take a look at the country. I thought if I was ever going to make a cross-country drive, I had better do it before gas rationing starts."

"Do you still want to do this book?"

"Oh, yes, definitely," Faust replied. "I wouldn't have come back if I didn't want to do the book."

"We'll have plenty of time to work on it," Jesse said. "Nobody has called me yet, and this war is winding down." He showed Faust the article he was reading. "Have you seen this? We bombed Japan and not a single airplane was lost."*

"Oh, I think the war will last a little longer," Faust said. "At least long enough for us to finish the book."

"Did you bring all your notes with you?" Jesse asked.

"I did. The last thing we spoke about was the raid on the Denver Mint. You and Billy got fifty thousand dollars apiece from that, which is an awful lot of money. Did you retire from the business after that?"

"I didn't exactly retire, but soon after that, the United States got into the Great War."

"They're now calling that war World War One," Faust said. "And they are calling this war World War Two, as if it is a sequel."

"Damn, if they start numbering them, I guess that means we'll just keep having them," Jesse said. "But to answer your question, we didn't do anything after the Denver Mint job. For one thing, we didn't have to; we got enough money from that one job to last us for several years, and for another, it just didn't seem right to be doing things like that during the war.

"It wasn't until after the war was over, and the government passed the prohibition law, that we got back into the business. Billy always did like fast cars."

---

*The news release intimated that the Doolittle Raid was without cost, but this isn't true. None of the aircraft was shot down, but all the aircraft were lost. One aircraft crashed into the sea, fifteen reached China, and one landed in the Soviet Union. Eight crewmen were captured by the Japanese Army in China; three of those were executed, as were thousands of Chinese as punishment for helping the American flyers.

West Plains, Missouri—June 17, 1922

The still was in the Ozark mountains, and though it could be reached by automobiles, the road that led from the major road up to where the still was located was one that had been privately cut. It showed on no maps. The exit off the highway was concealed by shrubbery, which, from the road, looked as if it were growing from the ground. In truth the bushes were attached to a swinging arm that could be pushed open, disclosing the road beyond.

Billy hopped out of the car, a Marmon 34, the fastest production car money could buy. In addition, Billy had souped up the car with dual carburetors and twin exhausts. On a paved road the car could do more than eighty miles per hour.

Billy swung the gate open and Jesse drove the car through. Billy closed the gate behind them and hopped back into the car for the drive up to the still that was run by the Morris twins.

"Was there anybody on the road when you come through the gate?" Travis asked.

"Nobody saw us come through," Billy said.

"They damn well better not have," Troy said. "If the law finds our still because you blundered through it—"

"You want the money or not?" Jesse asked. "Because if you don't, there are a dozen other moonshiners who'll take our business."

"Yeah, we want the money," Travis said.

"Then quit your bitching about whether or not we gave away your still," Jesse said. "I've been in this business a lot longer than you have."

"How could you be? Prohibition didn't start until 1920."

"There are more illegal things than drinking alcohol," Jesse said. "Now, get the car loaded."

The backseat had been taken out of the Marmon and was replaced by a one-hundred-gallon holding tank. Billy backed the car up to the two converted large oaken barrels that held the recently distilled liquor. Travis put the hose into the opening of the tank, and Troy began pumping.

"How much do you get for this up in Kansas City?" Troy asked.

"What does it matter to you?" Jesse asked. "You're getting paid fifty cents a gallon."

"I heard once that it was sellin' in the speakeasies for a dime a shot. Is that right?"

"I don't sell in the speakeasies, I sell to the speakeasies," Jesse said.

"The reason I ask is that we know there's about twenty shots in one quart, which is two dollars, and there's four quarts in a gallon, which means it's eight dollars a gallon," Troy said. "You got yourself a one-hundred-gallon tank there, which means this is eight hundred dollars' worth of whiskey, but we're only gettin' fifty dollars."

"You're just real good at math, aren't you?" Billy said.

"Well, does that seem right to you? I mean we're getting fifty cents a gallon, and we have to come up with the corn and the yeast and the sugar. And we're the ones takin' the chances on cookin' it."

"Like I told you, we don't sell *in* the speakeasies, we sell *to* them," Jesse said. "And we aren't bitching to them about what they pay us. Now, do you want to keep doing business with us or not?"

"Yeah, we got no choice."

"Sure you do. You could shut the still down and go back to raising pigs."

"Are you serious? We're makin' two hunnert dollars a week sellin' shine," Travis said. "That's near ten times what we can make raisin' pigs."

"Stop pumpin', Troy, the tank is runnin' over," Travis said, withdrawing the hose.

"Here's your fifty dollars," Jesse said.

"Be sure you check the road before you open the gate," Troy cautioned.

Halfway between West Plains and Mountain Grove, Billy was driving and Jesse was taking a nap.

"Pa," Billy said urgently. "Pa, I think there's law ahead, behind those trees."

"What makes you think so?"

"I saw a flash of light, like someone was walkin' around back there."

"Drive on by at a normal speed," Jesse said. "But if they come out onto the road to try and stop us, go around them if you can."

As they got closer, the trees began to reflect a flashing red light.

"It's the law, all right!" Billy said.

"All right, let's outrun them."

Billy pressed the accelerator all the way to the floor, and the car leaped ahead. The police car tried to come out to intercept them, but it was too late.

Billy was doing over ninety miles an hour on a road that, though paved, was narrow and twisting.

The police car, with its siren and flashing red light, was unable to keep up. Jesse looked around, then smiled as he saw the car falling away behind them.

"We've got him beat," Jesse said.

"They must have telephoned ahead," Billy said. "Look!"

Ahead of them two police cars, nose to nose, were blocking the road.

"Damn!" Jesse said.

"Look, there's enough room to go behind that car on the left. The side of the road is wide enough."

"It's barely wide enough," Jesse said. "If you go too far, you'll put the left wheels down into the ditch, and we'll roll over."

"Trust me, Pa, I can do it," Billy said.

At that moment, Jesse realized that their roles had changed. Billy was now the one who assumed the initiative.

"We don't have any choice," Jesse said. "Do it."

There were two policemen behind the car on the left, waiting for the roadblock to cause the approaching car to stop. When the policemen saw that the car wasn't going to stop, their first thought was to pull their pistols. Then they realized they wouldn't have time, and they leaped, headfirst, into the ditch that ran parallel with the road.

The Marmon sped by, a silver flash that passed so fast one could almost think it was a specter had it not thrown up rocks to slam against the police car, breaking out windows and painfully striking the policemen.

Billy whipped the steering wheel back to the right,

again onto the paved road, and the tires squealed in protest.

"Woowee! That was fun!" Billy shouted.

When they reached Kansas City, they knew the back roads and alleyways to take in order to reach the speakeasy that had agreed to take the load for four hundred dollars. They backed up to the back door, and the one-hundred-gallon tank was removed and the backseats were put in.

The owner of the speakeasy was a large black man named "Heavy" Hunt.

"You didn't have no trouble gettin' the hooch here, did you?" Hunt asked.

"Not really," Billy said. "Halfway between West Plains and Mountain Grove the police got a little curious, but we outran them."

"It ain't the police I'm talkin' about," Hunt said. "I'm talkin' about the Costaconti gang. He sent me a message, told me I couldn't operate anymore unless I paid him two hundred dollars for every shipment of moonshine I got."

"What kind of message?" Jesse asked.

"I'll show you."

Heavy Hunt went into his office in the back of the speakeasy, then returned with a cloth bundle. When he opened the bundle, Jesse saw a severed black hand.

"This hand belonged to Tibbie O'Neal," Hunt said. "He works for me, and Vernon Miller and Charles Arthur ran into him down in the park. They're the ones that brought me the hand. Tibbie damn near bled to death."

"Are you going to pay Costaconti?"

"Hell no, I ain't goin' to pay him," Hunt said.

"What if he, or one of his men, comes sneaking in here some day?" Jesse asked.

Hunt laughed. "Now, you tell me, Mr. Frank, how any white man is goin' to sneak into my place?"

Jesse laughed as well. "I see what you mean."

"Far as I'm concerned, you 'n your boy are the only white faces that can come in here without gettin' your asses shot off."

"Well I'm just real glad you think that well of me, Heavy."

"Hell, Mr. Frank, I don't think nothin' of you. You just another white man, but you the one that brings me my hooch. So as long as you do that, you're welcome any time."

Later that day, as Jesse and Billy were driving through downtown Kansas City, a police car pulled up behind them, flashed its red light, and sounded the siren. Jesse was driving, and he pulled over and sat patiently as two policemen approached.

"Did I run a stop sign, Officer? I know I wasn't speeding," Jesse said.

"Would you and your passenger exit the car, please?"

"Is there something wrong?"

"Please, just exit the car."

Jesse and Billy got out as the two policemen examined the car. They looked in the backseat, and one of them got under the car to look.

"Maybe if you would tell me what you are looking for, I could be of some help," Jesse suggested.

"There was a Marmon, just like this one, that ran a roadblock last night," one of the policemen said. "We suspect it was being used to transport illegal whiskey."

"Well, as you can see, I have no bottles of whiskey in the car."

The policeman laughed. "They don't transport it in bottles; they transport it in bulk."

"Ah, I see. So you were looking for a big tank, weren't you? Something to haul the whiskey in," Jesse said in as innocent a tone as he could muster.

"Harry, this isn't the same license number," the other policeman said. "This is a Missouri tag; the one we're looking for is Arkansas."

"All right, you can go," the first officer said.

CHAPTER THIRTY-THREE

The cabin on the Brazos—May 23, 1942

"You had changed the license plate, hadn't you?" Faust asked.

"Yes. If the cops had looked more closely, they would have seen a false top to the car. That was where I kept extra license plates. We had plates from Kansas, Oklahoma, Texas, Arkansas, Tennessee, Mississippi, Kentucky, Illinois, and Missouri. That's also where we kept our guns."

"You were still carrying your Colt .44?"

"Yes. And I still have that gun. But by the twenties, pistols weren't enough. If you got into a gunfight, you had to have something more. Both Billy and I had Tommy guns. That was before they were banned."

"What did you think about the submachine guns?"

"Other than the fact that they spit out a lot of bullets, they were as useless as tits on a boar hog. You couldn't hit a bull in the ass with the damn things."

"That sounds like you actually had to use them."

"Yeah," Jesse said, "we had to use them."

"Against the police?"

Jesse shook his head. "Anyone was a fool to go up against the police then. They were too easy to buy off. The real trouble came from people who were trying to horn in on your territory, or people who thought you were trying to horn in on theirs."

"How did you determine what territory belonged to who?" Faust asked.

"There were no real lines. You just decided what belonged to you, or what you wanted to belong to you, and if you had the guts and the firepower to defend it, it was yours."

Mountain Grove, Missouri—September 10, 1922

The place could be called a graveyard for old cars, because there were at least ten rusted out, window-less, and mostly wheel-less cars out in the ravine.

Jesse and Billy had parked their car on the road alongside the old auto graveyard. The Marmon was no more. Ninety thousand really hard miles on the car had completely worn it out. They had gone back to driving a Packard, and it was waiting for them in the alley.

"Maybe we should have brought the Marmon here," Billy suggested as the two of them got out of the car.

"No, I would no more put one of my cars here than I would sell an old horse to the glue factory," Jesse said.

Both Jesse and Billy were holding what some people called Street Sweepers. They were actually Thompson submachine guns. Both guns were equipped with a drum magazine that would hold fifty rounds of .45 caliber ammunition. They had just bought the weapons and came out here to test-fire them.

They weren't the first people to ever have the idea of shooting guns at the cars; there were dozens of bullet holes in all the car bodies. One, an old Buick, had the fewest number of bullet holes.

"That one," Billy said, pointing to the Buick.

"You go first," Jesse invited.

Billy pointed the gun at the car and pulled the bolt back. That not only put the first round in the chamber, it also cocked the gun so that all he had to do was pull the trigger.

Billy pulled the trigger and the staccato sound of the firing gun echoed back from the surrounding hills. Smoke streamed from the barrel of the gun, and pieces of metal flew up from the Buick as the bullets punched holes in the car.

"Sumbitch! That's really somethin'!" Billy said excitedly when the last bullet had been extended. "Pa, did you see that?"

"How many bullets did you shoot?" Jesse asked.

"All of 'em. Fifty," Billy answered.

"Look at the car. How many new holes did you put in it?"

"I put . . ." Billy started, then he looked toward the car. "Damn, looks like I only put about twenty new holes. That's less than half of the bullets I shot."

"I know that you are a good shot, Billy." Jesse held out the gun he was holding and looked at it. "That means these things aren't very accurate."

"Ha!" Billy said. "They don't have to be all that ac-curate. As many bullets as they put out, some of them are bound to hit. Hell, it's like squirting a water hose!"

Jesse cocked his weapon, then, like Billy, fired it at

the Buick. When the noise and the final echo were gone, he walked over to examine the car.

Like Billy, he had put less than half the rounds he fired into the target.

The Morris Still, West Plains, Missouri—September 15, 1922

"We ain't goin' to be sellin' you no more liquor," Travis Morris said.

"Why not?" Billy asked.

"We don't need no reason. We make the liquor, so I reckon we can do with it whatever we want. And that means we can sell to who we want, or not sell to whoever we don't want."

"You've got to sell your whiskey to somebody. Who are you selling it to?"

"We're selling it to Costaconti, if you have to know," Troy said.

"Costaconti? Come on, I happen to know that he pays ten cents less a gallon than we do."

"Money don't matter none if you're dead," Travis said.

"You've moved your still two or three times to hide it from the law. Why don't you hide it from Costaconti?"

"Costaconti is smarter'n the law," Troy said. "It don't matter where we move it, he'll find it. You ain't gettin' no whiskey from us."

As they drove away from the Morris still, Billy stopped the car just on the other side of the gate and started to get out.

"Leave the damn thing open," Jesse said.

Billy laughed. "Yeah, serves them right."

* * *

"They were pretty determined," Jesse told Heavy Hunt later that same day.

"I've got to have product," Heavy said. "You see the business I've got here. There needs to be some place for my people to go. Look over there at Leroy and Sally Mae. Can you see either one of them goin' to a white speakeasy?"

Leroy and Sally Mae were a young black couple who were so completely involved with each other they were not only unaware they were the subject of conversation, they were hardly aware of anyone else in the place.

"Nice young couple like that," Heavy said. "They deserve a place they can come to where they can be sure they ain't goin' to be poisoned by bad hooch."

"I'll look around and see if I can find someone Costaconti hasn't gotten to yet," Jesse answered.

"Find me somebody, Mr. Frank. If you can give me a steady supply, I'll give you five dollars for every gallon you bring in. It ain't just the money, you understand. I'm providin' a service here."

"We'll do what we can," Jesse promised.

Jesse shook hands with Heavy, then with a wave to Nippy Jones, who was getting his band ready to play, he and Billy stepped out the back door.

Eldridge, Missouri

Clyde and Arnold Butrum didn't have to take as elaborate measures to hide their still as the Morris twins did. That's because the nearest "town" wasn't a town at all. Eldridge wasn't incorporated; it had no mayor, no city government, and no police department. It consisted solely of a gas station, a grocery store, a feed store, and about twenty houses, which were built there because it was the only spot flat enough in this part of the Ozark Mountain range where one could actually build a house.

The still was three miles up a single lane so narrow that two cars couldn't meet on the road. Though, it could barely be called a road.

"Damn, looks like a traffic jam," Billy said when they arrived.

Billy's comment referred to a Chevrolet that was sitting next to an old, dilapidated truck.

"Billy, I don't like the looks of this," Jesse said. "When you get out of the car, have your gun in your hand."

Billy knew better than to question Jesse, so as he stepped out from the driver's side of the car, he was holding his pistol down by his side.

There were four men standing near the still. Two of the men were wearing coveralls, and the other two men were wearing suits. It was clear to Jesse that the men in coveralls were the Butrum boys, and the men in suits were Constaconti's thugs. All four had heard the car coming and were now looking back toward Jesse and Billy.

"Pa, they're Costaconti men," Billy said under his breath.

"Yes," Jesse said quietly. Then, he called out to the others, "Well, this looks like a busy place."

Suddenly, but not unexpectedly, the Costaconti men raised their hands and began firing. They were shooting Colt M1911 .45 automatic pistols, whereas Jesse and Billy were armed with revolvers, choosing them over the submachine guns because they couldn't use them without putting the Butrum brothers into danger.

Jesse felt the shock wave of one of the bullets as it snapped by his ear. The automatic cocked itself after each shot, so the two Costaconti men were able to get off three shots each. All six shots missed. Jesse and Billy got off only three shots between them, but all three shots found their mark and the two Costaconti men went down.

Jesse and Billy approached, still holding the pistols in their hands. Clyde and Arnold put their hands up.

"Put your hands down, boys," Jesse said. "We aren't the law, and we aren't your enemies."

With expressions of relief on their faces, the two brothers lowered their arms.

"Who were those two sons of bitches?" Arnold Butrum asked, pointing to the two bodies. "They said they was goin' to kill us if we sold our liquor to anyone but them. And they was only goin' to give us thirty cents a gallon."

"They were Costaconti's men," Jesse said.

"Costaconti? I've heard of him. He's some big shot in Kansas City ain't he? Some sort of mob guy?" Arnold asked.

"Yes. He controls most of the speakeasies in town. Not all of them, but most of them."

"And he only wants to pay thirty cents a gallon? By the time we pay for ever'thing, gettin' only thirty cents a gallon means we won't hardly make no money at all," Clyde complained.

"Actually these men weren't only cheating you, they were cheating their boss. He's paying forty cents a gallon, not thirty."

"Forty cents? That's no good, either."

"What about sixty cents a gallon?"

"Sixty cents? You'll pay sixty cents?"

"Yes."

"I don't know. Didn't you say that this man Costaconti was running things in Kansas City?" Arnold asked.

"I said most things, not everything."

"Will you be hauling the hooch?"

"Yes."

"Who for?"

"A man named Heavy Hunt." Jesse didn't tell the Butrums that Hunt was a black man.

The two brothers walked off some distance and discussed it among themselves, then they came back.

"We want to come into Kansas City and take a look at his operation," Clyde said.

"Why?"

"According to these two men, if we didn't sell to them, they was going to kill us. I expect Costaconti may have the same idea. We just want to make certain that whoever you're selling to is stout enough to stay in business."

"All right," Jesse said. "I'll make the arrangements." He nodded toward the two men he and Billy had killed. "Can you take care of them?"

"Yeah," Arnold said. "About half a mile on up the road here is a thousand-foot drop-off into a real deep ravine. We can put 'em in their car and push it off, and there won't nobody discover 'em for a hunnert years or more."

Jesse gave each of the men a one-hundred-dollar bill. "This is for your trouble."

Clyde smiled. "This'll more'n pay for our trip to Kansas City."

CHAPTER THIRTY-FOUR

The cabin on the Brazos—June 2, 1942

"Did the Butrum boys show up in Kansas City?" Faust asked.

"Yes, they showed up."

"What did they think when they learned that Heavy Hunt was a black man and it was his speakeasy they would be providing whiskey for?"

"They were a little surprised, but I think they would have been more than willing to work with him."

"Would have been willing to work with him? You mean they didn't work with him?"

"No."

"Why not? Why didn't they work with him?"

"It was my fault," Jesse said. "I had spent my entire life being aware of everything around me, no matter how small. I could tell if a rock was in the wrong place, if a tree limb was bent in the wrong direction, if the birds were acting different. I should have seen it."

Jesse was quiet for a moment.

"I did see it. I saw it, and that's what has bothered

me all these years. I saw it, but I just didn't pay attention to it."

"What did you see, Jesse?"

"I saw a green Plymouth parked where a car shouldn't have been parked."

Kansas City—September 29, 1922

Jesse, Billy, Heavy Hunt, and two of Heavy Hunt's men were waiting at Union Station to pick up Clyde and Arnold Butrum when they arrived on the eleven o'clock train. They met the two brothers on the platform.

"Clyde, Arnold," Jesse said. "This is Heavy Hunt, and these are two of his men."

The Butrum brothers looked at Heavy and the two men with him.

"I came down here myself because I wanted you to see who you will be working with," Heavy said. "I want to know if my color bothers you. Because if it does, there ain't no need in goin' any further because I can find someone else to give my money to."

"What color is your money?" Clyde asked.

It took Heavy a moment to catch what Clyde was saying, then a broad, white-toothed smile spread across his round, black face. "It's green," he said.

"That's the only color I'm concerned with."

"Tell me, gentlemen, do you like barbeque ribs?" Heavy asked. "Or is that just something my people like?"

"I don't know a Missourian, black or white, who doesn't like barbeque ribs," Clyde said.

"Then why don't we discuss business over a big mess of ribs, potato salad, baked beans, and coleslaw?"

"Mr. Alexander, I already like doing business with this man," Arnold said as they started toward the two cars, Jesse and Billy's Packard and, parked just behind the Packard, Heavy Hunt's Cadillac.

A green Plymouth was parked a few feet away on the right side of Heavy's car. Jesse had seen it when it arrived a few minutes earlier, but he had taken no particular notice of it. Now, though, as the seven men started to get into the two cars, four men suddenly ran from behind the Plymouth. All four were carrying Thompson submachine guns.

"Pa, look out!" Billy shouted, and stepping between Jesse and the armed men, he shoved Jesse down.

"Let 'em have it!" one of the armed men shouted.

When the four men opened fire, they were no more than fifteen feet away and diagonally to the right of the Packard. Clyde and Arnold Butrum were killed instantly and fell to the ground. The two men who were with Heavy Hunt were armed, but Heavy was not. They managed to get their pistols out, but they were badly outgunned and the chattering machine guns continued to fire. Heavy Hunt and the men with him went down as the Cadillac was peppered with holes.

Billy opened the front door of the Packard and reached under the seat, trying to get his own machine gun, but Jesse saw him jerk back, then spin around, with half a dozen bullets in his body. One of the bullets was a fatal head wound.

Billy fell on top of Jesse, which saved Jesse's life, not only because Billy's body absorbed more bullets, but also because his blood covered Jesse.

"They're all dead! Let's get out of here!" one of the

shooters shouted, hurrying back to the Plymouth.
They sped away.

There had been several witnesses to the shooting,
and vaguely, Jesse was aware that some of the women
had been screaming.

Now, it was deathly quiet.

The cabin on the Brazos—June 3, 1942

Faust asked, "Do you feel like talking this morning?"

"Yeah," Jesse said. "But there's not much more
to tell. After Billy . . . well, I quit the whiskey-running
business. In fact, I left the outlaw trail altogether.
That is, after I took care of one more thing."

"One more thing?"

"Actually, you might say five more things," Jesse
said. "But since I took care of all five things at the
same time, you might say it was just one more thing."

Kansas City—October 8, 1922

"The bastard actually wants my band to play in his
joints," Nippy said. "He killed my best friend, but
I'm s'posed to just forget about that because his customers 'like colored music' when they're drinkin'."

Jesse had come to talk to Nippy Jones, ostensibly
to offer his regrets for Heavy being killed. In truth,
it was to find out what he could about Rico Costaconti. Costaconti wasn't one of the men who killed
Billy, but Jesse knew that the men who had done the
job were working for him.

"You see, what happened was, Costaconti sent two
of his goons out to bring some sweat on the Butrum
brothers, but you showed up while they be there, 'n
you off 'em. Costaconti blamed the Butrums for

that, so he sent his button men to the depot when the brothers come to town. He figures that if he kills them for crossing him, that'll teach a lesson to anyone else that might decide not to do business with him."

"So you are saying his target was the Butrum brothers, and not Heavy?"

"Yeah. Heavy, Julius, Lorenzo, you and your boy, you just happen to be there when it all goes down."

"Are you going to meet with him this Sunday?"

"I got to make a livin'," Nippy said. "You understand that, don't you?"

"Yes, I understand. A man has to do what he has to do. Is he coming here to meet with you?"

"No, he wants me to come to his warehouse but not until after two o'clock. You know why he wants to wait until after two o'clock, don't you?"

"No, why?"

"Because Sunday is the day he meets with his button men. That's the day he tells them who to go put some hurt on, you know what I mean?"

"The same men who killed Billy, Heavy, Clyde, and Arnold?"

"Yeah, and Julius and Lorenzo."

Costaconti didn't allow any of his speakeasies to be open on Sunday. It wasn't because of any religious obligation that his speakeasies were closed; it was because he needed one day when he could gather his key people to conduct important business.

On this day, Costaconti was having a meeting in the office at the back of a warehouse that advertised itself as Sicilian Olive Imports. Sicilian Olive Imports was a legitimate business, owned by Rico Costaconti and used by him as a front for his much more lucrative liquor business.

The warehouse district was quiet when Jesse drove by a building that had a large sign out front identifying it as Sicilian Olive Imports. In addition to four trucks, which had the same sign painted on the doors as was on the warehouse, there were two cars. One was a black Cadillac, and one was a green Plymouth. The green Plymouth was the same one that had been at the depot on the day of the shooting.

Jesse parked his car down the street at another warehouse, tucked in between two trucks so as not to be immediately noticeable. Then, with a pistol in each hand, he walked down to Sicilian Olive Imports.

So confident was Costaconti in his invincibility that the front door was unlocked.

Jesse walked through the shadows of the warehouse area, dimly illuminated only by the dust mote–filled bars of sunlight that came through the narrow, dirty windows at the top of the walls.

At the back of the warehouse a door was open, and light splashed out onto the floor. He could hear laughter and talking coming from inside.

"That black son of a bitch was so fat I thought he'd split wide open when I shot him, but the bullets just poked holes in all that fat."

The comment was met with laughter.

"You boys did a good job," a weasely looking man at the head of the table said smugly. "Killin' those hillbilly bastards who wouldn't do business with us will bring all the other bootleggers in line. I don't think we'll have any more trouble."

Jesse instinctively knew this was Constaconti.

"Oh, you've got trouble all right," Jesse said, stepping in through the door.

"Who the hell are—" Costaconti shouted, though he didn't have the opportunity to finish his question.

Jesse fired both guns, and it was all over within a matter of seconds. Costaconti and his four button men, the same ones who had killed Billy and the others, lay dead before him.

Jesse turned and walked away.

Granbury—1942

"I'm sorry," Faust said, leaning forward in his chair. "I didn't realize that Billy had passed. I'm sorry for your loss, Jesse."

Jesse wiped his eyes, even though they looked dry to Faust. "Well, so am I, Faust, so am I. More sorry for that than I ever was for anything in my whole life. And I had a lot to be sorry for. Ain't easy outliving your own children," he said.

"I kinda lost my taste for life," he said. "Crawled into a whiskey bottle and stayed there for a spell. Whiskey ain't a cure for pain, though—it numbs you to be sure . . . but as any drunk will tell you, the heartache is still waitin' for you right around the corner when you sober up."

"I apologize, Jesse." Faust said. "I didn't mean to upset you. Perhaps we should stop for the day?"

"You know," Jesse went on as if he hadn't heard Faust, "maybe I shouldn't have encouraged Billy. If he hadn't gone law-breaking with me. If he had settled down, met some nice girl—he wouldn't have caught that bullet. Things might've been different."

"It's no use thinking like that," Faust said. "We none

of us can change the past. Not even the legendary Jesse James." He smiled weakly.

"I know," Jesse said. "That's what I tell myself. Sometimes I lay awake all night, just telling myself that . . . but that's why I wanna join this war! Don't you see, Faust? I could help these young fellas. Do right by them. Like the way I shoulda done for Billy."

"I understand. And I agree. I think there's a lot you have to offer."

"Like my story?" Jesse raised a silver eyebrow.

"Well, it's quite a tale." Faust laughed. "If this story was published, I don't think there is a man, woman, or child who wouldn't want to know the *real* Jesse James."

Jesse stopped smiling and stared into the distance. "Right. The real Jesse James. Whoever he is."

Faust leaned forward in his chair, a concerned expression on his face. "Are you all right, Jesse? Can I get you something? A glass of water?"

"No, thank you," Jesse answered, snapping back from reality as if being pulled out of a dream. "But I reckon I'm plum tuckered. Getting old'll do that to you. You don't mind if we call it quits for the day?"

"Not at all. Can I walk you home?"

"Heck no! You think an outlaw like Jesse James needs anyone for to walk him home?" But he was smiling as he said it.

Faust laughed. "Okay, Jesse. See you tomorrow?"

Jesse nodded, a strange light in his eyes. "Tomorrow."

Jesse left. Faust watched from the widow as the noble old figure walked down the dusty street until he disappeared from view. Somehow he just knew that he would never see the man they called see Jesse James again. He'd seen it in the man's eyes.

Faust couldn't blame him for that. Jesse was a man who lived life, not one to sit around talking about regrets. Faust knew Jesse'd had a bellyful of reminiscing and just wanted to live out his days in peace. Seemed like the way it ought to be.

Faust turned away from the window and stared at the piles of papers and notes stacked neatly on the table. His manuscript. His masterpiece. The true life story of Jesse James.

He walked over to the papers and picked them up. Amazing that an entire man's life could be captured on a few pieces of paper. More than a man's life, really. A legend.

Maybe he wouldn't turn in this manuscript to his publisher after all, Faust thought. Oh, it would mean giving up a fortune. A damned-near gold mine— that was if he could find a publisher who actually believed he wasn't making the whole thing up, or wasn't going crazy.

But there was something else nagging at Faust. Another reason he didn't want to turn in the manuscript. The legend of Jesse James was too big to ever be put down in one book. It was a legend that lived on, in the hearts and imaginations of Americans young and old. And legends never die. Why try to change that? Maybe that's what Jesse was trying to tell him all along.

With the manuscript still in his hands, Faust walked to the fire and threw the papers into the flames. He watched as the orange tongues devoured the pale leaves. Ashes to ashes.

"Good-bye, Jesse."

EPILOGUE

In the Granbury Cemetery in Granbury, Texas, there is a tombstone with the following inscription:

CSA – JESSE WOODSON JAMES

Sept. 5, 1847–Aug. 15, 1951

Supposedly killed in 1882

A small Confederate flag is etched above the inscription. But who lies buried in this grave is something none of us may ever know.

Turn the page for an exciting preview!

**BY THE GREATEST WESTERN WRITERS
OF THE TWENTY-FIRST CENTURY**

*A bold, sprawling epic of the American West, the Jensen
family saga has captivated readers for nearly three decades.
Now comes the untold story of Smoke Jensen's long-lost
nephews, Ace and Chance, a pair of young-gun twins
as reckless and wild as the frontier itself . . .*

THOSE JENSEN BOYS!
Their father is Luke Jensen, thought to be killed in the
Civil War. Their uncle, Smoke, is one of the fiercest
gunfighters the West has ever known. It's no surprise
that the inseparable Ace and Chance Jensen have a
knack for taking risks—even if they have to blast their
way out of them. Chance is a bit of a hothead, good
with his gun and his fists. Ace is more of a thinker,
sharp as a snakebite and just as deadly quick. Their
skills are put to the test when two young ladies ask
them to protect their struggling stagecoach line from a
ruthless bloodthirsty mine owner with money, power—
and enough hired killers to slaughter half the territory.

Those Jensen boys have to ask themselves:
What would Smoke Jensen do?

THOSE JENSEN BOYS!
by William W. Johnstone
with J. A. Johnstone

First in a new series!

On sale now, wherever Pinnacle Books are sold.

CHAPTER ONE

Wyoming Territory, 1885

The atmosphere in the saloon was tense with the potential for violence. All the men around the baize-covered poker table sat stiffly, waiting for the next turn of the cards—and the trouble it might bring.

Except for one young man. He sat back easily in his chair, a smile on his face as he regarded the cards in front of him. He had two jacks and a nine showing. He picked up some greenbacks from the pile next to him and tossed them into the center of the table with the rest of the pot. "I'll see that twenty and raise fifty."

Most of the other players had already dropped out as the pot grew. The bet made them look even grimmer.

The player to the young man's left muttered, "Forget it," and shoved his chair away from the table. He stood up and headed for the bar.

The game had drawn quite a bit of attention. Men who had been drinking at the bar or at other tables drifted over to see how the hand was going to play out.

The young man said, "Looks like it's down to you and me, Harrington."

"That's *Mayor* Harrington to you," said his sole remaining opponent.

"Sorry. Didn't mean any disrespect, Mr. Mayor." The young man's slightly mocking tone made it clear to everyone around the table and those standing and watching that disrespect was exactly what he meant.

One patron who seemed to be paying no attention at all stood at the bar with the beer he'd been nursing. He was a man of medium height, dressed in range clothes, with sandy hair under his thumbed-back Stetson. At first glance, not much was remarkable about him except the span of his broad shoulders. He took another sip of his beer and kept his back to what was going on in the rest of the room.

Harrington's pile of winnings was considerably smaller than that of the young man. He hesitated, then picked up some bills and added them to the pot. "There's your damn fifty." He was a dark-haired, well-dressed man of middle years, sporting a narrow mustache. "Deal the cards, Blake."

The nervous-looking dealer, who happened to be the owner of the saloon, swallowed, cleared his throat, and dealt a card faceup to the young man. "That's a three," he announced unnecessarily, since everybody could see what the card was. "Still a pair of jacks showing."

With expert skill, he flipped the next card in the deck to Harrington. "A seven. No help to the mayor, who still has a pair of queens."

"We can all see that, blast it," Harrington snapped. "Who the hell bids up the pot like that on a lousy pair of jacks? It's not good enough to beat me and you know it."

"I thought we'd already been introduced," the young man said as his smile widened into a cocky grin. "The name's Chance."

He was in his mid-twenties, handsome, clean-shaven with close-cropped brown hair. The brown suit he wore had been of fine quality at one time, It was beginning to show some age and wear, but the ivory stickpin in his cravat still shone.

"I know who you are," Harrington said coldly. "A damn tinhorn gambler who should have been run out of town by now."

The grin on Chance's face didn't budge, but his eyes turned hard as flint. "I think everybody here knows this game has been dealt fair and square, Mr. Mayor. They've seen it with their own eyes." He put his hand on the pile of bills and coins and pushed it into the middle of the table. "And I reckon I'm all in."

Before Harrington could react, another man pushed through the batwings into the saloon and started across the room toward the poker table. He was the same age as Chance but bigger and huskier, with a thatch of rumpled dark hair. He wore denim trousers and a pullover buckskin shirt. His black hat hung behind his head from its chin strap. A Colt Peacemaker rode in a holster on his right hip.

A couple hard-looking men got in the newcomer's way, but a flick of Harrington's hand made them move back.

"I need to talk to my brother for a second," the dark-haired young man said.

"Ace, you know better than that," Chance drawled. "You don't go interrupting a fella when he's in the middle of a game."

"It's all right," Harrington said. "Those cards stay right where they are, though."

"Of course," Chance said smoothly. He stood up, and he and his brother Ace moved a few feet away from the table. Chance continued to smile and look relaxed, but his voice was tight and angry as he asked under his breath, "What the hell are you doing? I've got the mayor right where I want him!"

Ace kept his voice low enough that only his brother could hear him. "I heard over at the general store that you'd gotten into a game with him. The mayor is crooked as a dog's hind leg! Those are his hired guns around the table. You can take that pot off him, but he'll never let you leave town with it."

Chance tried not to appear as shaken as he felt. "How'd you find that out?"

"The fella over at the general store likes to gossip. Seems like Harrington's got everybody around here under his thumb, and some folks don't like it."

"Well, that's just too bad," Chance insisted. "I haven't done anything wrong, and I'm not gonna throw in my hand now. That's what you want, isn't it? You want me to quit? What would Doc think if I did that?"

"Doc wouldn't want you getting killed over a poker game."

"I don't know about that. Seems like he always knew what was important in life."

From the table, Harrington said, "Are you going to play or jaw with your brother all day?"

Chance was as self-confident as ever as he turned back to the table. "Why, I'm going to play, of course, Mr. Mayor. I believe the bet was to you." Chance settled back into his seat while Ace stood a few feet away, looking worried.

"And I'm going to call, you impudent young pup. I'm not going to let you bluff me." Harrington pushed his remaining money into the pile at the center of the table. "I'll have to give you a marker for the rest."

"Well, I don't know. . . ." As Harrington's men loomed closer to the table, Chance went on. "Of course I'll take your marker, Mr. Harrington."

The mayor turned over his hole card, which was an eight. "My queens beat your jacks."

"But they don't beat my jacks *and* my threes," Chance said as he flipped over his hole card, which was the second trey. "Two pairs always beat one pair."

Harrington's face was bleak as he stared at the cards on the table.

Chance said, "I believe you mentioned something about a marker. . . ."

Harrington's breath hissed between his clenched teeth. He shoved his chair back and stood up abruptly. "You think you're so damn smart." He looked around. The two men who had tried to stop Ace from talking to his brother had been joined by three more big, tough-looking hombres. "Teach these two a lesson and then dump them somewhere outside of town. Make sure they understand they're never to come back here."

"Wait just a minute." Chance's right hand moved

almost imperceptibly closer to the lapel of his jacket. "Are you saying you're not gonna pay up, Harrington?"

"I don't honor debts to a cheater," Harrington snapped.

"It was a square deal," Chance insisted. "What'll your constituents think of you welshing like this?"

Everybody in the saloon had started edging away. The feathered and spangled serving girls headed for the bar where they could duck behind cover. In a matter of moments, nobody was anywhere near Ace and Chance to offer them help.

Harrington smirked at the two young men. "Why in the hell would I care what they think? Nobody dares do anything about it. They all know I run this town." He gestured curtly, and his hired toughs started closing in around Ace and Chance.

The sandy-haired man who'd been standing at the bar, seemingly paying no attention to what was going on, turned around then. "Hold it right there, gents."

Harrington stiffened. "You don't want to get mixed up in this, stranger."

The man ambled closer, thumbs hooked in his gun belt. "You're right. I'm a stranger here. So I don't care if you're the mayor and I don't care if these hombres who think they're tough work for you. I don't like to see anybody ganging up on a couple young fellas."

One of Harrington's men said, "We don't just think we're tough, mister. We'll prove it if we have to."

The stranger stood beside Ace and Chance. "I reckon you'll have to."

"Get them!" Harrington barked.

Five men charged forward. Two headed for the stranger, two for Ace, and one lunged at Chance and threw a looping punch.

Chance ducked under the blow and stepped in to hook a left into his opponent's belly. His punch packed surprising power. As the man's breath gusted out and he bent over, Chance threw a right to his jaw that landed solidly. The man's head jerked around and his eyes rolled up. His knees unhinged and dropped him to the sawdust-littered floor.

A few feet away, Ace had his hands full with the two men who had tackled him. One of them grabbed him around the waist and drove him back into the bar. He grunted in pain. Stunned, he couldn't stop the man from grabbing his arms and pinning them. Grinning, the other man closed in with fists poised to deliver a vicious beating while his friend hung on to Ace.

As his head cleared, Ace threw his weight back against the man holding him and raised both legs, bending his knees. He straightened them in a double kick that slammed into the chest of the man coming at him. The kick was so powerful it lifted the man off the floor and sent him flying backwards to crash down on a table that collapsed underneath him and left him sprawled in its wreckage.

The move also threw the man holding Ace off balance. His grip slipped enough for Ace to drive an elbow back into his belly. As the man let go entirely, Ace whirled around and planted his right fist in the middle of his opponent's face. Blood spurted and the man's nose flattened as he reeled against the bar. Ace finished him with a hard left that knocked him to the floor.

While that was going on, the broad-shouldered stranger dealt with the two men attacking him. Moving almost too fast for the eye to follow, his hands shot out and grabbed each man by the throat. With the corded muscles in his shoulders and arms bunching, he smashed their heads together with comparative ease—about as much effort as a child would expend to do the same thing to a pair of ragdolls. The two toughs dropped as limply as rag dolls, too, when the stranger let go of them.

Clearly furious at seeing his men defeated, Harrington uttered a curse and clawed a short-barreled revolver from under his coat. He started to lift the gun—only to stop short as he found himself staring down the barrels of three revolvers.

Ace, Chance, and the stranger each had drawn a weapon with breathtaking speed, Chance's gun coming from a shoulder holster under his coat. All it would take to blow Harrington to hell was a slight bit of pressure on the triggers.

Harrington's hand opened, the pistol thudded to the floor, and his eyes widened in fear. "P-Please, don't shoot. Don't kill me."

"Seems pretty foolish for anybody to die over a stupid saloon brawl," the stranger said. "Why don't you kick that gun away?"

Harrington did so.

The stranger went on. "I was watching in the bar mirror, and as far as I could tell, this young fella beat you fair and square, mister. I'd like to hear you admit that."

"O-of course," Harrington stammered. "He beat me."

"Tell him, not me."

Harrington swallowed and looked at Chance. "You won fair and square."

"That means the pot's mine," Chance pointed out.

"Certainly."

He replaced his gun in the shoulder holster, then began gathering up the bills and stuffing them in an inside pocket of his coat.

"I-I'll make out that marker," Harrington went on.

"Forget it. What's here on the table is good enough. My brother and I are leaving, and I'd just as soon not have to come back to this burg to collect."

"That's very generous of you."

The stranger said, "I'd advise you fellas to saddle your horses and ride on out as soon as you can. I'll hang around here for a while just to make sure the mayor doesn't get any ideas about sending his men after you to recover that money."

"I wouldn't do that," Harrington insisted. His face was pale, making his mustache stand out in sharp contrast.

The stranger smiled. "Well, a fella can't be too careful, you know."

Ace and Chance looked at each other.

Ace asked, "You ready to go?"

"Yeah." Chance turned to the stranger. "We're much obliged to you for your help, Mister . . . ?"

"Jensen. Smoke Jensen."

That brought surprised exclamations from several people in the room. Smoke Jensen was one of the most famous names in the West. He was a gunfighter, thought by many to be the fastest on the draw who had ever lived, but he was also a successful rancher in Colorado, having put his notorious past behind him, for the most part. His reputation was still such that nobody in his right mind wanted to cross him.

Ace and Chance exchanged a glance when they heard the name, but they didn't say anything else except for Ace expressing his gratitude, too, as they made their way around the unconscious men on the saloon floor. When they left the place, they headed straight for the livery stable in the next block. They had already gotten their gear from their hotel room and settled the bill, since they'd planned on leaving town, anyway. Their restless nature never let them stay in one place for too long.

Quickly, they saddled their horses, a cream-colored gelding for Chance and a big chestnut for Ace.

Chance tossed a silver dollar to the hostler and smiled. "Thanks for taking care of them, friend."

The brothers swung up into their saddles and headed out of the settlement.

When they had put the town behind them, Chance said, "Smoke Jensen. How about that? We had an honest-to-goodness legend step in to give us a hand, Ace."

"He's mighty famous, all right," Ace agreed. "We've talked about him, but I never really figured we'd run into him someday."

Chance grinned. "You reckon we should've told him that *our* last name is Jensen, too? Shoot, we might be long-lost relatives!"

"I doubt that," Ace said dryly. "You really think a

couple down-on-their-luck drifters like us could be related to the famous Smoke Jensen?"

"You never know," Chance replied with a chuckle. "Stranger things have happened, I reckon. Anyway, we're not down on our luck right now." He slapped the sheaf of money through his coat. "We're as flush as we've been for a while. Let's go see what's on the other side of the mountain, brother!"

CHAPTER TWO

Denver, Colorado Territory, 1861

"Jacks over tens, gents." Ennis Monday laid down his cards. "I believe that takes this hand."

"Dadgum it, Doc!" one of the other players exclaimed. "You're just too good at this game."

Monday smiled slightly. "That's how I make my living, Mr. Tucker—being good at what I do."

"Well, I don't begrudge you." Alfred Tucker slid a small leather pouch full of gold nuggets across the table to the gambler. "Everybody in Denver knows that Doc Monday is a square player."

"I appreciate that." Monday tucked the pouch inside his coat and gathered up the cards to shuffle them. "Another hand, gentlemen?"

One of the other players nodded toward a woman across the room. "Looks to me like you might have something more interesting to turn your hand to, Doc. That lady over there's been watching you mighty keenly for the past few minutes."

Monday had been concentrating on his cards or

he would have noticed the woman. As he met her eyes across the room, she started toward him.

She was a little on the short side, dark-haired, and curvy. Most of the females who ventured into this establishment in Denver's red-light district were no better than they had to be, but this young brunette had a certain air of respectability to her.

Alfred Tucker chortled. "She's comin' over here, Doc. You got an admirer, all right."

"Or else she's looking for someone who loved and left her, eh, Doc?" another card player gibed.

"I believe I'll sit out the next hand." Monday gathered up his winnings. "Best of luck."

"Oh, it'll improve once you're gone," one of the men said.

Monday's eyes narrowed. "You wouldn't be implying anything by that, would you, Clete?"

Quickly, Clete held up his hands and shook his head. "Not a thing, Doc, I swear. Just that you're too good at this game for the likes of us."

"In that case . . ." Monday gave the men at the table a friendly nod, then moved to meet the woman coming toward them.

"Excuse me," she said as she looked up at him. "Would you happen to be Mr. Ennis Monday?"

He touched the brim of his hat. "You have the advantage of me, ma'am. I am indeed Ennis Monday. But my friends call me Doc."

"I'm pleased to meet you, Mr. Monday." Her voice was a bit pointed as she addressed him formally. "My name is Lettie Margrabe." She paused, then added, "Mrs. Lettie Margrabe."

Something about the way she said that struck him

as being off, but he didn't press the issue. "It's an honor, Mrs. Margrabe. What can I do for you?"

"Perhaps if we could sit down at a table where it's quiet . . ."

"We're in a saloon, ma'am. There's only a certain level of privacy and decorum we can hope to attain. However, that said"—he gestured toward an empty table in the corner—"let's try over there."

Once they were seated, Monday took a better look at the woman. She was dressed in a decent traveling outfit, but it wasn't anything fancy or expensive. A waiter came over and Monday asked her if she'd like anything to drink, but she shook her head.

"Bourbon," Monday told the waiter, who left to fetch it. "Now, you obviously know who I am. Were you given a description of me?"

"That's right," Lettie Margrabe replied. "An old friend of yours told me to look you up. Belle Robb."

"Belle . . ." The memory brought a smile to Monday's lips under his neatly trimmed mustache. "I haven't seen her in a long time. How is she? As lovely as ever?"

"Yes, I suppose so. She, ah, provided me with a letter to give to you."

"A letter of introduction, eh?" Monday cocked an eyebrow. "Are you in the same line of work as Belle? Looking to get into that game here in Denver? I must say, with all due respect to Belle, you don't really look the sort."

In fact, even in the shadowy confines of the saloon, he could tell that Lettie was blushing furiously at the suggestion she might be a lady of the evening like Belle.

"We were friends, back in the town where I come

from in Missouri," she said. "That's all. I . . . I taught school there and helped Belle by tutoring her with her own reading."

"I see. Belle always did enjoy improving her mind," Monday said with a sardonic smile. "About this letter . . . ?"

"Of course." Lettie reached in her handbag and brought it out. "Here."

Monday unfolded the paper. As he read what was written in Belle Robb's extravagant hand, his expression grew more solemn. He looked up from the letter and said, "My apologies, Mrs. Margrabe, and my sympathy, as well. I didn't realize your husband was dead. And to be killed in the very first battle of the war that way."

"Yes, it was . . . tragic," Lettie agreed. "You can understand why I wanted to leave. I had to get away from all those . . . bitter memories. Belle suggested I might come to Denver and make a fresh start."

"She thought I could help you with that?" Monday murmured.

"She said you were a good man, Mr. Monday. She said you would treat me well."

His eyebrows arched. "My God. You're not thinking that I'll marry you, are you? Not even Belle would suggest—"

"No. No, marriage isn't necessary. I just need a place to stay, perhaps a job . . ."

"I spend practically all my time in saloons," Monday growled. "All the jobs I know of for women aren't what you'd call respectable. They're not anything a former schoolteacher would want to do."

"Perhaps a former schoolteacher who is desperate enough would," Lettie said.

Monday studied her in silence for a moment. "You're plainspoken. I like that in a man, and I find that I appreciate it in a woman, too. I'll tell you what. I have a room in a boardinghouse where the landlady doesn't ask many questions. You can stay there for now." He held up a hand to forestall any protest she might make. "I'm not suggesting anything improper. There are plenty of other places I can stay for the time being."

"With other women, I suppose."

Monday laughed. "You go beyond plainspoken to blunt, but I don't mind. It's a pretty refreshing attitude, to be honest. Anyway, you can stay there, and I'll ask around and see if I can find something for you to do. Agreed?"

Lettie hesitated, but only for a second. Then she extended her hand across the table. "Agreed."

"We'd drink to it," Monday said as he shook her hand, "if you drank . . . and if that slovenly waiter had come back with my bourbon. At any rate, we have a deal. I hope you knew what Belle was letting you in for."

"Salvation," Lettie Margrabe said.

Ennis Monday was good as his word, for which Lettie was exceedingly grateful. He allowed her to stay in his room at the boardinghouse without ever making any improper advances, and he found her a job keeping the books for a store on Colfax Avenue. Her knowledge of arithmetic gained from being a teacher came in very handy.

Within a few weeks of her arrival in Denver, however, two things began to be obvious. One was that

Ennis, or Doc as he preferred to be called, was smitten with her.

The other was that Lettie was with child.

The letter from Belle Robb had given her a perfectly reasonable excuse for that, of course—the dead "husband" who tragically had lost his life at the Battle of Bull Run. In truth, Lettie had never been married, and while it was certainly possible the father of her child had been killed in battle, she didn't know that. It was just as possible that Luke Jensen was still alive. She hadn't seen him since he'd joined the Confederate Army and gone off to war.

That blasted war had played a part in her current predicament. The night before he left, Luke had come to Lettie's room to say good-bye, and their passion for each other had caused them to get carried away. Luke had spent the night and was gone the next day without ever knowing that he had planted new life inside her.

Once she'd discovered it, she hadn't written to tell him. He had enough to do, trying to stay alive in the madness of war. He didn't need anything distracting him. Someday, when the terrible times were over and if he came home safely, she would let him know he was a father.

When her belly had swollen enough that only a blind man could miss it, she finally said something to Doc when they were out to dinner one evening. Two or three times a week, he took her to dinner in one of Denver's better restaurants. As he was chewing a bite of steak, she leaned forward on the other side of the table. "Mr. Monday, there's a subject we should discuss."

He swallowed. "Let's discuss why you still resist

calling me Doc. It's what my friends call me, and I think we're friends by now, don't you? You don't object when I call you Lettie."

"I could hardly object. You've been so kind to me—"

"So you really do mind, is that it?"

She shook her head and reached out to rest her hand on his. "No, I don't mind. In fact, I like it . . . Doc."

"Good. That's settled," he said with a grin.

"But that's not what I want to talk about."

His grin disappeared and was replaced by a frown. "Blast it, you sound serious. You know I'm not fond of serious matters. That's why I spend most of my time in saloons, playing cards."

"You spend most of your time in saloons playing cards because you're a rapscallion."

He inclined his head in acknowledgment of her comment. "Guilty as charged, ma'am."

Lettie drew in a deep breath. "What I'm talking about is that I . . . I'm in the family way, and you know it, Doc."

He shrugged, but Lettie wondered if he truly felt as casual as he was trying to act.

"You were a married woman until recently. There's nothing unusual or unexpected about a married woman being with child."

"I know that. It's just—" Her hand still rested on his.

He turned his hand over and gripped hers. "Do you think it really matters to me, Lettie? I'll be honest with you. I've grown quite fond of you in the time we've known each other. Why, if I had anything to offer you other than a wastrel's life—

No, best not go down that path, I suppose. The facts are what they are. But the fact that you're expecting doesn't change the way I feel about you. Not one bit."

Her fingers tightened on his as she smiled. "You are a dear man, Ennis Monday."

"Don't let my enemies hear you say that. They'll laugh themselves silly." He took her hand in both of his. "Let's just put this behind us, shall we? When the child is born, I'll be there for you. Whatever you need, I'll provide, if it's in my power to do so."

"All right," she whispered. "Thank you."

She knew she ought to do something to express her gratitude in a more tangible manner. He had hinted that he wanted to marry her. In many ways, that would be a good thing to do. Her child could grow up with a father and would never have to know the truth . . .

But what about Luke? If he lived through the war, didn't he have a right to know about the child? Besides, in many ways she still loved him. Luke Jensen was a good strong man from a decent family. Back in Missouri, Luke's younger brother and sister, Kirby and Janey, had been in Lettie's class. Janey was a bit of a flirt but a decent girl at heart, Lettie believed, and Kirby was a fine young man. Lettie would have been quite happy to be part of the Jensen family by marriage . . . if only the rest of the world hadn't gotten in the way.

But as Doc had said, the facts were what they were. Luke was gone and might not even be living. Lettie was in Denver, growing larger by the day, and Ennis Monday's friendship had proven to be the salvation for which she had hoped.

That night when he took her back to the boarding-house, she took hold of his hand as he started to turn away at the door and told him that he didn't have to leave.

"You can stay if you like," she told him.

And so he did.

Not many more weeks passed before Lettie knew that something was . . . well, not *wrong*, exactly, but not the way she expected it to be.

Doc, despite his nickname, had no medical training whatsoever. He found a good physician for her, and after an examination, the man told her, "It's my considered opinion, Mrs. Margrabe, that you're carrying twins."

"Twins!" Lettie gasped. "But that's . . . I started to say impossible, but I suppose . . . Are you sure, Doctor?"

"As sure as I can be at this point in time." The man frowned. "It's a bit worrisome, too. Let me phrase this carefully. You're somewhat of a . . . delicate woman. Giving birth to one baby may be rather difficult for you. If we're talking about two . . ." He spread his hands. "But we'll give you the best of care, you have my word on that. Do everything I tell you, and there's every chance that in a few more months you'll be the proud mother of two infants."

"Sons," Lettie said, surprising herself.

"Well, there's no way to know that until the time comes, of course."

She knew it, though. Somehow she knew that the babies inside her were boys, and she didn't question it.

* * *

Winter had settled in on Denver, bringing with it cold winds and blowing snow. Doc leaned against the wall just outside the door of his room in the boardinghouse and smoked a cigar. He heard the pane in the window at the end of the corridor rattle as the howling wind struck it, but he was really listening for something else.

He was waiting to hear a baby's cry.

The sawbones had run him out of the room, making some excuse about how the place wasn't big enough for the doctor, the nurse he had brought with him, Lettie, and Doc. He knew the man just wanted him out because he was afraid Lettie was going to have a hard time of it.

Judging from the screams that had sounded earlier, that was what had happened. The cries had twisted his guts. Even worse was the knowledge that he couldn't do anything to help her. Being one of the best poker players in the territory didn't mean a damn thing.

Doc puffed anxiously on the cigar. Over the past six months, he had grown closer to Lettie than any woman he had ever known. He had done his best to talk her into marrying him, but she steadfastly refused. She said she couldn't marry another man until after the babies were born. That didn't make any sense to him, but he hadn't been able to get her to budge from her decision.

Now it might be too late. He tried not to allow that thought to sneak into his brain, but it was impossible to keep it out.

He straightened and tossed the cigar butt into a

nearby bucket of sand as a wailing cry came from inside the room, followed a moment later by another. Doc's heart slugged hard in his chest. He was no expert, but to him it sounded as if both babies had healthy sets of lungs. That was encouraging.

But he still didn't know how Lettie was doing.

After a few minutes that seemed like an eternity, the door opened. The doctor looked out, and the gloomy expression on the man's face struck fear into Doc's heart. "You can come on in, Mr. Monday, but I should caution you, the situation is grave."

"The babies—?" Doc asked with a catch in his throat.

"That's the one bright spot in this affair. Or rather, the *two* bright spots. Two healthy baby boys. I think they'll be fine."

Doc closed his eyes for a second. He wasn't a praying man, but he couldn't keep himself from sending a few unspoken words of thanks heavenwards.

But there was still Lettie to see about. He followed the doctor into the room.

She was propped up a little on some pillows, and her face was so pale and drawn that the sight of it made Doc gasp. Her eyes were closed and for a horrible second he believed she was dead. Then he saw the sheet rising and falling slightly over her chest.

There was no guarantee how long that would last, however. When the doctor motioned him closer, he went to the bed, dropped to a knee beside it, and took hold of her right hand in both of his.

Her eyelids fluttered and then opened slowly. She had trouble focusing at first, then her gaze settled on his face and she sighed. A faint smile touched her lips. "Doc . . ." she whispered.

His hands tightened on hers. "I'm here, darling."

"The . . . babies?"

"They're fine. Two healthy baby boys."

"Ahhhh . . ." Her smile grew. "Twins. Are they . . . identical?"

Doc glanced up at the physician, who spread his hands, shook his head, and shrugged.

"They look alike to me," Doc said to Lettie, although in truth he hadn't actually looked at the babies yet. They were in bassinets across the room, being tended to by the nurse. Of course, to him all babies looked alike, Doc thought, so he wasn't actually lying to Lettie.

"That's . . . good. They'll be . . . strong, beautiful boys. Doc . . . you'll raise them?"

"We'll raise them. You've no excuse not to marry me now."

"No excuse," she repeated, "except the best one of all . . ."

"Don't talk like that," he urged. "You just need to get your strength back—"

"I don't have . . . any strength to get back. This took . . . all I had." She paused, licked her lips, and with a visible effort forced herself to go on. "Their name . . ."

"We'll call them anything you like."

"No, I mean . . . their last name . . ."

"Margrabe," Doc said. "Your late husband—"

"No," Lettie broke in. "I'm ashamed to admit it . . . even now . . . but I was . . . never married to their father. His last name is . . . Jensen . . . I want you to name them . . . William, after my father . . . and

Benjamin, after my grandfather . . . William and Benjamin . . . Jensen."

"If that's what you want, my dear, that's what we'll do," Doc promised. "I give you my word."

"You'll take care . . . of them?"

"We—"

"No," she husked. "You. They have . . . no one else . . ."

Lord, Lord, Lord, Doc thought. This couldn't be. He'd barely spent time with her, barely gotten to know her. She couldn't be taken away from him now.

But he couldn't hold her. He sensed she was slipping away. A matter of moments only. He felt a hot stinging in his eyes and realized it was tears—for the first time in longer than he could remember.

"Take . . . take care . . ." she breathed.

He could barely hear the words. Her eyes began to close and he gripped her hands even tighter, as if he could hold on to her and keep her with him that way. "I will. I'll take care of the boys. I love you, Lettie."

"Ah," she said again, and the smile came back to her. "And I love . . ."

The breath eased out of her, and the sheet grew still.

Doc bent his head forward and tried not to sob.

The doctor gripped his shoulder. "She's gone, Mr. Monday. I'm sorry."

"I . . . I know," Doc choked out. He found the strength to lift his head. "But those boys. They're here. And they need me."

As if to reinforce that, both babies began to cry.

"Indeed they do," the doctor agreed. "Would you like to take a look at them?"

Gently, Doc laid Lettie's hand on the sheet beside her and got to his feet. He turned, feeling numb and awkward, and the doctor led him over to the bassinets. Doc had seen babies before, of course, and always thought of them as squalling, red-faced bundles of trouble.

Not these two, though. There was something about them . . . something special.

"William and Benjamin. Those are fine names, but . . . so formal. I'm not sure they suit you. We'll put them down on the papers because that's what your mother wanted, but I think I'll call you"—he forced a smile onto his face as he looked at the infant with darker hair—"Ace. And your brother . . . well, he has to be Chance, of course. Ace and Chance Jensen. And what a winning pair you'll be."